I0535411

Outliers of Speculative Fiction
L.A. Little, Editor

ACKNOWLEDGMENTS

My thanks go first and foremost to the authors who took a chance and submitted to a brand new anthology that came with no imprimatur and no established brand—just a mission to help authors and add new voices and ideas to the universe of speculative fiction. We had submissions from authors in all stages of their careers, across speculative genres, and from around the world. To those who are in this edition and to those who submitted but I was not able to include this time, I offer my sincere and profound thank you!

Naturally many thanks go as well to all of the fans who will read this collection and those who have helped get the word out through the web and social media, even going so far as to recruit their favorite authors to submit. It has truly been a measure of the passion speculative fiction fans have, not just for the stories, but for the community. Thank you to all of the fans, friends, and family members who have supported all of the authors and the broader community.

Credit of, course, has to be given as well to the platforms which make a project like this possible and to the innovators and leaders who have proven the model. To be sure, the modern publishing industry had been wildly disrupted over the last two decades and that has had mixed results in terms of quality. However, there have been authors who could not enter the field through traditional portals and who have yet proven that their stories deserved to be told and could be told effectively from outside the normal sphere. Without them, the technologists and the authors they liberated, this project would not have been viable and could not possibly have drawn this stunning array of talent.

Also, I must thank all of the editors, authors, and organizations past and present who are not among the current Outliers of Speculative Fiction: those who blazed the trails and created the genres, those who started the magazines and publishing houses and created the ideal of an editor to which I have aspired, those who carried the genres into the mainstream, those who have pushed the boundaries to make the field more diverse and dazzling in story with every decade, those who have battled for other kinds of diversity and to have new voices heard, and those who have weathered the storm publishing has endured during this century and found ways to not just keep speculative fiction alive, but to see it grow to unprecedented heights of reach and popularity. Their work has inspired and motivated me to push for even more voices to be heard and without them I would not be bringing you these stories and visions.

Finally, but not least of all, I wish to thank every author, editor, teacher, and reader who has taken time over the years to help me on my never ending journey to become a better writer.

TABLE OF CONTENTS

Introduction

I find myself writing this introduction in the last hours before we go to press. Of course it makes sense to hold off until I see the book coming into its final form before I comment on it, but, truth be told, I've procrastinated longer than I should have. I think I've been delaying partially because I'm intimidated by the task. It's not the challenge of writing a few paragraphs that gives me pause, of course. On average I write over 100,000 words per year. What has caused me to miss a step has been the momentous nature the book has taken on, the velocity with which it has already gained support and fans, and the truly humbling array of talent that has stepped forward—and all in just a little over 10 weeks.

This project began as a reaction on my part to what I perceived as a loss of productive interaction between authors trying to publish and the editors who make the publishing decisions. I expected this to resonate with other authors who, like myself, have been through what I think of as the "submissions mill" that has arisen in response to the truly mind boggling amount of content being produced. I wanted to provide an outlet that gave the sort of useful feedback and deeper relationship between author and editor that is so hard to come by these days. I did not expect so many authors, with such widely varied careers, nor so many fans to add their voices to the effort. It has both been a vindication and humbling.

Now, little more than two months later I've read a couple of hundred thousand words worth of stories, replied to every one, offered edits both mild and extensive, and arrived here. Some of the stories appear virtually unchanged from what was submitted, but I'm much more proud of the ones that I helped the authors refine, so that they could tell their story and have it be received as they intended. Not every suggestion I made was accepted (by any means) and not every story I edited appears here. Some simply didn't work for the anthology and at least one author disagreed with my changes strenuously enough to withdraw. I admire his conviction in his vision. Two authors who have stories in this volume were originally rejected but came back with an entirely different tale that made it. I think that says something about the openness and value of the process. It was all very hard to do, but well worth it, as I believe you, the readers, will see in the coming pages.

I chose the stories herein based on just one consideration—whether or not I thought the story was, or could be by the time it was published, excellent. And yet, the authors you will read come from wonderfully diverse points of view. I believe that proves the inherent value of diversity, not as social engineering, but for the sake of opening ourselves to the most and best possible stories and ideas, to give ourselves the best chance to experience the wonder of human excellence from wherever it may come.

Our youngest author is 21. The oldest is…well, not 21. Nine of the authors are women, eight are men. They come from the U.S. the U.K., including Scotland, Canada, Germany, Netherlands, India, and Philippines. They are straight and LGBTQ. They represent different races—though I confess I don't know how many since I didn't ask and I haven't even seen some of their faces. Some have been widely published, some are being published for the first time. Some have built solid reputations in the small press or self-publishing while others are well known in the mainstream industry, but for their own reasons are not often published.

More than all of these they are each individual, with unique experiences and influences, and therefore each with a unique lens through which to view worlds real and imaginary. They are not Outliers for reasons of demographics or publishing history, but for their ideas, their voices, and their vision of what speculative fiction can be and do in our world by showing us the worlds of their minds. Their stories are humorous and heartfelt, insightful and whimsical, deadly serious and fun, and above all they are wonder-full. I've been reading spec fiction and been a particular fan of the short story for more than three decades. This collection includes some of the best and most memorable tales from that broad experience.

That, I think, is why I've been slow to introduce the Outliers of Speculative Fiction—I doubt I am qualified to do them justice. I hope that, from this broad and deep selection of styles, topics, and voices, you too will find at least one story that gets into your marrow and travels with you for years to come. I honestly feel like you must, that it is unavoidable given what these authors have laid before you. So, read on and enjoy.

L.A. Little
November 7, 2015

Stepping On Sand & Gods

Cory Skerry

Mila's first contraction woke her from a dreamless sleep. Golden dawn limned the grey bulk of the Sierra Madres. She heaved herself to her feet and grabbed her satchel, sneaking through the house of secondhand lumber. If anyone saw her leave, they would try and stop her.

She looked back once, at the tiny village of Indians who had slowly become Mexicans. Angular plywood hovels had replaced their traditional cottages, and old cars had been gutted for porch furniture. Ranks of two liter soda bottles filled with clean water stood under her family's porch, where the wind had flattened less useful garbage into the crevices of the cinder block supports. The last thing she passed as she left town was the broken pickup truck that the boys always tried to lift when they'd had a lot of corn beer.

They were strong, perhaps, but they would be stronger if they gave up their *chabochiado* t-shirts, their Texan hats, their instant pasta and greasy potato chips. If they said *no* when someone wanted to dump the raw sewage from their hotel into the canyons or grow drugs in what used to be a cornfield.

The outside world had poisoned Mila, too. When her grandmother said there had been a time without scavenging, where people made something if they needed it, Mila craved that life so much she wanted to fight for it. Fighting had never been the way of the Rarámuri, the Fleet of Foot. So Mila would run instead, run back in time, to a place where she didn't scorn herself.

The path into the canyon was no hardship, even with Mila's distended belly. Sunlight warmed her face until one step took her into shadow. Shadow cooled her skin where it prickled with sweat until she climbed back into the sunlight once more. The cycle went on as she hiked deeper into the canyons, stopping every once in a while to clench her fists at the contractions. It was like having her period, but deeper, stronger. She imagined the baby clutching at her muscles and impatiently yanking on them.

When she had not passed a piece of litter for a couple miles, not even a Styrofoam cup or a faded soda can, she stopped. The canyon was small, a baby brother to the easily-accessible vistas the tourists liked most.

Mila's child would not meet the world in a claustrophobic box like the clinic in Creel. "It's safer," Mila's aunt had said, but all Mila could think was that a baby's first breath shouldn't be the same air as the last breath of a sick person.

She removed her skirts and tucked them neatly in the tree, then hesitated. Should she deliver while nude? She wasn't entirely certain how it was done-- traditionally, her mother or sister would have helped her--but she was alone. She decided to keep the shawls, which her mother had sewn by hand, as a substitute for her mother's presence.

The force of the next contraction took her by surprise, and she cried out.

For the first time, Mila wondered if she had been wrong, if this lonely birth would kill her or her baby. Once the pain ebbed away, it was easy enough to convince herself that she had made the right choice. After all, the Rarámuri had lived and birthed and died in the same way for hundreds of years, before plastic and tourism and drug lords.

"Nothing was easy, but it was ours," her grandmother had said. Mila felt the meaning as firmly as she could grasp a rock, and she held it close to her heart like a god made of seven words.

When Mila delivered her perfect, healthy, beautiful baby, they would go to live deeper in the Barranca del Cobre, in the caves, in lean-tos against cliff faces. They would tend arid desert gardens and small orchards of tenacious fruit, and they would hunt fat little mule deer and pebble-eyed rabbits. If it was a daughter, Mila would bury the birth cord here to ensure she grew clever; if it was a son, she would drape his birth cord on a tree limb, to ensure that he became a skillful hunter.

Mila positioned one shawl beneath the acacia, where the baby for which she had such hopes would first touch the world. She lounged beside it and ate a peach while she talked to her child. Just before noon, her water broke.

"When you are born," Mila said, "we will be old Rarámuri together, even if no one else comes with us."

***

El Chupacabra's scaled belly hissed over the hot stone of the Chihuahua desert as he fled Mexico City. Once, when he rested on a particularly large rock, he realized it was the dried corpse of a god.

To a human, perhaps this would appear only an inanimate desert sculpture, but El Chupacabra felt the echoes of the god's thirst ebbing through his bones. Its skin had hardened with the absence of sacrifice; its innards had solidified with the dearth of prayer.

He leapt free, shivering, and angled north, toward the arrogant peaks of the Sierra Madres.

He passed another god several nights later, a decrepit creature hunched over a rural roadkill. The god spread its greasy-feathered raven wings like a tent to hide the desperate way in which it stripped meat from the balding deer's bones. Rulers of the desert for hundreds of years, but now they starved just like the upstart chupacabra, the goat-sucker, the meanest of gods.

He sneaked past the Raven-god.

Mankind had yearned for something new to fear, but, newborn, El Chupacabra was quickly shouldered aside by a legion of smooth steel deities decked in blinking lights. They hummed incomprehensible tunes as they starved him, replacing his short reign of terror with poisonous disdain. He almost preferred the Raven-god, though he didn't even dare think that until he was miles away from its curved claws.

He lost count of the thirsty days, but the terrain became his calendar. Fat, saw-edged agave replaced the fire-barrel cactus, followed closely by fields of crunchy creosote bushes. The desert cement gave way to thin soil and then cliffs of bare rock streaked with bird feces and studded with stranded acacias.

He imagined he felt his skin hardening already, becoming a sedimentary crust. Desert plants would soon take root in the cracks of his body, in his armpits and the fold of flesh between his tail and anus.

One morning, in the rising heat, a shriek of pain cracked through the canyon, leading its echoes like a delicious grouse parading a string of chicks. The wind-borne aroma of wet blood caressed El Chupacabra's snout. His knife-shaped tongue rasped against the roof of his mouth in anticipation as he wended his way through the scrub.

An embroidered shawl the same blue of the morning sky was rumpled high on the shoulders of a human female, leaving bare the rest of her copper-brown body. Her arms, covered in soft fuzz, stretched toward the sun; her hands gripped the acacia's branches.

Her blood sang through her veins in a complex symphony, echoed by a tiny chorus inside her.

She was different from the humans who called him and then abandoned him. He could taste her faith on the air, as strong as the mess streaking down her thighs.

He kneaded the earth with his long claws. He had never tasted faith.

The mother-to-be's breath came faster, and she cried again, unaware of El Chupacabra. When a sack of demulcent flesh finally slid from her loins, El Chupacabra darted forth and snatched it in his jaws.

Sweet, living heat radiated through his bones from the contact, like having the sun in his mouth. He tried to run, but something yanked his prize back into the dirt. There was a funicle joining the infant to its mother. He snapped through the thin flesh with his teeth and picked up his meal again.

As he escaped into the scrub, pain struck El Chupacabra's haunches. The infant cried as he swung his head to glance over his shoulder.

The mother had thrown a knife. It protruded from his hide, almost to the hilt. She stumbled toward him across the uneven ground, wild-eyed with anger, her burnished cheeks plumped by a snarl. Her sweat stank of sour rage, but the only sound she made was the slap of rubber-soled *huaraches* on desert soil.

El Chupacabra limped away.

The infant's wail reverberated down his throat, ghostly thin, like wind passing through a cave. The sounds of the mother faded behind.

A thin film of blood leaked from the punctures made by El Chupacabra's teeth. The intoxicating scent lifted his feet farther and faster. He didn't dare put the infant down here in the open, where a hawk might snatch it away, so he would pluck the knife free once he reached cover.

***

Mila tripped and fell to her hands and knees, unbecoming of Rarámuri, but her abdomen felt swollen and thick, as if she needed to pass stool. She clawed at the hot dirt and pushed. After long minutes, the afterbirth began to peek its way forward.

When it slopped against the ground, she gathered the damp mess into her shawl, careful to keep the spiritually precious birth cord.

She clambered to her feet. Her body wavered as if it were merely heat on the horizon and not flesh at all. Tears blurred her vision, trying to convince her to sit down and cry, but she knew this for a test.

"You want to be Rarámuri?" the desert taunted.

"I *am* Rarámuri," Mila said, and she stumbled forward for a few steps, finding a rhythm on the balls of her feet. She willed herself to feel light, like a seed floating on a breeze. And she watched the ground for droplets of quickly drying blood to mark the path of the mysterious creature that had dared to steal her baby.

She had never before seen anything like it. The monster was the shape of a coyote, but bigger. Thin bones stretched under its skin like an ill-fitting tent of weathered copper scales. It ran on lizard-feet tipped in bouquets of badger-claws.

And it held her precious daughter in its canine jaws.

***

Each breath filled El Chupacabra with the scent of the infant's dwindling life. The sun blistered its delicate flesh, and it ceased crying. His once-vital prize now barely clung to its soul. El Chupacabra's tail lashed against hot rocks as he passed, the beat of an angry drum warding away a chorus of meddling flies, attracted by the scent of blood.

Even if he had been starved by men, he would *not* clutch at the dried up carcasses of mule deer the way some black-feathered gods did. He had never known a true sacrifice, as they once had. There had never been fawning humans for El Chupacabra, only his own wits and luck. So he would make a sacrifice of his own.

El Chupacabra paused. He curled into a circle and plucked the knife free with his fangs before probing at the wound with his tongue, until a crimson froth clustered along its length like an ugly flower. He thrust this foamy gift into the infant's mouth, humiliated by the indignity, but the desert was empty of gods, so there was no one to witness his shame.

The ungrateful baby murmured, disappointed with the mere blood of a god when it could have had its mother's nasty, oozing breast, but as it suckled at his tongue, its heartbeat grew stronger. When it finished consuming El Chupacabra's generosity, with the heat of godblood shining in its veins, it accepted the pain of his teeth with barely a murmur.

He'd barely gone two steps when a rock bounced off of his rump. And then another.

El Chupacabra hissed, peering through the brush to find the mother's determined face staring back. She was naked now, with her stained, meat-stinking shawl in her left hand. Every few seconds, she pulled another rock from within and threw it at El Chupacabra.

He snatched the infant again and dashed deeper into the canyon.

Every time El Chupacabra thought he had lost the mother, she caught up to him, and in this way they rolled through the rough terrain as the sun rolled through the sky.

Even in the waning heat of the afternoon, the mother didn't falter. Her fear fed him some, tiny prayers making their way to his gut from behind him, but her thoughts were less like pleas and more like indigestible hate and determination.

At last, dusk fatally wounded the canyon. The walls bled shadow in great black stains, reaching for El Chupacabra. Behind him, the mother rustled through the brush without care for scorpions or snakes, blind and desperate.

With his reptilian eyes, he could still see the baby, but in the darkness it now seemed a misshapen gourd with many wounds marring its pale surface. The drug of his blood and the rhythm of his gait had lulled it, and it now slept in his jaws.

The mother rustled off to the northwest, so he angled straight east, toward the welcoming darkness.

He would be glad to leave this land without horizons, bordered by forest-clad cliffs and filled with crazy humans who could run like gods.

Suddenly, warm metal pressed against his neck, and a rubber sole crushed his tail against the hard earth. She must have thrown more rocks, to trick him into thinking she was elsewhere.

"Put my baby on the ground, or I will kill you, kuchíwari," the mother said. She spoke in a language older than El Chupacabra, older than the trees that surrounded them.

With a sigh, El Chupacabra relinquished what would have been his last meal.

The rock beneath them, he saw, had once had eyes, though they had been closed long enough to collect seams of yellow dirt. Perhaps some day another god would die on top of El Chupacabra, and in this way, they would build a monument to their collective defeat.

***

Mila's foot felt huge on the monster's knobby tail. She felt she might crack his fragile bones beneath her weight.

"The desert is vicious," she said to the desert's agent. It was important that it carry this message. "But I *want* it that way."

Her knife hand shook as she collected her daughter, because she had to put both her hands near the monster's face. When she had her baby safely tucked under her left arm, she stepped off of the monster's tail.

Between them, illuminated by metallic moonlight, Mila caught sight of a pair of identical seams in the rock. Outcroppings jutted up like bones; ridges on the side could have been ribs. There was a weathered beak and stubs where two ears had crumbled away in the weather.

The monster crouched on top of this stone carcass, its body tortured into the same angular shape. In the settling dark, its coppery scales were as dim as the stone on which it perched.

"Go back to the city," Mila commanded. "Go back to your father and his wicked children."

The little god shook its head.

Mila's stomach hurt. Not a mere beast, then, but another outcast, a sentient being.

The heat of the ground was still rising, but within the hour, it would be deadly cold.

"I am sunburned and thirsty and I have nowhere to sleep tonight and only one dry shawl to keep my baby warm. Instead of losing her, I've perhaps lost myself as well, because of you."

No wonder her people shrank away instead of standing their ground. Understanding blossomed in her heart, and she shivered. Maybe fighting would make her strong, but for how long?

If they survived this, perhaps she wouldn't settle quite so far from her people. Her tears escaped and rolled off of her face.

The little god suddenly looked down at the dead god upon which it stood.

The earth trembled.

Mila backed away, her daughter clutched tightly in her arms. The awakening desert god's stone body shuddered. It shed a hail of black pebbles, silhouetted against the lighter blue of the night horizon.

The little god leapt free, landing near Mila.

"You thought you were finished?" the desert taunted.

Mila set her teeth and picked her way through the brush, trying not to turn her back on either of the gods.

When the desert god moved, the rock crumbled and exposed raw, dark flesh beneath, bled cascades of thin black fluid onto the hard soil below.

The little god placed itself between the desert god and Mila, its mouth open, its fangs bared. Something warm stirred in her heart, but she crushed it with hate. That little thing had tried to kill her daughter. Had poured out her child's blood, or maybe its own blood, and the red song had soaked deep into the stone and awakened something terrible.

The desert god wheezed a breath that stank of dusty meat and forgotten stories. A faded red glow floated in the darkness. It was an eye, creaking open against the weight of ages.

***

The stupid human wasn't throwing rocks now, El Chupacabra noticed, not when it would be useful. The awakening god dusted soil from its lanky arms, each movement cracking its stone skin. The oily mess of its ancient blood flooded toward him across the ground, shunned by even the thirstiest of desert plants. It was the milk of death, and El Chupacabra winced as it stung his claws.

He had been born and discarded, suffered and fought, but he'd survived. And now someone who had already lost the game would cheat his way back in. The dead god would drink El Chupacabra, would suck the goatsucker. The dead god, the cheater, stepped out of the earth. Its head angled down, staring at El Chupacabra with a hunger he didn't ever want to know.

El Chupacabra howled as he leapt forward and sunk his fangs into the red smear of the cheater's eye. The cheater shook its head, trying to fling El Chupacabra free. The violence shook loose a cascade of stone scabs, bouncing off El Chupacabra's hide and scattering like the pellet shot of disrespectful farmers. El Chupacabra hung, his fangs hooked in the dead god's eye socket, and scrabbled at its neck and throat. His claws peeled off the rock where it had clotted old wounds. Thin black godblood poured down his belly. It burned, but he kept digging his long claws into its dense, clay-like flesh.

The cheater swiped at him with its broken finger stubs. His foot ripped away another slab of immortal meat. When the cheater slapped at him, it struck itself in the face. Its petrified skeleton was too brittle to take the force of its own blow, and its head came off with El Chupacabra still attached.

They slammed into the dirt together. When El Chupacabra lifted his head, he realized one of his fangs was gone. One left with which to suck goats. And only three legs to chase them, because one of his hind legs was pinned beneath the stone skull of the cheater. The light in its red eye was extinguished.

El Chupacabra bled into the desert, tired and defeated and still faintly smug over his unlikely victory. Perhaps the mother would tell tales of his prowess. His ghost could sup on that small adulation.

She approached, her footsteps hesitant at first, but gaining in confidence. The godblood must not sting her the way it had stung him.

She kicked the skull off of his leg, and everything went white.

***

Mila crouched beside the motionless little god.

"I came out here to be part of the desert. Maybe you did too."

The little god nodded. Mila hoped it wasn't lying, that it meant this, that it wanted to take the place of that desperate monster they'd awoken together.

Her throat hurt, but it let her words by. "We might die, but we'll do what we came to do."

Mila cut the trailing birth cord from her daughter's belly, and collected the other from her soaked shawl. She held both halves out to the god.

"Honor us by swallowing this. I want my daughter to run between the worlds as you do, *chabochiado* yet a part of the desert. She will be clever and a hunter, a Rarámuri who can survive what may come."

***

El Chupacabra thrust his chest forward and tipped up his chin. As the funicles slid down his gullet, a warmth spread through his guts. His worship had been fear and blood, but now, tangled in this limp bit of flesh, he tasted something else.

His leg mended in that wave of purity. He didn't grow a new fang, but the hole stopped aching. He poked it with his tongue for a few moments, then followed the woman as she strode through the brush.

As long as the pair of them lived, he would never starve.

Cory Skerry lives in the Pacific Northwest, where he goes exploring with his sweet, goofy pit bulls and any friends who can keep up. He writes impossible things and paints what he shouldn't. When his current meatshell begins to fall apart, he'd like science to put his brain into a giant killer octopus body, with which he'll be very responsible and not even slightly shipwrecky. Pinky swear. For more about him and his work, visit coryskerry.net.

While I did my best to research and respect the culture of the Rarámuri (also referred to as the Tarahumara), this is a work of fiction and not an accurate reflection of real Tarahumaran people or life. Anyone who feels like reaching out to me about what I may have gotten wrong (or right) will be doing me a greatly appreciated favor.

No Other

Tim Jeffreys

All that I've done, I've done for her.

Since we can live anywhere we choose to now we decided on a house by the beach. It's a huge rambling house which must once have been occupied by a wealthy family with a lot of offspring, as quite a few of the rooms are painted in bright primary colours only a child could tolerate. Of course, nothing works anymore. There's no heating – which is partly why we travelled as far south as we could before meeting the ocean; and for light we have to rely on candles which are increasingly difficult to source. The plumbing worked for a while, until one day I pressed the toilet flush and heard an ominous bellow from the pipes throughout the house. Now we dig holes in the back lawn and use those, filling them in after we're done.

Also, some of the walls in the house feel wet to the touch. Damp will set in when winter comes. We might have to move on then. Despite the wealth of space, we've ended up occupying only two rooms on the top floor. These two rooms hadn't been furnished when we arrived, so had - in our minds - belonged to no one before us. It made us feel a bit less like intruders, I suppose. In truth, the idea that anyone could ever have *owned* anything I now find absurd; but after we settled here Dawn said all the other rooms in the house felt haunted. She especially avoided the children's bedrooms and asked me to make sure the doors to these rooms always stayed closed. I had no problem with this. It's not the size of the house I like, but the spectacular views it allows across the sea from its highest windows. There are days when I can sit and stare at the view for hours. I think about the family that used to live here; all those children running and laughing down on the beach on sunny days. That makes me smile. I wonder if Dawn and I will ever have a child, or children, which Dawn says is our duty even though I can see the idea scares her half to death. She says she always thought her mother would be with her if she ever had a child. Nothing's happened yet though, despite all the unprotected sex. Sometimes I wonder if it's our fear that prevents a pregnancy; or perhaps there's something physically wrong with one or both of us that stops it happening. Wouldn't that be a kick in the pants for the human race? Only two people left alive after the outbreak. As luck would have it they were a man and a woman, but ironically they were both infertile. How *funny*, right?

Why us? Out of all the billions of people that had once lived on Earth, why us? Dawn says that statistically there have to be other survivors out there, maybe in another country, somewhere cut off from the rest of the world, somewhere the virus hadn't found its way to. Or, most likely – she says – there are other people with immunity. Why, she says, should there have only been two survivors, who lived a relatively short distance apart so that they'd been able to find each other, a man and a woman, a new Adam and Eve? Didn't that seem incredible? I would admit to her that it did seem incredible, but the world feels different to me these days. It feels the same way this house we live in felt when we first arrived. I hadn't needed to check every room to know that there was nobody home. I just sensed it.

Returning to the house today as the sun sinks into the sea at my back, I glance up at the window of our bedroom and see Dawn. Catching her attention, I smile and hold up the day's catch for her to see: a good sized bass. In my other hand I'm carrying a plastic bottle I've filled from the freshwater stream we discovered in some woodland a few miles away. All this foraging and hunting has toned up my body some. I wonder if this makes me more appealing. From the window, Dawn only watches me. Her face and her stance remain pensive. It's as if she's forgotten who I am. More and more these days she's prone to melancholy moods and weeping. She's fixed on the idea of finding other people. "There *must* be more people out there somewhere!" she says. "Maybe we can take a boat and cross the Channel. Maybe there are people left alive in Europe. Somewhere! It *can't* just be the two of us."

Though I know she doesn't say these things to hurt me, I can't help wondering why I'm not enough for her. I know it's stupid to think that way. Personally, I've never been a people person. I'd be quite happy for Dawn and I to live out the rest of our lives alone. Let the human race end. I don't long for conversation. All I have is this diary, which I hide under a loose floorboard and scribble in when Dawn's asleep. It's a way of communicating; but only with myself. It helps me make sense of things. Maybe what Dawn really wants is to find another man who can give her that baby she so desperately thinks she should provide. Just thinking about her with someone else fills me with a kind of cold, impotent fury. When we first met I thought she would fall for me. I thought it was inevitable. I'm older after all. I've seen the world. I know how to take care of her. I see no sign of love though, unless you count the sex which I know she does more out of duty and a need for comfort rather than any deep feelings. Instead, it's me who has fallen deeply for her. The physical attraction was immediate, but I initially took her for some airhead blonde. Every day, though, I peel away new layers and find something unexpected underneath. I hope sometimes that it's the same for her, that she looks into me, finds something new in me. Other times, I think I'd prefer to remain a mystery. Keep her wanting to discover more. It's easy for me as I've never been much of a talker. "Every man's a chasm. It makes you dizzy when you look down in." That's a quote Dawn told me from some German writer from the nineteenth century. I forget his name. You wouldn't think to look at her that she could have such things just floating about in her head.

When I reach our rooms on the top floor, I find her mood has improved and she's sitting on the bed with her arms folded.

"The sirens in the cove," she says before I can speak. "Did you find them?"

This is a game we play. Dawn found a big book on mythology in the library downstairs and read it from cover to cover. Then she invented these games. One week she was Danae and I Zeus, come to shower her in gold. Another week I was a besotted Lancelot returned from a quest and she my queen, Guinevere. Today I am an infatuated Ulysses and she Circe on her island. Perhaps out of respect, she avoids the myths from my own culture. I will never be Rama come with my army of monkeys to rescue Sita from the demons. That one I think I'd quite enjoy. Sometimes it occurs to me how all these stories from the past, all these myths, could now so easily be lost. If I was to burn all the books in the library downstairs, which I might have to do when the cold weather sets in, and let all the other books out there in the world rot we could turn the page, and let it be blank. Start again. But these games, this play-acting, it makes Dawn happy. Sometimes I wonder if it's her way of not acknowledging me, the real me – pretending I'm someone else, a knight, a hero, someone more desirable.

"I found them," I tell her, setting the fish and the bottle of water down on a low table. "They had the bodies of birds, but the faces of women. Unspeakable things they were. I slaughtered them all and left their corpses lying there amongst their treasure."

"But why? Why did you slaughter them?"

I shrug. "Their screeching bothered me."

Dawn's face shows a hint of amusement, but she remains in character.

"But were they not beautiful? Were their faces not the most beautiful faces you had ever seen?"

"Not as beautiful as yours."

Dawn smiles. After this, she beckons me to the bed and lets me lie down beside her. Gingerly, she removes the hunting knife from my belt and tosses it to the floor. Then, slowly, we undress each other. We stay in character until it's over. There was a time, I know, when Dawn would not have looked at me twice. Back when she was a student of English Literature and a part-time swimwear model. At just twenty-one, or so she estimates, she's twenty-two years my junior. But calendars are obsolete now; days and weeks and years unchecked. We could be any age. I wonder, though, what Dawn might have said if I'd hit on her in our previous lives. *Not if you were the last man on Earth?* Ha! More irony.

When it's over, Dawn rolls on to her side and gazes at the dead fish lying upon the table on the other side of the room. Other days I have brought back rabbits, birds, once a squirrel, all of which she helped to cook and ate, despite telling me she'd been a vegetarian before the outbreak. Thankfully the virus didn't affect the animals.

"You kill so easily," she says. "I don't think I could ever kill anything, even if my life depended on it."

I never told her that I used to be a soldier, that I was trained to kill, trained to survive. Lieutenant Nishi Kapoor – that was me. I thought it wouldn't suit her ideas about me, so I lied and said that before the outbreak I was a primary school teacher. So not only does she force me to pretend and play her games, I've reinvented myself in order to please her. Well, why not? There's no one left to point out the lie. I can be anyone I want to be, anyone *she* wants me to be.

"It's survival. Self-preservation. If I wasn't here, you'd be surprised at what you'd do. What you'd have to do."

"Oh no, I couldn't kill anything. I couldn't do it. I think I'd rather starve."

"Then you're lucky I'm here."

She makes no response to this. In time she takes up another subject. A familiar subject.

"Have you thought anymore about that idea I had, about finding a boat and sailing to France? I'm sure between us we could work out how to sail. There might be people alive on the continent. Maybe in Spain…"

"Neither of us have the first idea how to sail a boat." Secretly I'm ashamed at how easily the lies come. "We'd end up drowned. Is that what you want?"

"But how hard can it be? Really?"

"Do you want to drown, Dawn?"

There's a long silence before she huffs and says: "It might be preferable. At least I'd have *hope*."

These words are like a knife twisted into my chest.

How did I end up this way? How could I have fallen so deeply in love with her? How could I have put myself in a position where I can be hurt by a few careless words? I am the last man living.

At some point during the night she shakes me awake.

"What? What is it?"

Leaning over me, she says: "I need to ask you something. I don't know why I've never asked before. Were you married once? Before the outbreak?"

"Married?" I stare into the twilight dark, searching for her face. "Yes. Yes, I was married." The truth for once. It must be my half-sleeping state. She caught me off-guard.

"What was your wife's name?"

"Deepa."

Dawn is silent a moment. "Did you have any children?"

"Children. No. No, we had no children. It was an arranged marriage. We never really…she wasn't really…" I am regaining my senses. "She died. She got sick and…What is all this?"

But Dawn doesn't answer. With a sigh, she falls back against the pillows, muttering something to herself. It sounds like what she says is: "We are the damned."

None of this makes any sense to me, until I wake the next morning. Dawn is already gone from the bed, but I notice a few drops of blood on the sheet where she'd been lying.

For the time being, there will be no baby.

The next day's mission is to visit some of the houses on the far side of the wood to see what I can find that might be useful to us. I've already ransacked all the houses in the immediate vicinity. I make a mental note of what essentials to look for as I set out: soap, candles, tinned food, medicines, weaponry. I haven't yet shown Dawn my cache of weapons, which I keep in one of those brightly painted bedrooms she insists she'll never enter. I doubt it's ever occurred to her that if by some miracle there are other people left alive, chances are they won't be friendly. Today, as always, I have my hunting knife tucked into my belt. Dawn thinks it's just for hunting. It would never occur to her to think otherwise.

Dawn watches from our bedroom window as I walk away. She doesn't ask about my forages anymore, just reels of a list of things she'd like me to bring back for her – tampons and toiletries and such. Today, she emphasised tampons. It's as if she thinks I'm nipping out to the supermarket. I don't know what I'll find. She'll have to learn to make do. There was a time when she used to ask me questions when I returned. "Were there…bodies?" she'd say. What could I tell her? I'd usually just shrug.

The woods are quiet. It gives me an odd sort of comfort knowing I won't encounter another human being. It's just me and the birds. This calm brings back memories of a time when it was not so calm. The virus spread so quickly. For a time we only heard about it on the news. It was contained to certain parts of India. Nothing for us to trouble ourselves over. In the west we were safe, or so they said. An outbreak was impossible. Our health systems were too strong. Then westerners started getting sick. A case in Spain, a case in America. They said they could contain it, but soon more people started showing signs of contamination and after that it couldn't be stopped. People were panicking. Self-preservation. It's amazing what a person will do, just to survive. I try hard not to think about those times, but every so often the memories swarm over me like a migraine.

What I told Dawn about my wife, Deepa, wasn't strictly true. She never got sick. Never showed any signs. She was injured though in the panic. Damaged her leg. She couldn't walk. I kept her at home and cared for her. Until that day. That day when I was out on my own looking for supplies and instead I found Dawn.

It was an arranged marriage. It wasn't love.

The virus changed everything. All the rules and constrictions we'd formally lived by were wiped away. What is marriage anyway except a conceit?

Before we were introduced Deepa had loved someone else, even become pregnant by him and been forced to have an abortion. I don't think she ever recovered from this. She too longed for a child.

I wonder sometimes what became of her. Sometimes I imagine she's still lying there in bed waiting for me to come home.

But that can't be. Something would have got to her by now. The virus. Something.

Once I've left the wood, I search a few of the houses I encounter until I come upon a pretty little cottage. Apart from the overgrown garden, you'd think someone still lived there. It looks so perfect I'm reluctant to break a window in order to get inside. Luckily, I find one window at the back of the house is already broken. Entering, I find that the place immediately feels homey. I can imagine myself living here with Dawn. But no. We need high places, vantage points. There's a smell inside that I can't describe, but which I've smelt before. It grows stronger as I approach a particular room; a room I decide not to look in. Turning I enter a small bathroom. There are rust stains around the taps on the sink and spider's webs in the shower cubicle. Without pausing to think, I toss what I find into my holdall and then I'm on to another room. It's a sitting room. My rummaging unearths nothing useful. There's a thick book about art on the coffee table, which I think Dawn might enjoy. I wonder if it's worth taking the book at the cost of something more practical, just to see Dawn's face when I hand it to her. It's as I'm deliberating that I hear a noise.

Holding my breath, I turn about on the spot. I listen. What I'd heard had seemed to come from the next room which I imagined was the kitchen, my next port of call. Kitchens were where the real bounty's often lay. I usually looked for them first. As quietly as I can I set the art book back down on the coffee table, and pluck the knife from my belt. Then I move to the kitchen with the knife held out in two hands in front of me. When I reach the kitchen, I'm so shocked by what I find there that I stand for a few moments blinking, unable to believe what I am seeing.

Staring back at me with wide eyes and palms held out in front of them in a gesture of *don't shoot* are two boys. One is tall, and perhaps eighteen or nineteen years old, although his face has a scruff of beard which makes him look older. The other's shorter, younger – not quite old enough to miss shaving. Both have long, unwashed fair hair which hangs over their eyes and down to their collars. Their clothes are ragged, dirty. My guess is that they are brothers. They look so alike. Though undernourished, they look strong, the kind of boys who preferred sports to books, although who knows? Maybe they liked both. Once. They press against the work surface at the end of the kitchen, leaning back and staring at me. Maybe they too had thought themselves that last people alive on Earth. Or maybe it was the knife in my hand.

"Don't hurt us," the older one says. "Everything's cool. This your house, mister? Is this your house?"

"No."

"We were looking for food. Something to eat. There's nothing here. We've looked. There's nothing."

"How many of you are there?"

For a second the older boy, after glancing at his companion, looks at me as if he thinks I'm crazy. Then he realises what I mean.

"We're alone. I'm Dan. This is George. We're from Kendal. You know Kendall, in the Lake District? We've walked all the way here. It took months. I don't know how long. You're the first person we've seen in all that time. Alive, I mean. We should stick together, man. Help each other, you know?"

Standing there, I think about how happy Dawn would be if I returned home with these two boys. Here was something better than books, better than tampons and toiletries and perfume. People. Other people. How her face would light up. But then my mind is immediately besieged with unpleasant ideas, things it pains me to think about.

"We cool?" asks the older boy again.

It's late when I arrive back at the house by the beach. Upstairs, I discover Dawn lying on the bed, in no mood for role-play. She doesn't look at me, her eyes are far-away and glassy. Standing over her, I reach into the holdall and take out the art book.

"Here," I say, dropping it down on the mattress beside her. "I found this. Thought you might enjoy it."

She doesn't look. Doesn't raise her head. As I turn away, I hear her speak.

"There must be more people, Nishi. Somewhere. There must."

"There isn't."

With my back to her, I remove the hunting knife from my belt. Unsheathing the blade, I examine it for a few seconds, then wipe it on my pants a few times for good measure before re-sheathing it and setting it down on the table. It's amazing what a person will do, just to survive. When I turn around again, I see that Dawn has raised herself a little and she's watching me very closely with a look almost of suspicion on her face. I stand still until she drops her eyes.

I decide to try something. "The sirens..."

"Don't."

There are a few long moments of silence then.

"Tomorrow *I'll* go looking," she says. "I have to do something. I'll go crazy sitting here by myself day after day. I need other people. Someone to *talk* to."

This time, her words seemed chosen to inflict hurt. Little atomic bombs.

"You're wasting your time. There's only us left. Anyway, hell is other people. You told me that, remember?"

"I didn't say that. It's a quote. From Sartre. From his play, No Exit." She's silent for a while then, her face thoughtful. Then as if an idea had sprang into her mind, she sat up, her eyes searching the room and then settling on the table where I had placed my hunting knife.

"It's true though," I say casually, hiding my unease. "Don't you think?"

"No," she says, lifting herself up off the bed. "This. This right here. This is hell."

She rushes at me then, but no – not at me, at the table. Grabbing up my hunting knife, she pulls off the sheath and turns the blade on herself, intending – I see at once - to plant it into her own chest. I can see the fierce determination in her eyes. I only just manage to stop her, to get the knife out of her grasp. Then she screams at me and falls face down on the bed, sobbing and flailing hysterically.

I do what I always do at times like this. I sit down beside her and stroke her back until she calms.

"It's all right," I say, soothingly. "Don't worry. You've got me. Everything will be all right. We don't need anyone else. We can be happy, just the two of us. I'll look after you. I'll take care of you whatever happens. I'd never leave you."

My gaze shifts to the window. I watch as the sun drowns in the wide ocean.

Tim Jeffreys is the author of five collections of short stories, the most recent being 'From Elsewhere', and a couple of novellas, 'The Haunted Grove' and 'The Foundering'. Another novella, 'Voids', co-written with Martin Greaves will be published by Omnium Gatherum Media in early 2016. His short fiction has appeared in various small press anthologies and magazines. He also edits and compiles the Dark Lane Anthologies where he gets to publish talented writers from all over the world. In his own work he incorporates elements of horror, fantasy, absurdist humour, science-fiction and anything else he wants to toss into the pot to create his own brand of weird fiction. Tim is also a talented artist and gained a university honours degree in Graphic Arts and Design in 2000.

Originally from Oldham, UK, Tim moved 'down south' over a decade ago and now lives in Bristol with his partner Isabel and his two daughters. He remains a northerner at heart, misses the rain, and, like most other writers he knows, dreams of one day giving up the day job. Visit him online at www.timjeffreys.blogspot.co.uk.

Reflections from Mirror World #57

Cat Rambo

I picked the wrong superpower. Superspeed, you'd think that was pretty cool and it was -- in theory. You could get a lot done -- in theory.

But in fact? Not so. Everyone else is moving and speaking so slow that you could read an encyclopedia in the time it takes your neighbor to say hello. So much for that.

Sure, if you didn't have to interact with other, slower people, that'd be fine.

But the fact of the matter is, you have to deal with them, have to wait what seems like a few decades in the line at the post office or a week watching the laundromat lady give you your change.

So much isn't fast, so much of life would be a thousand times better at superspeed, but it's not.

Physics, plain old physics, hems even the fastest turtle in, corrals a speedster and sends him down a long dull corridor called Time.

Superspeed? Superyawn, more like it.

***

People are tired of Super. Everything is the awesomest, the bestest, the cats-pjs-est. Instead, we're going plebian with our noms de guerre. Meet Anonymous and Dirt Lass, Captain Dung and everyone's favorite, Lowly Worm.

***

It was a wham-bang, whiz-snot of a breakfast, stacked with buckwheat pancakes guaranteed to make you impervious to snoop rays and to keep you regular as Clockwork Lad as well.

There were carrots for sharp eyes and iron for strong teeth and element 236 – 64 for stray psychotelepathic abilities. There were eggs harvested from the great Tiki-Tiki Bird, gathered on the slopes of the sun and garnished with hummingbird bills like monochromatic needles.

Space Age Bliss Juice! Coffee strained with runes, toast as black as the heart of evil. Satan's jelly strawberry bright in a teaspoon.

Captain Ajax shook cereal into a bowl and read the box.

"Fantas-tee-ohs!" it said. "Guaranteed with Vim and Vigor in every Vite!"

"Vite?" he wondered, and poured in milk strained through promises of nightmares, white as charity, pure as lambchops, unprecedented as a triple-off coupon, and settled in to read the news and see which villains had been released from prison that morning.

***

The thing is this. We've run out of names. We can pretend, but really it's ridiculous: Captain Courage, Madam Courage, Mr. Courage, Sister Courage, Courage Chum and Courage Jones.

Sure, there's the nonsense crowd: the Jellicle Bum and Stumblin' Adam. Mrs. Mixadoodle and the Lalalamster. But they're so hard to remember, makes Justice Legion rollcall like yelling out a Mother Goose rhyme.

My proposal? Consolidate. All the Courages can be just Courage. It'll make the Fantasy Leagues more complicated, sure, but that's just a bunch of fans living basements. As for the government stipend, they can sort that out by Social Security number.

Let the villains be as complicated as they like. It just trips them up, in the end.

***

The saddest superhero was Mr. Miracle, because people didn't believe in miracles anymore. They rationalized it all, talked in terms of scientific breakthroughs, ergs and lumens and memes.

They said what he did could be explained when you looked at the subatomic particles. They didn't say anything about angels dancing there, which was how he'd always imagined his powers. Tiny angels dancing, spinning, generating the force that fueled his punches, his leaps, his eye blast, which were certainly tiny angels flying forward like microscopic bullets, hands clasped together in front of themselves as though diving, falling into the face of evil to barrage it with a red and burning glow.

No angels. No one said anything about that. But he still wanted to believe in them. So he pretended to believe in science but didn't tell anyone he was pretending, which made him sad.

But he would have been even sadder to see the tiny angels go away.

***

Look, the names thing is important. Here's why.

How else is a hero to know they're a hero? How else is it that they're going to know what they do, who they are? Abstract names are all very good and well, but they don't give any sort of instructions.

Without names, it's all the same really. As though they were just reflections of us. Their masks more colorful, that's all.

That's all.

Cat Rambo lives, writes, and teaches high on a hill in West Seattle. Her fiction publications include stories in Asimov's, Clarkesworld Magazine, and Tor.com. Her short story, "Five Ways to Fall in Love on Planet Porcelain," from her story collection Near + Far (Hydra House Books), was a 2012 Nebula nominee. Her editorship of Fantasy Magazine earned her a World Fantasy Award nomination in 2012. She is the current President of SFWA (the Science Fiction and Fantasy Writers of America). For more about her, as well as links to her fiction, see http://www.kittywumpus.net

Story notes: Superheroes fascinate me. I'm a long-time comic book reader and that fascination led me to make them one of my foci in grad school. I've managed to throttle back the weekly addiction, but I still love to write about them, and recent developments, like G. Willow Wilson's Ms. Marvel and new stuff like Spidey-Gwen seem to be luring me back.
This piece centers on the idea of superheroes, names, and identities, which play out differently for the superpowered, yet in a way that still illuminates our own less costume-dependent lives

.

Liminal Hill

Kelly Dwyer

"You smoke that shit, your skin gonna fall off."

Lim, taking a long drag, was pretty sure that was a load of crap. These new bio-neutral synthetics had come out while he was down in the deep freeze. His flesh had suffered through nicotine withdrawal in those five years, but his brain had defrosted still craving the real stuff. The stuff that turned your lungs that classic shade of black. These tasted sweeter, like those fruity designer analogs they'd tried marketing to desperate celebrities a long while ago. Like you were smoking a fucking rose bush.

"Yeah, yeah. And my teeth will turn green and my kids will have four eyes. You're just jealous, Raul. Get out here and light one up, or leave me alone."

The janitor leaned against the open door and shook his head. "Naw, can't do it, man. Mites in the lungs, ya know? Shouldn't even be breathing your dirty air. And you shouldn't be out here neither, Lim. It ain't on your rounds."

Lim ignored him and concentrated on his aim. The squirrel's body hung on one of the cables that suspended the fly-over cameras above the parking lot and around the perimeter of the lab building. One of the cameras was repeatedly bumping up against the sizzling, blackened rodent corpse and emitting a piercing beep every time it was unable to complete its loop. Lim didn't really care whether he hit the camera or the squirrel, just as long as it shut that noise up. The perfectly chiseled lump of volcanic rock from the building's immaculately sculptured landscaping flew true and knocked the carcass in the head, sending it splattering to the ground. It was something Lim was all too familiar with - how juicy death could be.

He stubbed out the cigarette on the arch of his new boots; steel-toed, reinforced, with slick rubber treads that scuffed up the polished lobby floors when he did his rounds. Pissed off Raul to no end, finding ovals of long black lines across the pale pink granite. Antagonizing his ever-present babysitter had become a moral imperative for Lim over the past month.

"Quit checking on me. I'm fine." Lim yanked the door shut on the way in and brushed past Raul's obese form with difficulty in the narrow back hallway.

"Electrical's been surging because of that thing shorting out the line. Wasn't able to get the game on downstairs." Raul tapped the back of his neck. Lim was sick of the janitor bragging about the cheap-ass network he set up to stream soaps and porn via his link while he worked. "Didn't know if you were fixing it or just scarecrowing out and walking into a wall over and over again tonight."

"I told you, I'm fine." Lim ground his teeth and spit the words over his shoulder. The clattering sound of the cleaning cart, sloshing mop water and bouncing aerosol cans, followed him out into the lobby. Lim shrugged toward the handheld TV on the security desk. "Be my guest. Slum it up here old-school."

When his parole officer had suggested that working private security might be his only option, Lim had been less than pleased. His grip on reality might have been thin, but it still pissed him off to be the poster boy of success for the Cryopsych rehab/replay program. Problem was, there wasn't any gainful employment to be found in his former line of work. The criminal underworld had dried up while Lim had been frozen, and it made him very, very nervous. He had to admit that the job wasn't really that bad, decent medical benefits and all. He knew he'd have to suck it up while he put his head back in order, if he ever could, but the idea of going straight chaffed him almost as much as the wool blazer and tie. *I hate this fucking tie.*

It felt good to walk after sitting in the stiff-backed chair at the security desk, staring at the same blank walls and windows, out into the dark of the night for hours on end. He didn't have to go far on his rounds, just a loop around the outer perimeter of the building, and then up the elevator and down the primary emergency stairs, checking each floor as he went. If he wasn't so sure that he'd be hassled all night by Raul and cited by his boss for breaching job protocol, he would have walked up the stairs instead of down. Cryopsych was a stickler for rules. The one time he'd tried to sneak into the company gym in the basement, the whole building went into lock down, strobes and quick drop metal doors and all that song and dance. Trying to get back into shape after the years of being popsicled was killing him. He felt like his lungs were going to explode just climbing up the ramp to the front door.

They'd given him court-ordered physical therapy once he'd been paroled. Mostly consisted of a cute young nurse stripping him down to his inadequately-sized prison-standard boxers and pasting electrodes over his major muscle groups. If it hadn't hurt so much, he would have enjoyed himself a lot more. She'd been the first woman he'd seen in half a decade. Well, besides Dani, in the replays. Lim bit his tongue hard and tasted bile in the back of his throat. *Shut that shit down, you idiot.*

15 minutes around the perimeter, keeping his mind focused on multiplication tables and saying the alphabet backwards to clear his head, and he was inside nodding to Raul at the desk and up the elevator. Check the roof, check the door, check the lock, check, check, check. The metal edging on the stairs clanged under the toes of his boots. Open door, 10th floor, check.

The silver paint of the company logos was flecking off the walls of the stairwell, revealing strange curving patterns underneath. His nails picked at the paint, his eyes seeing the silver teeth on Dani's zippered jumpsuit, dotted freckles on smooth blushing skin just underneath. Dani, tangles of red hair floating in the hazy light of sunset streaming through broken glass, her eyes wide but not seeing him, that trickle of sweat between the tensed tendons on her neck, turning, gone.

Damn it. His head exploded with stabbing pain and he grabbed the railing and squeezed his eyes shut. It was getting worse. Every time he tried to reach back to some time before it all, to put the pieces together of who the hell he was, what the hell he was supposed to be doing, Lim felt his grip on reality slip a little further. It was harder and harder to stop the playback shock when it took over. Scarecrowing, frozen stiff and hung out to dry, stuck in a nightmare with crows pecking your eyes out. One of these days he was going to scarecrow it right down several flights of stairs.

Itching the bandaged plug at the base of his skull, Lim wished there was a way to activate it out of observer-only mode, to prove that there really was something wrong with his head and that he needed help. No one believed him though, not his PO, not the discharge doc at the jail. Of course the Cryopsych replay/rehab program works perfectly, they said. And who cares about another ex-con who deserves every ounce of misery he gets. Or all those other ex-cons who scarecrowed themselves right into oncoming traffic. Or a bullet in a firefight. Just like...

9th floor, check. 4096, 8192, 16300 and four or something. Even though he was walking down the stairs, his lungs were starting to wheeze a bit. Resting against the railing on the 8th floor, he tried to remember what it was like to have a six pack and the endurance of a street runner. His body didn't feel like it fit him anymore, this sagging, bulging, weak blob of flesh. He cursed the wardens for skipping the legally required exercise breaks and nerve tune-ups. Hadn't been cost effective for them to unplug him every month for a walk around an empty prison courtyard. Just left him slotted in there to rot. Even the cheap rinky-dink tracking anklet that Cryopsych forced him to put on every night to evaluate his performance and efficiency was too tight on its largest setting, threatening to pop off every waddling, jiggling step he took.

Lim was aware of the sonic reverb of a single gunshot from the bottom of the stairs before the metallic ping of it reached all the way up to where he stood. The sound was too distorted for him to peg the exact weapon, but it was certainly something high powered. Something nasty.

He considered his options, and they weren't looking great. If someone was down there shooting, they'd probably have picked this exact time to come in the front, thinking that the security desk would be unmanned. The lab rooms on all the floors were locked, and he figured opening a door would tip off anyone who had linked into the security system. Stranding himself on the roof was a suicide move, as was taking the elevator down. That just left the stairs then, though they'd surely know he was coming. Quietly and slowly.

Reaching the bottom floor, lungs burning, he took a steadying breath and slid along the wall closest to the entry door to the lobby. His fingers had just grasped the door handle when a bright voice from behind him piped up.

"Well, that's just about the ugliest fucking tie I've ever seen.

***

They were an organized crew, as far as Lim could tell. Worked together like they'd been doing this a while. The little one that had caught him in the stairs was hefting Raul's furiously thrashing and cuff-bound body into a chair like it weighed no more than a bottle of whiskey. He looked closer at her arms bulging out of the black T-shirt she was wearing. Grafts, and lots of them. Or a hyped up adrenal. Or both.

Lim was loath to admit it, but he was rather enjoying watching the four of them work. Two of the crew were linked into the security system and cameras. The little one secured his hands in front with an effective depilatory combination of duct tape and plastic cuffs and sat him in the second swivel chair behind the desk.

And the leader was trying to coerce him to give up the security codes for the labs. Lim almost smiled. Just like old times. Except he was on the wrong side of the firepower this time.

"Why are you wasting our time? Give me the codes, or I will..."

"Sure, sure." Lim cut him off cheerfully, over the sounds of Raul's duct tape muffled moans. "Happy to help however I can. Of course, it would be a lot easier for you and me both if the company had actually given me the codes."

The leader looked remarkably like Lim's Uncle Chip, with the same snarling curl to his mouth, and the same tendency to perspire under pressure. Nothing nastier than a very hairy man drenched in sweat sitting at the kitchen table, drinking his father's beer and cussing out his mother for raising a fuck up of a kid. Yeah, Lim felt an affinity with this guy from the second the asshole had peeled up that absurd face mask and hood.

The leader exchanged a look with the little one that Lim couldn't read. "I don't think you understand what's going on here," the leader's voice was sharper, filled with implicit threats of torture and pain.

Lim was enjoying himself immensely by this point. "Did you stuff that badass hood into your ears as a fashion statement? 'Cause it sure as hell ain't helping your interpersonal communication skills. The company doesn't give security guards access to the labs."

It might have been the one time Lim actually recognized the benefit of having a little padding around the middle. The punch landed just under his left ribs, with enough heft to knock the wind out of his lungs. He'd had far worse. And that extra fat just diffused the blow. But he doubled over anyways, giving the impression of being incapacitated.

The leader leaned close. "Get with the program, you idiot. We need those codes." And with that, he and the two-man team working on the security network swept out of the lobby and up the elevator.

That left just Lim and the little one. And Raul, bleeding and sobbing in the chair next them.

She grabbed his pack of cigarettes from the top of the security desk where all of his gear had been tossed after she'd patted him down. Did something downright naughty with the tip of her thumb scraping along the gloved underside of her forefinger to produce a spark. He could really use a smoke.

"You smoke that shit, your skin gonna fall off." He didn't know why he said it.

She tipped her head at him from her crouch beside the desk, bracing a fantastic looking compact SMG across her thighs. "Yeah, yeah. You really believe that?"

"Naw. Was just something a friend of mine used to say." Lim's eyes flicked involuntarily to the bubbles of blood oozing out of the bullet hole in Raul's thigh.

She caught his glance and held out the cigarette to his lips. An apology, professional to professional. He leaned forward and took a drag.

"Thanks."

She regarded him from her crouch with critical eyes. Dark black, with no differentiation between pupil and iris, they looked downright devilish against her cherubic face. Rounded cheeks and a generous mouth. Somebody who liked to smile, with teeth like a rabid wolverine. He felt that familiar tug in his mind of a memory trying to worm its way out. The spasming, spreading pain behind his eyes of an oncoming playback. Clamped it down. *Z, Y, X...*

"Man, that tie's really throwing me off," she said as though they were old friends.

*S, R, Q...*Lim let out a nervous laugh. "Come here often?"

She joined him in the laugh, cigarette hanging from that big smile. The smile froze as all movement in her eyes stopped, fuzzed out. He felt a pang of jealousy at how easy it was for her to link, knowing that he had a long road of conditioning and recovery from the damage to his plug, not to mention all the rest of the mess in his head. She rose fluidly from her crouch, practically instantaneous. He blinked at the implications. Those weren't just grafts in her muscles. Girl was coiled.

And damn if she didn't look familiar to him too.

She casually clipped the side of Raul's head with her elbow, and Lim heard the hollow crunch of bone hitting something harder than steel, and the squelch of wet flesh smacking the floor as she kicked his body under the desk.

"Come on. We're needed upstairs."

***

Lim knew that every team had their limit with hostages, and he knew that his wisecracks downstairs were the only opportunity he was going to get to have a little fun tonight. It was time to get down to business and start looking for some openings to get out of this mess. He really didn't care whether or not they opened the place up. His pay grade wasn't going to get cut as a result. Hell, maybe he'd even get a few days paid leave out of the whole debacle. He could use a vacation. And a couple of stiff drinks to make this headache feel less like someone was playing basketball on a bed of nails with his skull.

She trained the gun on him in the elevator on the way up to the 4th floor and directed him around the hallway to the very last room on the northern side. The systechs had some swooshy looking equipment out on the floor. Sniffers, he thought. Too bad. If they'd been dumb enough to open the lab doors without them, the building would have had a few fun surprises for any would-be infiltration team. Of course, it was a double-edged sword for Lim. Labs with their own counter-intrusion security meant that the company didn't arm their guards, which was just downright criminal in Lim's mind, considering the current circumstances.

Uncle Chip's clone stepped forward and put on his best death-is-imminent face before pulling out his pistol and aiming it at Lim's forehead. He opened his mouth, no doubt to spout something about blowing Lim's brains out if he didn't talk.

Lim beat him to it. "Yeah, yeah. The codes. No problem." He listed out a twelve digit string of numbers. Lucky for Lim, he was a quick study and a sneaky bastard. All the mental gymnastics to avoid playback shock left him with a rather good short term memory for numbers, and a penchant for peaking over shoulders at keypads everywhere he went.

The entire team looked at him as though he was nuts. Lim smiled, apologetically.

"What? You thought I was going to put up a fight? I was just playing around downstairs. I'm really not paid enough for this shit."

"Told you so," the little one chuckled behind him. Uncle Chip snapped out of it and glared at her.

The systechs typed the numbers into their system. The door lock blinked green and the team packed the sniffers up and lead him inside the lab. Lim wasn't really sure what the Cryopsych technicians did up here. It didn't seem like there was any place to even sit down amongst the hulking white and blue boxes of electronics and equipment. Everything was automated, nowadays. Hell, they probably gave lab tech degrees to anyone who could tell a red button from a green button.

Uncle Chip followed the systechs to a terminal at the back of the room and set up beside an enormous refrigeration unit with hefty security locks. They got to work with a single-minded focus that he'd seen before in people deeply linked into the data. Lim was impressed. These guys hadn't been fried out by the security bots yet. They might actually get what they were looking for. Good for them.

The little one leaned back against the closed door to the lab and motioned for Lim to stand in front of her.

"So, nice night for a little corporate espionage, isn't it?" Lim said.

She rolled her eyes at him and shoved the half-smoked cigarette in his mouth.

He shifted it to the side. "Yeah, yeah. I get it. Shut my mouth."

Lim heard the refrigeration unit slide open behind him, and the accompanying cusses and growls from Uncle Chip.

He leaned closer to the little one. "You know that they move everything to the basement biovault every night, right? I mean, how embarrassing is it that your intel didn't include that important piece of data?"

Her eyes expanded and flicked over to Uncle Chip and the wonder twins, data parsing through their links instantly.

The pistol was out again as Uncle Chip stalked over to Lim.

"The basement?"

Lim nodded amicably.

"You have access?"

Lim shrugged his shoulders. Uncle Chip attempted to make the slide on his gun sound particularly threatening.

Lim smiled broadly at the assembled team, feeling rather like an older, wiser brother helping out a sibling who'd just gotten himself in a bit of a jam. "But, you know the funny thing about Cryopsych is that they trust the janitors more than us security grunts."

"You're saying the janitor can access the basement?"

"Well, his thumb and access card get you in the door, but you're on your own with the vault. Hurts my feelings a little, you know, that they'd trust a janitor more than me. Made me just angry enough to peak over his shoulder now and then. I'm very resourceful, you know. Have a good head for numbers, I do."

The little one sighed in exasperation.

***

They rode down to the basement with the anesthetizing sounds of smooth jazz and the anticipation of violence. The little one braced Raul's mumbling, half-conscious body above her shoulders in the cramped elevator, his boots nudging the side of Lim's shoulder.

Lim's head was starting to really hurt, in a way that made his skin prickle with chills and sweat. He could see it happening, any minute now. The next memory would split his whole head open and ooze his brain out on to the floor and that would be the end of Lim. He tried to breathe slowly and get it together, but all he could focus on was the overpowering smell of blood and those black, black eyes in front of him. It was almost enough to tip him over. Almost.

She dumped Raul out of the elevator after her team proceeded down the short hallway. To the left was Raul's supply closet sanctuary, and ahead of them, the locked access door to the rest of the basement.

She pointed to the open doorway of Raul's closet. "Stand. Don't move." Lim complied. She crouched beside Raul and sliced off the necessary digit. The gun never wavered from Lim's chest as Raul began to scream, the duct tape bubbling off his mouth with the ooze of blood and spit down his chin. She tossed Raul's finger and access card down the hallway to Uncle Chip where the systechs were preparing a compact blowtorch and several dozen feet of wiring.

Lim leaned back against the door frame, willing his heart to slow so that he could think his way out of this mess. He needed an edge, anything that could help him, like aerosols or a homemade chemical explosive from Raul's closet. Lim snuck a look in the room behind him.

It was absolutely not a janitor's supply closet. Behind Lim was a security setup that rivaled most military grade surveillance rooms that he'd ever broken into in his previous life. Screens lined the walls with video feeds from cameras that Lim had never known were in the building. He scanned the monitors with a sinking feeling, seeing lists of names crossed out in red. So many names. And there it was - a little blinking dot on a map of the lab building that said Liminal Hill. To the right on the wall was a larger map. 355 Fourth Street, Lim's half-way house. 41 Main Street, the transit center in town. Central City Shops, Lim's favorite noodle shop. And even the corner of Wilson and that other unnamed alley where the black market clinic doctor told Lim that it would cost him three years pay to get his plug linked up again.

Raul's voice across from him was remarkably coherent for someone who had lost so much blood. "Fuck you Lim. You called them in, didn't you? You did this. You just couldn't let it go."

"What the hell are you talking about?" Lim felt his mental hold on the surety of his place in the world start to break apart. There were spots swarming his vision as he started to hyperventilate from the pain in his head, the panic. "What is going on here?"

Waverly delivered a brutally well placed kick to Raul's injured leg sending him rolling across the hallway, next to Lim. She shook her head at Lim, her voice tinged with something near compassionate sympathy. "For your sake, I hope you're messing around with us for fun, and that you don't really have holes in your head as big as a tank. You're all sorts of messed up in there, aren't you?" She said it slowly, every word emphasized frustration. "We are here to help you."

Lim couldn't stop shaking, his major muscle groups shivering uncontrollably, his breath coming in shuddering gasps. "No, stop. Just stop. Please."

Raul spit blood at her and hauled his body around to look at Lim from the doorway of the closet. "You're just going to die like the rest of them. I had a bet on how long it would take you to scarecrow out for good. Not long now, eh Lim? Your buddies, all you mercs, are just running into unfortunate accidents after you get out of the deep freeze. How nice that Cryospsych keeps their perfect zero recidivism rate. Especially when every ex-con ends up flattened under a truck or at the bottom of a lake. Whoopsies. Or a splattered on a sidewalk, like your girl, right Lim? Just like her."

Lim used to have this little hand-crank lantern by his bedside as a child. Bright red and clear plastic in the shape of a balloon. He'd wind it and wind it and switch it on, and watch the tiny bulb fade out, dimming each second until all he could see was a pinprick glow of orange, like the opening of a tunnel getting farther and farther away.

Right then, reality felt like it was dimming, pulling him down that gravitational tunnel of black, and there wasn't any lantern to wind when he hit bottom. *Oh fuck,* Lim thought. *Here we go.*

The playback-shock hit him as hard as a grenade hitting an armored chest-plate, freezing his body and seizing his mind. The endless hours of conditioning and replay triggered, throwing him straight into the memory of that night so many years ago. He knew every millisecond of detail, every color cataloged, every hair counted, every bullet fired. He knew how much he needed to piss, and how his heart would lurch as his boots slipped, trying to get to her.

The gun in his shaking hands, the Cryopsych high-rise headquarters downtown. Seeing Dani, scarecrowed, damaged from her time in the freeze. Watching her unable to move, just at the edge of the blown out window, bullets flying, the data center behind them just out of reach. That feeling of hopelessness knowing that they weren't going to be able to find a fix for what Cryopsych had done to her. The blossom of blood spraying from under her collarbone as the bullet tore through her, tipping her over the edge. Watching her fall. The smell of damp concrete and the sound of his own screams. The sirens.

Lim didn't remember much after that. A blur of police brutality, court appearances, tired public defenders and failed attempts to get his link recordings admitted as evidence. Too easily hacked, they said. With no other way to prove his innocence, Lim didn't come off as the most upstanding citizen to the judge or jury. So they stuck him on ice and triggered his link to replay the timeframe of the crime over and over, just like they'd done to Dani, in the hopes he would have an epiphany about the preciousness of human life and the importance of obeying the law. Lim didn't need that lesson. Spending five years watching your lover slowly die from torture inflicted by a crooked corporation, and then being set up for her murder and tortured by the same group did strange things to the brain.

He watched her fall, over and over, in a nightmarish timeline that reversed and warped uncontrollably. Somewhere, there was yelling. He remembered yelling Dani's name. But this was different. Someone was yelling his name. Yelling it loud. He felt the replay shift sideways, as though the

TV set he was watching had been knocked on its side. And again, a yell, and a lurching impact as the memory of that night went spinning in and out of focus.

"Shit! Snap out of it!" He heard a voice, a woman's voice, and felt pain blossom somewhere in a corporeal place that he hadn't remembered belonged to him.

I think someone's hitting me. Lim thought. And he was immensely proud of himself for the first coherent thought that made sense in a long time. *Good job, brain. That's a good start.*

And then she hit him again, hard, and the smack felt like the most real thing in the world. The most grounding, stabbing, throbbing feeling that made him nearly cry with relief. "Wake up! Don't do this now! Damn it, we're so close! Wake UP!" She screamed.

Lim turned, bent in half and threw up all over the floor. The curdled taste in his mouth and the acid burn in his nasal passages were enough to snap him out of the last vestiges of the playback-shock. The little one took a few steps backwards down the hallway to avoid the splatter of his puke.

Lifting his head felt like bench pressing an elephant, with all his muscles still seized and tightened from the playback. He looked at Raul, ready to cuss him out.

And Raul smiled from the floor of his supply closet, his bound hands in front of him, bloody fingers on the panic keypad.

"NO!" Lim screamed, and stepped forward. Right into the puddle of vomit.

Lim's legs still hadn't started working right and his balance shifted too far backwards with the sudden movement, sending his stiff and lumbering body crashing to the ground and sliding backwards towards the elevator. The impact knocked the wind out of him and jostled every bone in his body. His feet hit the floor last.

That was all it took. With that massive impact on the ground, his monitoring ankle cuff finally popped loose and ricocheted off the floor, bouncing past the little one's feet, straight through the open access door to the basement. He met her widening eyes and saw her start to lunge forward.

And then the security doors dropped on the hallway, between Lim and everyone else.

The sirens and lights started a second later and Lim knew he didn't have much time. He hauled himself into the elevator just as the doors started to close, the car automatically recalled to the lobby as the evacuation protocols that Raul enacted were processed. The wailing noise buffeted his ears and he couldn't tell if the sirens were louder than the pounding of his heart.

The elevator shifted sideways slightly as the fire alarm system activated, blasting the entire basement with a particularly nasty cocktail of fire suppressant chemicals and foam. Lim was out and dashing forward to the lobby security desk as soon as the doors slid open, his body working at near deadly levels of adrenaline. Reaching underneath the long counter, he stripped off the knife that he'd taped there his first day at work. Lim had always told his crews, you never know when a big knife's going to be useful, guns or not. The plastic cuffs and tape cut like gristled flesh, resistant and taut.

The knife slipped out of his hands as the whole building jumped and groaned, chunks of ceiling tiles and glass raining down around him, and he knew what Raul had done. The explosives in the basement aerated the foam into an impenetrable toxic cloud, likely smearing every member of the infiltration team against the blast doors. Lim grabbed his cigarettes from the desk and then he was up and sprinting for the back hallway and the employee parking lot before the building had stopped shaking.

Almost home free.

The bullet glanced off the floor between his feet as he ran, fracturing the granite and embedding itself into the door ahead of him. There was no doubt that she'd fired it as a warning shot. Thinking back on it, this tiny hallway was probably the worst place that he could have chosen to make his escape. *Well, hindsight is 20/20 and all that shit.*

He turned around slowly, his hands raised to shoulder height, one fist gripping the cigarettes. He was pretty sure if he didn't sit down sometime soon, he was going pass out from an exercised-induced asthma attack or just the shock to his system from running for the first time in years.

She stood at the end of the hallway in the lobby, that sexy SMG pointed straight for his head, a portable breathing mask hanging loose around her neck. The remains of her blast shield were shredded, peeling like latex off her damp skin head to toe. She flashed that famous smile at him again, looking like one hell of an angel of death coated in foam, blood and carpet fuzz.

"What am I going to do with you, Liminal Hill? You're really messed up in that head of yours, aren't you? Don't you remember me? A long time ago, in a place a bit warmer than this one. I remember that little cafe on the delta and that unbelievable beer."

Maybe it was the way she said his name, or maybe it was the conduit that the replay shock had torn open in his brain to those deeper memories of a time before prison, before Dani, before the gun pointed between his eyes, before everything went horribly wrong and his life was destroyed. He remembered the orange clay on their fatigues, mud smeared over their skin, and two ice cold cases of beer on the ground between them as they sat on the roots of a mangrove tree by the water's edge and drank themselves stupid. That beer really had tasted like nothing on this earth.

She saw it in his eyes, the recognition.

"You know, it's a funny thing. My team has recently undergone a radical reorg, and I seem to have an opening for someone with significant infiltration and retrieval experience. I hear that you might be looking for a little more job satisfaction and a chance to get your life back. What do you say, Lim?"

He lowered his hands slowly and tapped the pack of cigarettes to his palm. He lifted one to his lips with a shaking hand and patted his pockets for a lighter.

Sauntering down the hall and lowering her weapon, she stared up at his eyes from the shadows. She lifted her hand to his face and flicked that magic thumb towards him, sparking. He cupped her hand to the end of the cigarette gently and took a long drag.

Waverly's voice was soft in his ear.

"I hear, you smoke that shit, your skin gonna fall off."

Kelly Dwyer is an instructional designer and learning technologist with a passion for all things cyberpunk, science fiction and fantasy. When not writing or reading, Kelly spends her days discussing complex number theory with her 8 year old, stomping in mud puddles with her 3 year old, and rescuing flocks of innocent spiderbots that roam the house from the tinkering of her boffin husband. She can be found online at www.digilutionary.net and @DeviousDwyer.

Poor Lim just can't seem to figure out how to get back on his feet in a world that feels like it's out to get him. A sympathetically pathetic former criminal can only take so much soul-crushing torture and failure before giving up and submitting to the bonds and (literal) ties of a straight and narrow life. Liminal Hill came about from my desire to write an old style pulpy cyberpunk heist story. In my head, Lim's comedic misdeeds were always set to a soundtrack that played somewhere between a Keystone Cops caper and a far-too-morose future noir tragedy. It was fantastically enjoyable for me to stick Lim into these impossible situations and watch him bumble, trip and hork his way through them with improbable, cringeworthy luck. I cannot wait to toss him back into the underworld. Keep an eye out for more adventures with Lim and Waverly at www.digilutionary.net.

When We Go Flying

Kama Post

Outliers of Speculative Fiction 72

If I write poetry on the crossword page of the in-flight magazine I won't think about crashing. The last poem I wrote was about how up here above the clouds it's bright and clear like paradise, while just below them it's bleak and gray and pouring rain. When I finished I tucked the magazine back in the seat pocket and imagined who might read it. Twice I've folded back the page to write a poem and was surprised to find one I had written. It was like proof that I existed. Anyway that's how much I fly.

JFK to Heathrow, so I was in for the long haul. They ripped the seats out last time and a couple of people ended up dead for the duration of the flight. I met a woman. Her name was Rachel. And I only know that because I looked at her license while she was putting on her clothes in 14C. Meanwhile I'm squeezing past a sleeping Italian and trying not to slip on the miniature empty plastic vodka bottles rolling around by his feet. It was my fault. I booked at the last minute. I can't stress how important it is not to get stuck with a window seat if you can avoid it. Especially on anything bigger than a 737. That's how most accidents happen. Aisle seat, you don't have to worry about that kind of thing as much. Because you know whoever's in the window is a newbie. You can almost hear their heart beat, though any real fear is tempered by an understanding everyone shares: whatever happens from the moment you walk wide-eyed down the gangway to the moment you touch down on the tarmac does not count against you. Quantum mechanics, time dilation, inertial frames, wormholes, parallel universes, whatever.

I only cared about finding Rachel.

She wore a brooch. She's the only twenty-five year old I've ever seen with a brooch. A gigantic, antique brooch. Gaudy as all hell. I said as much and she said she did it to get attention. It worked, I said. She just looked at me. She wasn't anything spectacular at first glance but because of that brooch you looked again. Looking again always does something to a man. She could have had ten of us that flight. You could see it in their eyes, arms draped over the backs of their seats like excited children, like chimps. You know they'd been puffing out their chests in the men's room mirrors before they boarded.

I tucked my briefcase into the overhead bin and assessed the situation. I was feeling good about it, got that flutter in my chest, you know. Adrenaline is a fine thing, though precarious, if you let it take you over. There were fifty of us on board, max, mostly a younger crowd. You don't want a younger crowd. That's when you see the animal in us. That's when you end up plunging your pen into someone's back, or watching someone do the same. Or watching everyone do nothing, shaking your head and going back to your own business. You have to make the decision that's best for you. Some of them, they learn that the hard way. Anyway Rachel. She must have been watching me, because I zeroed right in on her. You know how eyes draw eyes. They all watched me walk back. They all knew where I was going.

"Why are you wearing that thing?" I asked her.

"I wanted you to come back here," she said.

"Do you want to go in the bathroom?" I asked, because I always ask. It's just this thing I have.

She didn't even bat her eyelashes, she said she would like to sit with me a few minutes and then decide. I slid right in next to her. We looked at each other for a while because she told me she likes to do that. It gave me the chance to really get to know her eyes. Almond shaped and deep green with flecks of yellow. They grew more spectacular as I watched. I thought she might have been hypnotizing me. She let me kiss her a few times. It was so much better, drawing it out like that. It actually got me going.

Some of them, they just want you to get it over with, they'll take you by the hand or push up against you from behind and some of them don't even care about privacy. Of course I don't care either way. The bathrooms can be a pain. You have to time it just right. It's messy, or someone else less patient causes some big scene, banging on the door and all.

It's easier if you just move up to business class, put the armrest down. Sure you'll get rubberneckers but I'm up here I'm like air, like water. I have no conscience. I don't care. Neither does anyone else. Anyway, there's only so much you can do to spice it up anymore. I'm just scratching an itch, now.

This guy on my last flight, he was from Paraguay, and we got to talking. He was smoking a cigarette by the Emergency Exit and using the safety card to clean his weed. He wore a straw cowboy hat and his eyes were black. We upturned some of the seats lying around from earlier and made a kind of sweat lodge. When we were high he asked me if this was exactly what I wanted to be doing. I told him I didn't really know. I knew it was the wrong answer as soon as I said it. He told me about a flight he was on where someone shot himself in the head. I asked how he got the gun past security. His accent was thick, but I think he said Divinity. He parted his hair to show me the entrance wound. Not even a mark, of course. He remembers the searing heat.

I've never seen anything quite that extreme, but I've seen a lot of things. I don't dig the violence but I've been part of it. You just get carried away in it, a salmon in a stream. Still, though, I don't get off on inflicting pain. Not up here, not down there. Sometimes you have to keep your head down so the type doesn't notice you, or you have to say exactly the right thing, like you're right out of a movie. And believe it or not, it's usually a woman. I will tell you right now that they are much stronger than they look. They board, fists tight with years of repressed frustration, and in a consequence-free environment? Well.

That's why I don't wear jeans on airplanes. You never know when you might have to jump over people.

The brooch Rachel wore belonged to her grandmother. We had gotten to talking after we were dressed. In the aisle across from us a painter had taken out his brushes. He arranged them in the seat pocket, handles down, from thick to thin, then removed several tubes of paint from a canvas tote and laid them one by one on the extended tray table next to him. Rachel watched him too, leaning across me, her hand on my forearm. We shared the intimacy of two people who had just made love.

It was the only thing left in the jewelry box, she said. Everyone always hated this, she said, looking down at the black glass, then looking up, her eyes smiling darkly at me. It was impossible not to smile back. My mouth moved on its own. I could see the little girl in her. Those eyes so big and round, swallowing everything. The painter turned toward his window and closed the shade. I wanted to kiss her again but I didn't. We looked at each other for a time. I can only imagine the things she was thinking, looking at me like that, studying me. From the way her mouth turned down, I could tell she wanted to say something, yet she didn't. Just sat looking in my eyes while behind her the painter's shoulders moved in a sort of a dance.

The old people, they have different motives. I've seen them dance down the aisle, cheek to cheek. They do those sorts of things, the things you would think they'd do. They play checkers or they suck down Manhattans and pass out, snoring like buzz saws with their fluffy eyebrows and ear hair and no apologies. I always wonder why it is they still partake. They know what it is up here. They know the risk. They're an easy target for the violent ones. They are closer to death than any of us, or so we like to think. Why did the old man board the airplane? To get to the other side.

I sat next to one of them once - a retired pilot coming home from Costa Rica. Two dings means we're cleared to land, he told me. I listen for those two dings with dread in my gut. Sometimes I just don't want it to end. Then those two dings come and it's like when all the lights come on at the end of a party and you see everyone as bright as day, and you kind of sink into yourself and sneak out the back door, ashamed of who you were in the dark.

That's what I found myself telling Rachel. I didn't mean to say all of it, but what did I care. Chances are I wouldn't see her again. I could have told her anything. Her eyes returned to the painter, to watch what was emerging on the side of the plane, like a moonflower opening before our eyes. She would focus on me, listen intently as if absorbing everything I said, absorbing me, then look past me to him, to his creation. A landscape, it seemed, an expanse of ocean, and the horizon a bright orange line. One single stroke, I saw him do it.

"It's lovely," she said to him. He turned to us with a surprised look on his haggard face, as if he didn't know he had an audience, as if he was offended. Then he gathered up his supplies in his arms like he was afraid we would steal them, and moved to a different seat, leaving us an unobstructed view of his creation. I leaned across and opened the shade, and the sun poured in.

I had been looking for her. I wrote her poems. I forgot to say I'm no good at it. I only call them poems because they're short, and they more or less don't make sense. That's the thing with poetry. You make constant adjustments: a word here or there, a dot or a comma, striking out a useless article—constant, small adjustments, like balancing on a wobbling two-wheeler, each subtle shift making all the difference, changing the course. Now I always check the crossword page, and when the month is up and they change the magazines I get the same feeling as those two dings.

I thought maybe she'd write back. You just think you know things and then life proves you wrong. On one of my first flights, all angst and nerves and a forced recklessness, gathering up courage the whole time to make my mark, and what did I decide to do? In a pathetic effort to test boundaries, I launch a drink cart down the aisle. It hit a young boy. He couldn't have been more than five. His mother screamed and bent over him, trying to stop the bleeding. Others helped themselves to the scattered bottles. Not knowing what else to do, I grabbed three Skyy vodkas and moved up front.

Two men in business class took off each other's clothes. I sat in the jump seat watching everything transpire, breathing heavy, twisting caps, then propositioned a small beady-eyed woman in First Class who turned me down. I considered not flying again, but being on the ground gives you perspective, and the little boy and his mother deplaned with smiles, and those two men were clothed and business-stoic, and none of it had any lasting impact on anyone. That's flight. Takeoff to landing in some cyclic quantum state, then back to business.

After that first one I got into my rhythm.

I had been watching the last of the sun fade over the horizon, watching the slow emergence of white lights on the ground. I liked to know life still went on down there, but I rarely stopped to think about what they were doing below me, what I might have been doing. My wife Joanie taking out a fresh smelling armful of clothes from the dryer, perhaps, Little T wobbling hands-first into whatever new and exciting thing. They were like characters in a novel. You shut the book and they stopped.

"Do you mind if I sit?" someone asked. Female. It had been a quiet flight, apart from persistent turbulence. I did not choose the leg this time. I had a solid destination, a briefcase full of important documents, presentation notes. I was highlighting my speaking points. Each bump sent my pen flying across the page. I was tired. It took energy to turn my head.

It's funny how you come to think of someone, and they look entirely different when you finally see them again. She was not wearing the brooch this time. She tucked her skirt under her and sat down. What could I even say? I must have looked like some moron with my mouth hanging open, banging my knees together, my breath caught in my throat. This had never happened before. Sure there were a lot of us, frequent flyers, we saw each other all the time, we knew each other's names and proclivities and knew who to stay away from and who could supply rich conversation when we were in the mood for it. I had considered cutting down, but for some reason I couldn't. It was always next week, next month. What did I care. My wife, Joanie, she isn't a big flyer. She got worn down years before working as a flight attendant. Imagine the things she saw.

No, that's not how we met. You don't do that sort of thing. You don't bring them to the ground with you. I've never flown with Joan--wouldn't have it. You wouldn't throw your own wife to a pack of wolves, would you? Especially with her being a wolf as well. She's scared of crashing. Doesn't like not being in control. I ask her what she thinks she can control, and she just shakes her head at me like I'm a kid, like she knows the secret of the world and I don't. But I do, and it's this: the world doesn't have any secret. We're like those seeds that fall from maple trees, those helicopters, those whirligigs. Our life is the flight down. We're twirling and weaving at the whim of the air currents. Once you can admit that, you're free.

From the front of the plane a man's voice increased in tempo and volume. It didn't stand out from the other clamor at first, the shifting in seats, the zipping or unzipping of bags, clearing throats, the engines. God, I don't even hear the engines anymore. I wonder what other noises are present just beyond my reach. What other wonders. This guy's voice grew louder, other voices circled around it. Rachel leaned into the aisle. Her hands were folded in her lap, nails painted red.

"I think they're storming the cockpit," she said, maintaining watch on the lower numbers. A short angry man in a white t-shirt huffed up the aisle, banging his hands across the backs of the seats as he went.

"They can't get in," I said. A large bump and a sudden dip tightened my fingers around the armrests. You wouldn't think I'd mind about turbulence but it's the one thing that pins me to life up here. And now they have the nerve to be mixing it up in the back too, even with it feeling like we were in a damn popcorn popper.

While we fastened our seatbelts she said that with some difficulty she had decided to stop wearing the brooch.

"Free will," I said, my eyes roaming to the faces of the other passengers.

Rachel slammed her fist on the armrest. "That's exactly it! That's exactly what I mean. Free will. You think you can do anything you want up here? When it was my turn, my grandmother's jewelry box was practically empty. A couple of mismatched earrings and then there was the brooch. I was only ten. I'm thinking, well this is unfair. Everyone gets to pick what they want, but when your choices are a few mismatched earrings or a hideous brooch, is that really free will? Look around you." She fell back against her seat and remained quiet for several moments, watching the passengers up front. From my seat all I could do was listen. The airplane banged and bucked. My eyes must have been as big as plates.

"I think they're trying to fly the plane," she said, leaning out into the aisle.

We dipped, one of those freefalls where everyone exclaims, "Oh!" and their stomachs leap to their throats and they laugh nervously afterward, eyeing each other. She put her hand on mine.

"Why are you scared?"

A woman cried out from the back. I knew what they were doing but couldn't bring myself to look. This kind of thing was too common to be extraordinary. You looked straight ahead or you watched, or you went back to your newspaper or your alcohol or storming the cockpit or whatever aspiration you pinned to your momentary happiness, your release. We were unhindered by consequence. We could fight and fuck and drink and destroy and land as lighthearted as we boarded, smiling and waving at our waiting loved ones, renting our cars, going to work, mowing our lawns.

She squeezed my hand, moved her face closer to mine. "Ask yourself, what would you like to do in this moment?"

I opened my mouth to answer. I thought of the dark-eyed Paraguayan.

Smiling with pursed lips, she put her hand on my chest, undid my top button. The plane pitched and swayed. She held my eyes and lifted the armrest between us. The familiar sounds of fighting came from the back. They knocked each other against the walls. I craned my neck to look. Duck, I told her, and she did. The restroom door sailed like a disc over the tops of our seats. She kept unbuttoning.

"What are you scared of?"

"I am afraid of crashing," I said. "I am afraid of pain."

"The pain will be so brief, it won't even register as pain. Your nerves are a fraction behind. You'll be dead by that time."

I looked past her out the window. The view outside was dark gray. The praying was more of a reaction than a conscious effort.

"You're praying," she said, "for what?" She had come to the last button. I sucked in my stomach out of habit. The things people do.

"Survival," I said. That this wasn't the end. Maximum entropy. The whole phenomenon started suddenly. It could end just as suddenly.

She leaned back in her seat and laughed, stretched her legs out in front of her and slid her skirt down and over her shoes. We bounced up and down with the dips and jerks of the cabin.

"You're right. So this is it," she said. "It's finally here. What we've all been waiting for."

I asked her, "What have we been waiting for? What do you mean?"

"Haven't you ever seen the movies, the television shows? The plane is crashing and anything goes?"

"Yeah," I said, sure. "But we're not crashing. Are we?"

I dared to look. They had made it to the cockpit. The weary pilot leaned against the first class bathroom door, taking long drags of his cigarette, eyes far away. A mass of bodies struggled against each other for the controls. People bled.

"Anything goes," she said with enthusiasm. "This is it. Anything goes," she yelled, unbuckling herself, standing in a crouch on the seat, her hands on the ceiling. "Come on!" she said. "It's liberating!"

I glanced out the window once, don't know what made me do it. We had dropped beneath the haze. The horizon was turned on its side, and such loudness, like my head was stuck right up the engine, and over that, her yelling, others yelling, the cacophony of panicked males in the back screaming in angst, no this is not how we're supposed to end, we aren't done, we haven't found ourselves. All of them no older than thirty. Rachel standing on the seat next to me looking down and smiling, and that's what brought me back. I was closer than any of them. I exhaled everything.

"We're crashing," I said, so matter-of-factly it made me laugh. Thinking back on it, I was probably afraid of looking like a coward in front of her, in case we saw each other again. Who knows. Looking back does things to a man. Changes things. I undid my belt, threw my papers in the air. They fluttered like birds. I stood up next to her, rocking the back of my seat harder and harder, trying to tear it right out, kicking it, pushing at it with both legs, using the seat in front of me for leverage. Eventually I gave up, grabbed Rachel with vigor and threw her in the aisle, crawled on top of her, kissed her hard like a madman, hungry like you wouldn't believe.

"We're all going to die!" someone screamed. Rachel was still smiling, an everlasting smile, her eyes fixed on me.

We must have hit. She was right about the pain. Not a thing. A thud and black. I don't know how I got back to the airport. Someone came and tried to interview us but we were all a bit shaken and anxious to get home. They told us we couldn't fly again. Not until they did some testing. Something about out of phase matter, sensitive dependence on initial conditions. Rachel didn't look at me.

For most of my life when I'd glance up and see a plane in the sky part of me wanted to see it crash. See it catch fire and dip to one side and leave a dark plume of smoke as it headed for the side of a mountain. I wanted to see it but I didn't want it to happen, if that makes sense. I just wanted to know the feeling it brought. Now I don't look up at all, because feelings stay with you whether you want them to or not.

Kama Falzoi Post is an accomplished child-bearer who lives outside of Rochester, NY and works in pharmaceutical training. She has been published in a variety of online and print magazines, and is a semi-functioning member of society. When she is not working or writing, you can find her strumming a ukulele, chasing cats, or acquainting her progeny with the rapture of living.

Harbour

Amal Singh

Vyom came to my bar on a cold, moonless night. I was alone, cleaning up and singing to myself. My six year old daughter was sleeping upstairs in her room. She was very sick - Doctor Waqar had said pneumonia - and I was worried about her health. Singing was the only thing which kept me from falling into bouts of sadness. The night was beginning to turn harsh, and slowly I began to forget the lyrics of the song. After a while, and all that was left was a wordless tune, which I hummed as I began to scrub a deep, brown spot on the oak table, which wouldn't go away.

It had rained that night and the night before, first coming in sheets from across the ocean and then in a heavy but steady downpour. I was cleaning up after work, mostly glasses and mugs; there was hardly any business those days, so no one had made a mess, and thankfully no one had thrown up. No chit-chat, no fights, not even a casual romantic banter with my assistant, Betty-- just silent drinking and tuneless singing. Outside, the wind whistled and the rain tapped against the pavement. There was no one on the streets except Akram, the port watchman, and Mona, the tabby cat. Betty had left a while ago, bidding a hasty goodbye as she covered herself completely with her raincoat.

"Father…" I realised I had been staring absently at the wall ahead, my hand still scrubbing at the wood when my daughter called. She was out of bed and standing at the edge of the staircase, shivering violently. It was cold outside and cold inside, and she was just in her nightdress.

"Nafisa, what are you doing up? You should be sleeping." I rushed towards her and quickly wrapped her in my jacket. She was so little, so thin, so ill.

"I couldn't sleep," she said in a whisper, and fell asleep in my arms.

I realised I was staring at the wall ahead, my hand still scrubbing at the wood when she called. She wasn't standing at the edge of the staircase. She was calling from her room. It was cold outside and cold inside and I was afraid she didn't have enough blankets. I dashed upstairs.

She was sitting up, covered in enough blankets, staring at something outside the window, her eyes wide with interest. A flash of light brightened her room for a second and then it went dark.

Then came a thunderous sound which shook me from head to toe. Nafisa covered her ears and screamed; her voice was drowned by the sound which was coming from outside. The weather was harsh and it was cold, both inside and out.

When the sound subsided, I held her firmly as she sobbed herself to sleep again, this time for real. She was hot as furnace, and I could feel the heat through my layers of clothing. Outside, the rain had stopped suddenly. I tucked her in and walked towards the window. Through the misted glass I could make out a huge shape somewhere in the distance. I cleared the fog and peered outside. It was a ship.

How someone had managed to steer a ship in such treacherous weather was beyond me. The cold, dark port was suddenly illuminated and the silence was filled by the whirr and rumble of the engines. The ship bobbed in the water as the chain thundered down, the anchor hitting the water with a resounding splash. The glass rattled. I went to Nafisa and covered her ears with my hands, my own ears unprotected, the noise making me tremble. Soon, the ship berthed and it went quiet again for some time. I checked on Nafisa – she was asleep now, her breathing peaceful – and walked over to the window again.

I saw that the port was suddenly filled with people. The ship disgorged them into the city and they spread out like a wave. So many people meant good business for me, and for any other bar which was open at that time. But the people didn't look like sailors. They looked like foreigners, with very dark skin, and very long hair, shiny and braided, both men and women. The vessel bore no insignia, as far as I could make out--no discernible colour, some red, perhaps, but against the night sky and the glare of the ship's lights, it was hard to tell.

I checked again on Nafisa; she was fast asleep. Remembering I still had work to do in the bar, I hurried downstairs. There was someone already waiting for me. I hadn't realized that the 'Open' sign was still hanging by the Front door. He seemed to be one of the sailors, the dark skinned ones, except he was bald. Most of his face and almost half of his head was covered in what could only be described as tattoos. There was an irregular streak of black from his left eye to his chin, shaped somewhat like lightning. There were similar shapes on the right side, albeit more irregular, like the bare branches of a tree in autumn. He looked calm, and beamed at me when I arrived. His eyes were very black and his teeth were very white. "We are about to close, sir," I said to the new arrival.

"I just want a drink, if you don't mind, my friend. It is cold and it has been a very long journey." His manner of speaking was broken, a part of speech here, a dialect there. But his voice was mellifluous, gentle, and one could have listened to him all day.

A drink couldn't hurt. I realized I needed one too. The image of my daughter standing by the staircase was still etched in my mind; the image that wasn't.

I hung my cleaning cloth on a peg and took out two glasses, and a yet unopened bottle of Jack Daniel's.

"I wouldn't have guessed, you know," he said. "Such bad weather!"

"These parts, you never know."

"Yes, well. We had charted out the course and took ample measurements. Most of my crew got sick." I poured a generous amount of the whiskey in the two glasses.

"To the rain," I said and raised my glass. He did the same. We finished our drinks. I could have sworn I saw a tattoo glow-- just a faint trickle of light somewhere on his face along the lightning shaped tattoo and then it was gone.

"Bad air traffic. The entrance was tricky, and clogged by the Volko-fleet. We could have been killed, you know. So many last minute changes..." He used many strange words and terms. To my uneducated mind, all that sounded like normal things any sailor would say.

"Well, you're safe, and you're here. That's what matters," I replied when he finished.

"I suppose that's true." He finished his drink. "What is your name, my friend?"

"Rahim. Yours?"

"I am called Vyom," he said. More of his tattoos began to glow. My eyes grew wide, out of surprise, but not out of fear.

Fear came later.

"I don't suppose you'd let me stay here, Rahim, my friend?"

"I am sorry, Mr.Vyom. I don't provide lodging."

"I can rest on the sofa here. I won't intrude. Just a night-- we'll be gone our way
early tomorrow morning, and I won't be a bother anymore." It was an odd request coming from someone who had just completed a long voyage; ordinary sailors needed a good, snug bed, with hot food and drink, and some company.

"I am sorry, Mr.Vyom. You seem like a nice and honest person, but..."

"I can pay well, Rahim, and trust me, I intend no harm." Then he laid his left hand on mine, and his tattoo glowed again, this time with a blinding intensity. In that moment I knew what fear really was. Believe me, I was no stranger to it --two years in a senseless war had taught me that. But this was something else. I didn't feel anything cold gripping my heart or my spine, no hairs stood up on my neck. No death waiting two steps behind me with a sharp knife, no fear of getting blown up. Through his hand, a warmth flowed like a molten river of iron and traveled through my veins, all the way through my heart, reaching up to my mind, wrapping it in its fiery blanket.

***

Two suns. I was always fascinated by my two suns, our two suns. My planet is a warm, warm place. Was, I should say.

I destroyed it

They gave me my last set of graun – tattoos, in your tongue - about a year back. I became powerful, more powerful than Maun the Benevolent. My full name is Miir- Vyom Peretos the Third and I am from the planet Kox, which is, as per my calculations, nine light years away from Earth.

The Heradix field - constructed by the Council - was a problem. But I managed.

You see, soon after my initiation, the Council realized they had made a mistake. I wasn't to be trusted, they said. I was - unmanageable, they said.

Unfortunately, I confirmed all their suspicions.

Three tall spires made of gold and iron and silver, gleaming against the light of the two suns. My city sprawled in front of it, where a river runs through its middle, snaking left and right and left, culminating in the Ocean of Laas. The city itself is huge, all boxes - much like your houses, Rahim - connected with each other with a silvery rope. It's a giant residential meshwork.

Was.

How I regret doing what I did.

I'm not a bad person, Rahim. Really, I'm not. Are you still listening? I suppose you are. Your mind is still warm. You don't resist. You're a good person and I find myself trusting you. I expect the same of you.

After they gave me my graun, I was overjoyed. I had decided to take my son out to see the Trajectory, a great colourful arc which hangs over Obori river. Hung. I keep forgetting. Just as I was leaving the Korran tower, I was stopped by Vamor.

A little favourVyom. Could you do me a little favour?

Vamor, a friend, I couldn't say no to him. Even when my own son was waiting for me.

With pleasure, Vamor.

A knife, straight to your heart - with your attacker's eyes locked into yours - won't hurt as much as the one which crashes into your spine, unknown. Still, I could have taken betrayal, Rahim. Betrayal, I could have handled. I could have kept quiet and let Vamor and the Council do what they were doing and nothing would have changed, and I would still be home and the City would still be there and the Ocean wouldn't be seething and boiling right now, slowly eating away the land I called home.

And my son would still be alive. They took my son.

I feel your frail mind struggling, Rahim. I should stop. I shouldn't have gone this far…

***

I saw fields upon fields lit with fire, beneath a grey, smoke-filled sky. A sky which held two suns, their heat mixed with the heat below. I saw the ground cracking beneath my feet, and I heard the world groan.

And somewhere in the heat of the moment, I knew that the man spoke the truth when he said he meant no harm.

Then he lifted his hand and I was back in the cold, dark place I called my bar. I shivered slightly.

"What was that?"

"What was what?" Vyom said as if nothing had happened. Maybe I was imagining things, just like I had imagined my daughter, very sick, standing near the staircase earlier. She had fallen asleep in my arms.

"Where did you say you were from again?" I asked.

"I didn't tell you, but you saw it." He shifted a little. I still felt a little fuzzy in my head.

I looked around; there was a sofa just near the entrance where people lounged and had drunk conversations. I wasn't sure I had enough extra blankets to provide this strange man, but something told me he wouldn't need any.

In the end I found myself agreeing to his request. He smiled humbly, his tattoos gleaming once again. I hazarded a question.

"Your tattoos... why do they glow?" It was a strange question, now that I think about it. When you experience an inexplicable phenomenon, something which your mind's limited capacities can't comprehend, something which was quite possibly out of this world, you needed to keep your mouth shut.

"They're a part of me," his lips curved into a smile. It was a smile of realization, of amusement, of many things. He hadn't answered my question completely, but again, he had shown me too much of his world and I decided not to ask. The very idea that this strange alien, possibly a terrifying super-being, who could touch and destroy anything he wanted to, was having a hearty, chirpy conversation with a bartender was amusing to say the least.

I poured another drink for myself. I asked him, and he agreed. Soon we were talking and laughing like friends, making jokes and telling stories. With every laugh, his tattoos burned. With every frown, his tattoos burned.

Who was this stranger? I probed my memories, stories my abba had told me about creatures of the dark.

Maybe a *djinn*, or an *ifrit* for God's sake. Those creatures were not to be trusted.

But I found myself trusting this stranger, and so I agreed to let him stay the night.

***

I had decided to sleep in my daughter's room, just in case she woke up again. But she slept like the baby she was, and once my body fell like a heap on the rocking chair, I slept like one too.

I dreamt of Vyom and his strange world where two suns had shone-- the dying, abandoned world. I dreamt that Vyom was a criminal, an outcast, and he had fled from his world in that huge ship of his. I dreamt of many things. True things.

I woke up to the fierce tapping of Akram's stick and the soothing sound of waves lapping against the shore somewhere in the distance. The rain was gone and the sun was shining brightly. It seemed like a good day to be outside.

Nafisa was not in her bed. I rubbed my eyes hard and got up from the chair with a start. I called out her name, but she didn't answer.

I ran downstairs, skipping the bottom four steps. My stiff muscles complained but I ignored them.

I entered the bar. True to his promise, Vyom had left. The sofa looked hardly slept in, and everything was in its proper place. Nothing was missing.

Except Nafisa.

Painful and impossible thoughts of her discomfort ran through my mind. Once again, I saw her standing by the staircase, full of hot fever, and falling dead in my arms. Had Vyom…

No, no, no!

I ran outside, my heart pounding in my chest.

Nafisa was playing with Mona, the cat. Relief spread through me and my heart slowed to a steady rhythm. For a moment I just stood there and watched her play.

"Good morning, abba." She noticed me.

"What are you doing outside, Nafisa dear? You should be in bed. Aren't you ill?"

"I felt much better in the morning, papa. The rain was gone, the sun was up, so I thought…"

"You could have told me. I was scared."

"You were sleeping, papa." I nodded absently and waved towards Akram, who was standing idly by his guard post.

"Fancy a cup of tea?" he called out. I walked over to him, nodding in acknowledgement.

"It's like it never rained," he said as he handed me a steaming cup.

"True," I said. "So, when did that vessel leave?"

"What vessel?"

"That huge ship which anchored in the night."

"There wasn't a ship in the night, Rahim. What are you talking about?"

"Red, black, sailors with braided hair," I trailed off. Even as I said the words, I realised the futility of it all. My own words sounded strange to me. No ship could have travelled in such weather.

"You drank your own rum again, didn't you? I have told you it is very strong stuff, and can addle your wits."

"No, it was just Jack Daniels." I drank the tea and waved him goodbye.

I was just glad that Nafisa was okay now, and her fever had receded. She hadn't looked this happy in weeks.

"C'mon, dear. Let's go inside."

"Just a little while, abba."

I stared at her happy face for a while, relenting, and headed back inside. Just out of curiosity, I checked the bottom drawer of the oak table. That was where I had kept the bottle of Jack Daniels last night, before going to sleep.

It contained only about a gulp of the amber liquid. I felt a weird sense of satisfaction. At least I wasn't imagining things. I replaced the bottle.

Just then Betty walked in. After all, it was just another day. Just another day of work. Nothing had changed from last night.

"Good morning, Rahim," she said.

"'Morning Betty," I said.

"Looks like Nafisa is feeling a lot better. You look terrible though." I grunted. She placed her bags on the counter and started singing to herself. It was the same song I had been humming the night before.

"You start. I'll join you. Need to freshen up a bit. And keep your eyes on Nafisa."

I felt my face and realised it needed a shave. Already I was beginning to forget about Vyom and the conversation I had supposedly had with the stranger last night.

The water was hot, and it felt good against my rough skin. I applied some soap and took out my blade.

Akram may not have noticed it; he hardly noticed anything anyway. My daughter was too busy being cheerful to notice anything. Betty may not have noticed because she had just come from the sunlight, and it was comparatively dark inside, but as I began to remove tufts of hair from my sideburns, I noticed a strange blackness on the surface of my skin. Slowly, as I shaved off the left side of my face, the black streak seemed to grow, irregular, shaped like lightning, crawling all the way across my cheek.

Amal Singh is a Software Engineer by day and a writer by night. He's a cinema lover, a beer lover and writes for the site theCinemaholic.com. His fiction is forthcoming in Stupefying Stories. He lives in India with his family.

"Harbour" was one of the first stories I wrote. It was when I seriously gave a thought to writing short fiction. The story started out with a three-word prompt I gave to my brother for an illustration. He wanted more details for it, so I sketched out a first draft. I liked what I had written, so I went through with it.

Pandora's Toybox

Heather Harris McFarlane

A broken doll doesn't care who threw it away. It makes no difference to it who tossed it out the car window to get soaked by the rain in the gutter. It's only a toy, and a toy has neither compassion nor contempt for the sad sighs cast in its direction by passersby. It's only a lifeless thing, and it makes no difference to it whether or not it was loved by its former owner. A person is different. She can love a thing, even if it doesn't love her back.

Fiona walked among the piles of discarded scrap-iron and shrapnel that had replaced the wildflowers and birdhouses of suburban peacetime. She walked the same streets she'd been walking every day of the eight years since she'd left her family behind in Glasgow to take her dream job in the visual effects department of a new but much talked-about studio. She walked them without any specific aim because, though they'd changed, they were still her streets, and her husband's, and her daughter's. She didn't care how many news reports gave how many estimates of how many aliens were pouring into their cities. The "invasion" didn't exist for her; she had bigger problems.

Her husband did care about those news reports, and had made abundantly clear his desire to end their personal American experiment. Gary didn't care about the aliens. He'd be happy to live and let live. His problem was with the instant national freakout that began as soon as offworlder boots hit terra firma. The news he paid attention to alerted him to something scary, all right, but it came in the form of the neighbors he'd previously been happy to wave to when he went out to check the mail. All he could talk about was the increase in reports of violence, of how many citizens per capita now owned firearms, and more than anything, how much he wanted to move back home. Things might not be perfect over there, he'd say, but at least the United Kingdom's government wasn't sending brute squads with carte blanche to ransack suburban neighborhoods every time there was a rumor of an alien acting suspicious.

She turned it over and over in her head as she walked, and could come up with no answer to his demands to know why she was so resistant to leave. She was so busy chewing her lip and staring at the sidewalk that she walked straight into the NO TRESPASSING sign affixed to a chain-link fence that hadn't been there the day before. Once she'd recovered and her vision cleared, she stared through the links and wondered what was going on. There didn't seem to be anything amiss with that side of the neighborhood, yet there it was, barbed-wire-topped and bisecting the subdivision neatly and menacingly.

"Outstanding," she thought, "because there's not enough going on that makes no goddamn sense." Determined to find at least one answer that morning, she walked the length of the fence, searching for more signage, or a posted notice perhaps, just anything that would explain the sudden need for such a palisade. She found no balm for her piqued curiosity, and so it flared ever higher, leading her to a furrow under the fence. Some big dog must've been caught on the wrong side when they put the thing up and been pretty desperate to get home to leave that kind of crater. Kneeling down and peering through the space below the fence, she supposed she could probably fit through there if she didn't mind getting a little muddy.

"What the hell? Why not?"

On a normal day, she'd have told herself, "because there's a fucking NO TRESPASSING sign and the big, nasty dudes with the big, nasty guns like to shoot the Smart-Ass Liberals Who Think They're Too Good To Follow The Rules." It was nothing like a normal day. She shimmied under the fence and figured she'd have seen anyone likely to challenge her. After walking around for a few minutes, it seemed she'd figured right. There wasn't a soul to be found. Other than the lack of inhabitants and a noticeably greater amount of garbage left on the curbs outside every house, there wasn't much to distinguish this part of the neighborhood from the side where Fiona's family lived. Emboldened by the desolation, she decided to check out the inside of one of the vacant houses. Because it was tract-housing with only a handful of different models, it was easy to find one that looked just like her own. When she tried the doorknob and, finding it unlocked, entered, she thought this must be how Atreyu felt at the Magic Mirror Gate in the Neverending Story.

It was clear that until very recently, a family had occupied the house. All of the furniture had been dismantled, but it was still no work at all for a sculptor's brain to see the parts and imagine the dining room table they had once been, or the sofa, or the crib. In every corner were planks, poles, and piles of hardware. With everything sorted as it was, Fiona could only surmise that this was the doing of the latest government task force, engaging in some last-ditch effort to strip-mine civilian communities for supplies after burning through the existing resources. She was just about vibrating with anger at the thought when she stopped cold at the door to what had once been a little kid's room.

The walls were still cheerful yellow, but the bunk bed was a ruin of hacked plywood and torn linen. And then there were the toys - the dolls with smashed faces and dismembered teddy bears. There could be no weaponry created from these carcasses; they were ruined simply because they could be.

"Damn."

Fiona sank to her knees, finding too much in common between her own daughter's bedroom and this horrorshow. She sifted through the wreckage, recognizing princesses and fairy queens she'd seen glittering in shiny commercials, but stopped when she came upon an oddity -- something out of place even among abominations. For starters, it looked more like something one would imagine belonging to a much older child than the one who played with those other toys - a complicated figure full of unsafe sharp edges and points. It also appeared to be the only thing in the house left completely intact. She had never seen such a thing, a near-perfectly constructed skeleton done in metal -- stainless steel perhaps -- a tiny one, as if it belonged to a baby, or a young toddler who would soon be old enough to walk. She was unable to stop herself from rescuing it, clutching it to her chest as she bolted from the midden heap that had been a home.

"Where'd you go?" Gary called as she rushed into their house, but she ignored him and stalked the entire floorplan to make sure all was as it should be. She continued to wave off his further inquiries about what was wrong with her and what it was that she was carrying. He followed her around until she ducked into the garage she'd converted into her studio. She all but slammed the door in his face, then didn't exhale until his retreating stomps were too faint to hear.

She found him the next morning on the sofa, sound asleep but still dressed, with a half-empty mug of tea on the table next to him. She reached down to pick it up, but as she did, Gary's hand darted out and knocked the mug over, sloshing frigid tea all over her.

"I suppose I deserve that," she said, trying to blot her jeans with the bottom of her shirt.

"You said it," he groaned, stretching his arms wide. "Mmph time is it?"

"Half eight." She held out a hand to help him up, waiting awkwardly until he finally accepted it with a sigh.

"Wait, are you still up?" he asked, as the dominoes started to line up in his slowly-waking mind. "What are you doing?"

Instead of trying to explain, she just tugged him along to the studio and held the door open until he went in and surveyed her work. The metal skeleton Fiona had found abandoned in the bizarre mirror universe version of their home had been taken apart and supplemented with car parts, snapped-off screwdrivers, and mismatched cutlery foraged from the junkyards and construction sites that were her most common sources of materials. Encased in sculpted polymer, it all came together in the form of a little girl, about eight years of age.

"That's brilliant," Gary whispered, reaching out to touch the perfect overalls, the perfect strands of hair forming a perfect ponytail. "Really superb. She looks just like Gracie."

"You know how she keeps asking for a big sister," Fiona said.

"Aye, the wee dafty," he grinned at the memory of the circular arguments with the little girl who'd been smart enough to teach herself to read by the age of four, but was still unable to understand why it was impossible for her to gain an older sibling.

Fiona lifted it down and demonstrated how it bent at the joints. "You think she'll like it?" she asked.

"Aye, she will."

"Good. I'm thinking it'll be easier on her, having to leave her friends if she's got one she can take with her." Her eyes were glassy, but she managed to keep her voice steady. "We'll tell her when Denise brings her home."

"We'll tell her when we have everything sorted out. No need to spoil the time we have left."

"Sure. We'll tell her eventually."

Gary had the right idea, she thought. There was plenty of time to let Grace have more sleepovers with the girls in her scout troop without being stressed out about moving to a country that was strange to her, even if it was home to her parents. Yeah, he was right.

He was wrong. Troop leader Denise delivered Grace home as expected, and Grace was indeed delighted with her present. She named the doll Senga, after her granny, to the amusement of her mother and annoyance of her father. She cuddled her sculpted friend and announced that they would play outside. Fiona opened the front door for her, only to slam it immediately shut as Gary hauled his daughter into his arms, ignoring her wails as her Senga thudded to the hardwood.

With unspoken agreement, the adults ran for the back door, but they were met by a half-dozen well-armed and riot-geared thugs with government-issued authority to use whatever tactics they deemed necessary to neutralize a perceived threat. Fiona's mind reeled with the thought that this was her fault. Someone had to have seen her in the cordoned off area and reported her, and had damned her family just as she'd finally seen enough to make her willing to leave. Gary's irritation at her was apparently forgotten as he clung to her, keeping Grace firmly between them in effort to shield her from those who were shouting at them that they'd be vacating the premises immediately. No, not in a day so they could pack their things. Not in an hour so they could shower and change clothes. They would vacate the premises immediately and be escorted to the base for questioning. As the one with the bullhorn was telling them for the last time, no one noticed the sound of a pair of feet not clad in heavy boots marching through the house.

Fiona saw no merit to arguing. She'd done enough damage already by trying to circumvent this madness, and decided to just cooperate. She gently nudged her husband out the front door, doing her best to ignore the red dots from laser sights that were dancing across his body as they went. When they'd joined their neighbors on the sidewalk, the guns began to lower. Fiona turned for one last look. Grace did likewise, twisting and squirming to see over her dad's shoulder.

"Senga!" Grace shrieked.

"Hush, darlin," Gary hissed, but followed Fiona's pointing finger to a shadow moving past the thug standing in the doorway. None of them had no time to marvel at the doll's impossibly outstretched arms or wonder how they'd missed whatever motorized components propelled it forward.

Suddenly, the laser lights had a new stage to dance upon. Bullhorn guy started to laugh, until Senga took a clockwork step forward. He drew and fired in one seamless motion. Senga took another step. When the magazine was empty, they all stared, brute and civilian alike at the tiny corpse, watching as the plaster dust settled upon her, white against the pooling red.

Heather Harris McFarlane lives and works in the Seattle area, managing a comic shop and writing into the early hours of the morning. She's not actually a vampire, she swears. She prefers pen and ink to keyboards and backlit screens, especially for long-form fiction. Past publications include short stories in charitable anthologies, pop culture review and informational articles, and supplemental material for works of other authors. She is currently working on a dark fantasy comic script and a science fiction novel, due to be completed early in 2016. When she's not writing, she is a frequent panelist at conventions, recently appearing on the Women, Diversity, and Comics panel at Geek Girl Con, and the Meet the Valkyries panel at Emerald City Comicon.

Story notes: I created the original version of this story at the request of author Shawn Kupfer, as supplemental material for his dystopian series, 47 Echo. After it was finished, I knew that there was a lot more I wanted to do with one of the characters, so I have rewritten it to fit into the world of my own science fiction novel-in-progress. The easiest sell for me is a robot who can love. Bradbury's I Sing the Body Electric, Asimov's Bicentennial Man, Lemire and Nguyen's Descender - these are some of my favorites, and I aim to build my own to stand among them.

A Muse of Fire

Kayla Bashe

(This is a story; once, a king who decided to outlaw theatergoing burned a theater.

He had his men trap the actors and the audience inside. The actors, knowing that attempting to escape would be futile, continued the show even as tongues of flame ignited the walls around them- and the audience, who had been banging desperately on the doors, were entranced once again by their stagecraft. Instead of dying with desperate screams in their throats, they died in the midst of wild applause. But the fire was just as enchanted by the beauty of their performance, and it transformed the troupe instead of burning them. And they lived... forever.)

The troupe has three acrobats of varying sizes and a strongman, but no fire-eater. All of them, from beautiful old Ruthe who plays the grandmothers down to little Ainsley, the tiniest clown who plays boy princes and heroine's sons, could fill in for him.

They are all eaters of fire.

Today their queen is Oberon, the Queen of Shadows, and her night-dark hair is short and slick. With the addition of a starlight cloak, her customary black becomes the garments of fairy royalty. Her lover, the Brightling, performs Titania. Everyone laughs to see the beautiful performer, hir eyelashes long in sleep, awake and fall madly in love with an ass- and fondle both the donkey's muzzle and phallus enthusiastically. The audience howls, falls from their seats, nearly chokes.

Afterwards, their queen sheds her cloak, The Brightling removes translucent wings, and they come out to greet the crowd.

***

Whenever she tries to remember how the Brightling joined the troupe, her thoughts diverge down two strange paths.

In one memory, the clearer, Bright had rescued her from supreme boredom. Over and over, she'd tolerated the same lovers; the same distracted artists scribbling set-designs on her hipbones as if they'd forgotten she was living, the poets who sprinted from her rooms to fetch parchment and quill. The patrons, insipid beneath their riffs, eyes bugging as they questioned: "How do you learn so many lines?"

But then- a new face at the auditions, an elegant blonde queue draped over blue velvet and gold brocade. The Brightling juggled torches as serenely as breathing, then sang a ballad of lost love in a soprano pure as silver bells.

The Player Queen raised one dark brow. "You're new in the theater, aren't you? Your voice seems trained, your clothes drip wealth- I don't suppose we'll be plagued with some father or husband ranting down our doors and trying to take you back."

"Don't fret. I've no ties to the respectable world. I'm no young scion of privilege playing at art, either- I'll turn up when you need me, and I'll be satisfied playing so much as a servant." A smile, at once self-assured and innocent. "I'm here now, aren't I? It couldn't hurt to let me stay."

"All right," she said. "If you insist."

That's one way she remembers it. In the other way, she is screaming as her bones roast, and a blissfully cool hand wraps around the ruins of her ribcage, pressing her heart and lungs back in. *Hush, or you'll scrape your rich voice.* Lips press scorched air into her mouth. It hurts but she's breathing.

Her memory always skips over that part, even in dreams.

They searched through the ruins of the theater, pulling out costumes and props not too damaged by the fire. "Look, not all the gilt has melted from this crown." "If we cut off the burnt parts and sew on some trim, this cloak could become a capelet." Slouched against a pillar, she directed the process with hoarse words and limp gestures, her body cringing from the prospect of movement.

One person did most of the work, pushing aside the heaviest stone-blocks, smoothing ointment on scars; seemingly everywhere at once, with fire-white hair and fire-blue eyes.

Of course she knew everyone she'd ever worked with, but…

A pale hand resting on her shoulder; a soft voice, perfectly modulated. "You're thinking of sending me away."

She squinted, blinking ashes from her eyes. "Were you here before?"

The silk-clad youth knelt at her feet. "I'm here now, please. I'll promise I'll work. It couldn't hurt to let me stay, could it?" Fledgling innocence seemed to radiate from that upturned face.

"All right," she said. "If you insist."

If she considers it too deeply, the two stories twist around each other and make her throat clench, her head throb. Instead, she thinks about how well their hearts and talents match.

***

Ruthe, the character actress- grandmothers, old men, strict parents- gabbles and laughs with a gathering of women. She was aging well, even before the magic came. Someone, as always, is asking about how she keeps her figure; she waves surreptitiously at a young man passing by before answering. He's stunned, a little awed, but nods and comes closer. Ruthe loves her flirtations.

After an hour of accepting compliments, answering questions like "How do you do that?" or "Was that real magic?" with a smile and a finger raised to her lips, the Player Queen knows it is time to start clearing out the crowd.

And then it is time to strike the set, load everything into the carts, pack up and move on. By the end of the month, they will accomplish thirty-six performances in thirty-six different towns.

It is in town twenty-seven that something goes wrong.

"Open your ears, you." The Brightling calls, running into hir lover's tent with almost childish enthusiasm.

"Yes?"

"I heard there's a preacher in town, and I thought I'd listen to our competition. See if I can pick up any tricks of improvisation for our performances tonight."

"As long as you're back by curtain-up." She twines herself about the Brightling like a cat and kisses hir cheek before letting hir go.

The Brightling misses first call, which is all right, because ze wears the least makeup of all of them- just a bit of blush to bring out those already-rosy cheeks, a smudge of pigment to define the brows. The Player Queen always applies it, tilting hir chin upwards to look into hir eyes; and she knows that although ze could manage alone, ze likes the ritual. Sometimes they run lines. When the Brightling misses second call, though…

It seems as if everyone's trying to crowd into her tent at once.

"Calm down, calm down," the Queen says, getting to her feet. "Don't all speak over each other's lines. Let me understand what it is you have to say."

"Your dear heart's done a bunker," says Ruthe worriedly.

"I don't have the slightest idea what's wrong with that youth," rumbles Elbertus, who takes the older male roles.

Cattie's over-lipsticked bottom lip wobbles. "Are we going to have to cancel the performance?"

The Player Queen stands to reassure them. "We're not canceling the show. Have we canceled one yet?"

A resounding chorus of "No!" comes from her troupe.

"Then what show will we do?" Cattie queries tremulously. "As much as I'd love to see your Mephistopheles again, we can't do The Fall of Faustus without Faust."

Her mind is agile as her feet as she quicksteps through possibilities: what will play well in this town, and what can they manage without the Brightling? "Let's run 'Alfonso, or the Agnostic Old Fool,' put the tumbling in the interval, leave out the

Lazzi of Kisses and cut out all the swear words. Afterwards, we'll all go on a Brightling hunt. Change costumes, now."

"Alfonso, or the Agnostic Old Fool" is a commedia about a strict but non-believing father who wants to prevent his beautiful young daughter from marrying a poor but godly man. Two angels, Harlequin and Columbina, come down to earth to force him to believe in a deity by setting up coincidences that can be the work of none other but the Divine. They cut the part of the funny old woman by swapping lines around and give Columbina to Ruthie; Cattie, the aging ingénue, takes the female romantic lead. Cutting all but one of the soliloquies means the Player Queen can give the role of the male romantic lead to the Strongman, so she herself performs Harlequin with slick brilliance and dazzling flair, tumbling over her feet to make everyone laugh. But worry looms like a backdrop in her head: where is my Brightling, where in the world is my dear soft heart?

Too gentle for offstage combat, ze may have been waylaid by brigands- thrown into a well, or the river, or possibly worse. The members of her troupe do not die or age. They are hardly ever ill. But they can be harmed.

After the show, they roam the town and the roads beyond looking for the Brightling. They find hir by the crossroads out of town, sitting on the grass in a way that's sure to stain hir trousers. The Queen runs to hir at once, her actors following. Hir face is as openly confused as a child's, hir usual air of knowing playfulness somehow gone; when she takes hir hands, they are soft, but cold, like those of one dead. She keeps her startled gasp held tight and silenced behind a mask of friendliness. (Even if ze's fallen down and hit hir head, panicking never helps.) "Hello, love. Do you know who we are?"

"Who am I?" And then, hir words coming out in a rush as ze takes in the gaudy outfits of the people surrounding hir, "I'm not an actor, am I? The Priest said theater is immoral."

Everyone else just gapes, but the Player Queen improvises an explanation lickety-split, laying her hand on the Brightling's knee. "A member of our company. One who mends the sets and costumes, and tends to our horses and our gear."

"I think I can manage that," ze says. "Mending is an honorable trait in the eyes of our Lord, if it is useful. The Priest said so."

Later ze will shy away from touch; but now, hir new unthinking mind not fully formed yet, the Brightling lets her fall to her knees beside hir and wraps hir in her arms.

The Brightling she had known was all things. Pure and kind and graceful, a brilliant artist with an easy laugh who sounded like an angel when ze sang- and, when ze was crying out underneath her at the close of night, a creature of flesh and lusts indeed. This was a blank slate of a Bright, a tabula rasa, a hollow shell of her once dearest heart.

The Player Queen had never played Ophelia. There was too much of fire in her, a spirit too drawn to swiftness and the sword, yet now she quoted the Drowned Maiden: "Oh, what a noble mind here is overthrown."

She felt like Beatrice swearing her oath of vengeance: I will find who has done this to you, and I will eat his heart in the marketplace.

The Brightling is not only newly religious and an amnesiac, but entirely stripped of hir former intelligence and strength of character. Ze does exactly-exactly! – as ze's told. For example, if you were to instruct hir, "Go to the butcher and get a pound of raw steak for Caroline's face mask," you would have to make sure that you also told hir "And come back afterwards." Otherwise ze would just stand there outside the shop, like an abandoned puppy waiting for someone to take hir home. Sometimes ze sings to hirself, then stops suddenly, as if afraid to be noticed. In those moments, the soft, perfect huskiness of hir voice is just as the Queen remembers it, and longing swells and pains her heart.

While they unload the properties in a new stop, she notices that ze lifts boxes awkwardly, as if trying to avoid using hir right arm. "You're favoring that shoulder. Are you all right?"

Ze has to consider it. "I don't know, but the Priest said that those who believe will be healed."

"Get your shirt off. Let me see if you're hurt."

Inside her tent, after the Brightling shrugged off the garment, she seats hir on a crate and runs strong hands over hir back; ze stays obediently still. Palms press against skin, and the tension and pain she feels there make her wince. "When did you last stretch?"

Ze tilts hir head, confused. "Stretch?"

"Actors should always stretch before performances. Keeps us limber."

I'm not an actor, she expects hir to say. Instead, ze leans in and looks at her. Really looks at her. "Can I make you feel better?"

That catches her so, so off guard. "What makes you think I need help?" she asks warily.

"You look sad. I've seen you. You never look sad. Not with this strange stillness. You're always talking or moving or dancing. Like a tongue of flame from a bonfire, the way it flickers and leaps. Dangerous, but beautiful."

The adoration in hir eyes kindles old sentiments. "Don't move," she murmurs, moving towards hir.

"Will that help you?"

"It might help me if I kissed you."

The Brightling nods. "You can try that."

She slides a hand up hir thigh and leans in close.

Ze feels so damn cold, her perfect dear heart with sunshine hair, and she tries to kiss the fire back into hir. It would work, she's sure, if ze only knew how to kiss her back. But the fire won't catch. It's like ze's already left this world. Her pretty Brightling has become a marble statue, with all the stillness that implies.

Ze pulls back, shakes hir head. "That kiss felt like an act of lust. Lust is very, very sinful."

"It's not sinful. We're in love." The Brightling doesn't understand. How can she make hir understand? She seizes on a piece of poetry from an old tumbling act, reciting it with all the feeling she contains. "You are the lark to my magpie, the sun to my moon."

But ze doesn't understand the metaphor. "I can't be the sun. I would burn." When she moves towards hir again, ze pulls away. "Don't touch me. I knew you were dangerous- I just knew it!" Ze slaps the Player Queen across the face- not a stage slap, but a real slap that makes her face sting- and ze runs from the tent.

The Player Queen knows the proper ways to faint and fall. She's played Hamlet's death. But this collapse starts with an undignified loss of strength and ends with an ugly crumpling. *This bit would never do on stage,* she thinks. *We'd have to reblock this whole scene...*

Exit consciousness. Exit her.

Faces appear before her, sudden bright spots; she is in bed, and the sun through the window shines above huts.

"You missed first call."

"Can you do the show?"

She pushes words through a thick fog. "What kind of a Player Queen would I be if I couldn't manage a matinee?" Departing from blankets and bed makes her shiver. "Get my coat. And my gloves."

Ruthie looks worried. "They're in storage. You haven't asked for them in years, love."

"I'm doing the show with my gloves and my coat. They should be with the props from Richard the Third," she says, getting out of bed. Normally she is as limber as an ink-black cat, but her muscles feel stiff. Suddenly she staggers. As one, the strongman, Ruthe, and the acrobats all hurry to catch her and prop her back up on her feet.

"I'll be all right," she says sternly. To them, it's a way to reassure. To herself, it is an order. "I can do the show."

The matinee is like slow starvation; by curtain call she is trembling with chill, though she smiles through it nonetheless. Afterwards, sitting on a gilt-and-paint throne, she calls the troupe together. "We're changing the route."

When the troupe finds the Brightling at the priest's main temple, she can hardly bear to look at hir. Ze stands between marble pillars and preaches modesty, the eschewing of makeup and finery, spanking one's children, submission to God.

There are moments when hir abhorrent words seem almost believable, for ze is as every bit as beautiful and charismatic now as ze was on the stage, and the Queen has to recite speeches from the Alchemist under her breath to keep from crying out a soliloquy at the sheer wrongness of everything.

Afterwards, they enter the temple. They are a motley procession now; whatever chill infects her has spread to them. The age of years has started to show in their costumed finery, patterns fading to indistinguishable muddy shades. The Strongman's face is white with pain, and his muscles seem to visibly shrink, shrivel, atrophy. New wrinkles form like crawling vines on Ruthe's face. One of little Ainsley's legs dangles uselessly, and he seems very small and very crumpled; Cattie, in an uncharacteristic act of kindness, carries him. Her roots are showing, and she he can barely feign youth. Nevertheless, she holds her head high, seemingly invulnerable to stares and whispers. In that moment, the Player Queen admires her.

The priest, most of his face concealed, smiles at them. "Have you come to collect your creature? It's seen the light, so to speak."

He moves his hood back, and she recognizes him at last.

"You burned our theater. The Lakehouse. There were children in the audience."

"And hopefully the flames showed them the error of your ways," he says, with a too-sweet smile.

You played the king, she almost says. Then she remembers that most people don't live their lives in front of canvas backdrops, and corrects herself. "You were the king."

"Yes. And instead of giving you death, I gave you a strange sort of life. But I've worked how to remedy that. When this colleague of yours first came to hear me speak, I drew the flame from its heart and soul and bones. Now I will see all of you dead."

At a gesture, one of the priest's acolytes brings him a torch. The Player Queen feels her entire being straining towards the leaping flames.

"This bit of wood was taken from the ruins of your den of performative theatrical iniquity. Your fellow actor will refuse the torch, and therefore extinguish it- not only a symbolic rejection of the sin of theater, but also undoing the magic spell that keeps you alive. At last I'll see you made vulnerable. I'll see you burn out. "

She paces around him with all the contained power of a jaguar preparing to spring, seething with energy, drawing on the last dregs of the flame within. "Extinguish our lives, but the show will not stop. The music continues, the lights still shine."

He points at her, his expression grim. "At the end of your lives, you will suffer in hell for your devilish ways."

Technique and training does not fail. She will be brave- or seem so, at least. So, drawing on all practice and apprenticeship, she smiles slyly, as if the whole world was watching her and marveling at her art. "At least I've lived." People always say that hell is fire- but when she meets his eyes, she knows it's ice. Cold and dead and banal, so cold that no one wants to move or breathe.

"Give me the torch, please," her sometime lover says politely.

They cluster together, hold themselves as bravely as they can.

The Brightling takes a step towards the Player Queen and tilts hir head. Ze points at her; innocent curiousity peeks out of hir blue eyes. "Why don't you weep?"

An answer comes easily. "Because I'm not the sort to have regrets. When there was something I wanted to do- a role I wanted to play, a beautiful person I wanted to kiss- I did it. I didn't waste time mucking about with calling myself bad and sinful. I was happy." Softly, she added, "And so were you, Brightling. When you were mine."

Wrapping hir fingers around the torch, the Brightling meets hir Queen's dark eyes. The devil's eyes were blue as ice, but her lover's are as blue as the heart of a flame.

"Then let it be known," ze says, "that I choose to burn. I choose to sin. My life is mine; I will be glad." As gracefully as any veteran fire-eater, ze brought the torch to hir lips and swallowed the flame. Within seconds ze burns from within, doubled over and yelling out from what hir body interprets as pain. But then hir rictus of agony seems to change into a determined smile. The Player Queen can see hir mind working, like a child learning to walk for the very first time, as ze figures out how to stand up tall. Then, with a flash of light and a whoosh, the flames disappears under hir skin. Ze shakes hirself out and smiles, radiant.

Vigor and heat have returned to hir blood. Before, ze was as stone; now ze is the moon again, reflecting the sun. The fire ripples through them all. Faded costumes, bedraggled with holes, ravel and re-sequin and glimmer again. Colors brighten. The acrobats whoop with joy and turn handsprings, and the strongman lifts Ruthe.

The king-turned-priest tries to exit, but the Player Queen seizes him in her strong sinewy arms, spreads her long-fingered hands out over his red, sweaty head, and snaps his neck. He doesn't get back up afterwards, not even when Little Ainsley claps. This isn't stage combat, after all.

One of his followers creeps nervously forward; the others follow. "If you don't mind, can you please not kill us?"

Another hurries to say , "We were only following him because this area is poor in trade and land, and we didn't know what else to do.".

Vigorous nods from all of them. "We'll work for you now, if you want."

One who seems to be higher in rank raises his hand. "You can have the building, if you want. We'll even help you put on plays in it."

Stagehands! And more than just stagehands, she thinks as she scans the room's build- a proper trapdoor, a lift, a trapeze she can trust. A balcony. Tumbling silks for aerial dance- she hasn't gone up on the silks since

Verona, but she's sure she still has the knack for it. Already she knows where things will go.

"We'll have a theater," Cattie breathes, wide-eyed.

Ruthe corrects: "We'll have a home."

With a low sound of excitement, somewhere between an exhalation and a growl, the Player Queen beckons her lover close, and they kiss each other breathless. Everything is strength and heat and life again, bright as spotlights, bright as fire.

Kayla Bashe is a Jewish-American lesbian living in New York State. Her work has appeared in Vitality Magazine, Liminality Magazine, and Solarpunk Press, and her novellas- a Victorian-era F/F romantic suspense and a queer western- are available from Torquere Press and Less Than Three Press, respectively. She enjoys experimental theatre, listening to podcasts, and spending time with other peoples' dogs. Find her on Twitter at @KaylaBashe.

You can only say "theatre is my life" so many times before you end up exploring how a literal interpretation of that phrase would behave. The result was this grab bag of career-related influences- commedia dell'arte, the way theatre was treated during the reign of Oliver Cromwell, the theoretical queer production of Midsummer that I've been tossing around for ages, and my enduring love for Patina Miller.

Also, as a writing exercise, I wanted to explore possible reasons for consensually setting someone on fire.

This story was previously published in the inaugural issue of Vitality Magazine. It's come a long way since- just like me.

The Boomtown Slurry Snatch

Kristin Jacques

The explosion lit up the hazy evening sky, a star burst of orange and iridescent blues burned into the retinas of anyone unlucky enough to be looking eastward. Lowry dug the heels of her palms into her watering eyes as a hot wind hit her a second later. Good Glory, she was too close for comfort.

She looked up, blinking through the afterimage until she could follow the plume of smoke to its source. A thick coil of black spiraled into air already choked by factory smoke, blending in seconds. Lowry picked up the pace, determined to locate the crash site before the fire burned itself out. Her satchel thumped against her thigh, a muted clink in discordant rhythm to her steps. This was the abandoned section of the York 3 slums, buildings so run down and rotted even the rats steered clear. Good place to find forgotten materials.

The broken pavement nearly toppled her twice, each trip sending shocks through the wiring along her spine. She ignored it, her curiosity at full throttle when she finally found the wreck, an overturned transport. Its occupants were a lost cause. The crash had ignited the engine-side fuel tank and consumed the cab before hitting the stopgap of flame retardant alloys separating the containment unit. A goods transport, in the slum of the slums? That smacked of illicit activity. Lowry grinned, rubbing her hands together. What goodies had come her way?

Sparing a brief cant for the poor crispy bastards in the cab, she tiptoed through the field of debris, frowning as fluid leaked from the twisted back panel. Dark red, so dark it was almost black in the diminishing daylight. No, no way, it couldn't be. She scanned for the telltale sign, cringing as she caught sight of the unmistakable singed logo on the cab.

BioFuels Inc, the corporate titan and Local Authority of York 3's Production district and main producer of slurry. She contemplated turning around, abandoning the prize, and running like hell for the Workshop's panic room until the Local Authority came through and cleaned up the mess. Except, if the transport contained what she suspected, well, at the very least Sage would keep her stocked on miso packs for a year. The Workshop could settle its debts. They could fix up Ghost. That sold her.

Lowry darted forward before her nerve failed her, tugging the back panel open. Her breath left her in a gush as she counted. Nine, ten, no thirteen intact drums. One drum could keep the entire populace of Boomtown with functioning implants for months. How could someone pull off a theft this size? Except, they hadn't made it far. Not even past the district line. She could see bullet holes in the blackened metal. This was too big for her. There was nothing for it. She had to bring Sage here.

***

Lowry slammed through the Workshop door. Sage didn't even flinch, keeping her focus on her work. Her patient, however, a door buster of a man who ran the local greasy spoon, jerked in his seat, yelping as sparks shot in the air.

"Bronson, you scream like a six year old girl," Sage muttered, fixing the wire. "What gasket have you blown now, my little apprentice?"

Lowry bounced on the balls of her feet, not trusting the big man enough to spill in his presence. "I need you and the truck. Are you almost done?"

That made Sage pause, lifting an inquisitive brow at her apprentice. The truck was ancient, held together with a hope, a prayer, and about a gallon of Sage's special adhesive. Lowry only requested it for big finds.

"Give me two minutes."

***

Sage stood slack jawed before the untouched contents of the transport.

After three hours of swearing and several negotiating knocks with the sledgehammer they rode out into the night, coming to a wobbly halt beside the wreck. They left the truck running. One, for the weak headlights, and two, it was unlikely it would start again.

Sage counted and recounted the drums, absently tapping her fingertips together until a miniature socket wrench protruded from her right ring finger.

"Uh, boss, your tools are popping out-"

"We're taking it" Sage whirled on her with a squeal, wrapping Lowry in a tight hug.

"What about the Authority?" Lowry whispered, peering into the surrounding dark for any sign of movement. Sage snorted in her apprentice's ear.

"If they aren't here yet, they don't know where it is. Most of those thugs have never set foot in Boomtown, never mind the uninhabitable bits."

Her words were true enough, but they would come eventually. The Authority would bluster their way through Boomtown's residents with the only persuasive tactic they knew—violence.

The older woman could read the hesitation on Lowry's face. "Think of all the people we could help, like Ghost."

Lowry sighed. Trust the boss lady to zero in on the weakness that spurned her better judgement in the first place. "Let's load'em up."

The two strained to roll six drums into the truck bed until the undercarriage hovered dangerously close to the road. Sage cast one last mournful look at the remaining barrels. They wouldn't be back for them. She shoved Lowry into the driver's seat and climbed in the back to keep their cargo secure as the truck crawled the two miles to the Workshop through Boomtown's predawn streets. By the time they stored their haul in the Workshop's panic room, exhaustion sent them crashing to their shared pallet, closing their eyes to the first greasy streaks of sunlight.

***

Lowry plunked the mason jar of slurry on Madame Clare's scarred coffee table.

"Payment in full, May, with interest," Sage stretched her arms overhead with a groan. "Think you can work a little magic for me? Back's a right mess."

Mme. Clare's right eye whirred softly, examining the sloshing red liquid before she disappeared into the back room. A half-naked Mike Mulligan stumbled out a moment later, still fastening his belt beneath his generous paunch. His knee clicked with each heavy step.

"Gwarsh, Sage, can't wait ten minutes?"

The boss lady winked at him. "Come by the shop later and I'll recalibrate that knee," she patted his shoulder as she passed, "On the house."

Mulligan blinked after her, his jowls trembling as he rounded on Lowry. "She gettin' laid or somethin'?"

Lowry rolled her eyes, settling in the corner of Mme. Clare's questionably stained sofa. "Something like that."

She'd rolled off the pallet after two hours of dead sleep to find Sage divvying the slurry into a small horde of jars and bottles. Any empty vessel she could find was filled and loaded into Lowry's satchel.

The early morning streets of Boomtown clogged up fast as they set out to visit the Workshop's more frequent clientele. Lowry kept her bag cradled tight to her chest, keeping a watchful eye out for the presence of the Authority. The reactions to Sage's 'gifts' were powerful. It was hard to ignore the sobs of relief for a couple cups of grease.

Lowry wasn't old enough to remember the crisis a few decades back, hearing stories from Sage and the other elders. The global oil corps finally announced the exhaustion of the world's fossil fuels. A tried and true synthetic replacement failed to fill the void. The first winter was the worst. Biofuels Inc. rose to meet the need for affordable and plentiful fuel using an exceedingly available resource.

Slurry was rendered from human bodies. The company had their pick of corpse piles after that long deadly winter. Their product met little resistance, the dead rarely protest. The living want to survive.

The wealthier inhabitants of Old Manhattan in York 1's residential district were rumored to blow through a drum of Slurry in a week. Per person. Not the unrefined stuff either that reeked of rotten meat when it burned.

The poor, as usual, were left to scrape out a living in slums like Boomtown. Slurry was more heavily rationed than water, which meant Sage's little jars were a month's reprieve from begging at the distribution center. By the time they arrived at Mme. Clare's Parlor of Heavenly Delights, Lowry's satchel was considerably lighter and the Workshop was debt free for the first time in years.

The boss lady sauntered out an hour later, poking Lowry awake. "Want May to rub you down? Your joints must be aching." Sage pursed her lips. "Least let me realign your spine at the shop."

Lowry waved her off, wobbling as she stood. "Tired, is all." An arm slipped around her hip, Sage taking her weight. She gave her apprentice a gentle swat to the back of the head.

"Then nap. You've earned it."

The two women exited the Parlor, elated at their turn in fortune, and completely missed the Local Authority who passed behind them.

***

A wheezing cough woke her. Lowry reached out without opening her eyes, feeling around until she clasped the reed thin arm to pull Ghost under the covers. He settled in next to her with a sigh, snuggling his small body against her warmth. His hair smelled like lavender. Mrs. Bronson had coaxed him to bathe. She must have bribed him with those fabulous pop-overs she brought Sage from time to time.

Ghost was one of the many Boomtown foundlings. His mother bit it in a factory accident a couple years back. Even that poor girl didn't know who Ghost's father was. He was a beautiful waif, with bottomless brown eyes and a constant tangle of curls. Born with failing lungs, he was one of Sage's unspoken miracles. In the upper echelons of York's residential district, they would have swapped in clone organs. In the slums, you came to people like the Mulligans, purveyors of mechanical replacements, and Sage, the mechanics who implanted and maintained them. The hardware needed the addition of Slurry to function; the rich used it for convenience, the poor out of necessity.

"Sage check you out?" Lowry ruffled his hair.

"Yes," he giggled. He stilled, dropping his voice to a whisper. "I saw Finkin in town."

Lowry froze, her mind scrambling in a million directions before focusing on one important fact. Finkin, the sniveling punk, was now in the Authority. She cussed, rolling off the pallet to her feet in a dash for the shop's parlor. Empty. She ground to a halt, trying to force her heart out of her throat before she choked on it. Ghost caught up to her, slipping his hand into hers. She gave him a reassuring squeeze and opened the door to a crowded street.

"Think if I had your bleeding barrels I would be eating this slop?" Jacob Mulligan's thick drawl carried over the cacophony of gossiping voices. Those Mulligans, charmers every one. Mrs. Bronson looked ready to take her ladle to the back of his fat head, present Authority be damned.

The crowd was thickest outside Bronson's eatery, the flashy gold on black uniforms of the Authority stood out against rags and work stained aprons. Lowry spotted a familiar mop of white blond hair, fighting the urge to bolt or move closer. Finkin was a lot broader than the last time she laid eyes on him. A familiar hand gripped her shoulder as Sage's voice dripped in her ear.

"Easy, love, they want to search Mulligan's first." Her boss snorted. "Though Jakey boy's about two words from getting his face crunched."

Lowry was vibrating in her skin, wishing she had half the composure Sage possessed. "What do we do?"

"Pray they're too stupid to notice the extra panel in the wall."

Was she kidding? Gem Reed, one of the Authority's top dogs, stood right there observing all, and then, there was Finkin, the damn traitor. What local boy didn't know the community's secret places? She chanced a glance up, her stomach contracting at the beaded sweat on Sage's face. She turned back to find Finkin's dark eyes on her. They were doomed.

His gaze slid over her to Ghost at her side, to Sage, and back. He held her there, pinned to the spot before one eye dropped in an unmistakable wink. Finkin surged forward, planting a mallet sized fist in the older Mulligan's face. Hard enough they heard Jake's jaw crack from the shop stoop. He shook out his knuckles before facing the brother's stunned expression.

"Permission to search the premise of your shop for company property, Mr. Mulligan?"

Mike Mulligan weakly bobbed his head in assent, burying his chins in his porridge. Gem Reed stepped forward, moving the unit out with a gesture. They marched as one. Only Finkin turned toward them, nodding to her before dropping back in line.

"Used to be such a sweet boy," Sage murmured, looking a bit shell shocked as Lowry tugged her back into the Workshop.

"What would make the Authority stop their search?" Her blood hummed. He'd bought them time, she couldn't waste it. She shook her boss, forcing her to focus.

"When they find the product," Sage snapped

"What else, what would make them back off from Boomtown?"

The light of understanding sparked in the boss lady's eyes. "Clear evidence the product was destroyed." Her expression turned calculating. "How fast can you run there?"

"It will have to be fast enough. I'll need the torch." Lowry scooped up her satchel, loading it up with the required items.

Ghost tugged her sleeve. "I can stall them."

She dropped to her knees, wrapping him in a fierce hug. "I know you can. Give me as much time as possible without putting yourself in harm's way."

It would have to be enough.

***

Lowry ran.

She threw everything she had into forward propulsion—head down, chin tucked in, arms pumping at her sides, and her satchel slung over her back to prevent as much drag as possible. Two miles, that was all, two miles between the punishing grip of the Authority or the greatest coup Boomtown had seen in ages. She didn't slow for the pinch in her lungs or the vicious stitch in her side, not when her calf muscles seized and her compressed spine gave an ominous creak. Lowry pushed through all of it, determined to put her plan into play.

If the Authority found the panic room, it was over, not just for Sage but for all who relied on her. She was a fixture, one Lowry could not replace any time soon. Stolen contraband was a death sentence. She didn't have the breath to curse. They knew the Authority would come looking for it, but they got too caught up in helping those under their care. This had to work. She dug deep for a final burst of speed, her bag pummeling her backside with bruising force. There!

She dropped to the ground, yanking her pack around. Her numb fingers struggled to light the cutting torch. It would only need a good spark. The retardant alloys protected the slurry from outside heat, but punch through the barrier and the contents would ignite. If she lit up one of the remaining drums, all seven would go up. Her hands shook as the torch began to melt an uneven hole through the nearest one. Slurry began to drip from the breach, catching flame a second later. She stumbled out of the way on the last reserves of her energy as the drum buckled. The liquid burst upward in a fiery plume.

Lowry scuttled far enough to watch the spreading blaze, hugging her knees, regaining her breath in short pained gasps. It takes a long time for a human body to completely burn but slurry went up hot and fast, clogging the air with the rank smell of charred meat. She watched it burn, impassive, exhausted, until Finkin's shoes entered her peripheral vision.

"Such a small blaze for thirteen missing drums."

His shadow told her he'd come alone. She glanced sidelong at him, searching for the snot nosed kid who used to run the streets of Boomtown with her in the massive thug he'd become.

"Will you convince them?"

Finkin scuffed his foot along the cracked pavement, a gesture so familiar it made her chest tight.

"Gem will be a tough sell, but the others? Pfft. They want to wrap this up." He cleared his throat. "Plus some skinny little punk keeps luring them all over town with fake leads. Haven't even searched Sage's shop yet."

Lowry chuckled, climbing to her feet. She managed to stifle a groan as her spine emitted a chorus of clicks. Sage would have to recalibrate after all.

"Thank you," she said, not quite meeting Finkin's eyes.

"Hey, we gotta look after our own," he said. She looked up in time to catch another wink, the cheeky bastard.

Lowry was long gone before the rest of the Authority followed the smoke to the wreck. Even half a mile off she could make out Gem Reed's roar of displeasure. It made her smile.

The reports would note the stolen slurry as destroyed, never mind the time gap between the original crash and its discovery. The Authority would pull out, somewhat satisfied, and life in Boomtown would go on.

It would simply be a little bit easier for a while.

Mother, sci-fi enthusiast, lover of B-Horror movies, and chronic scribbler. Lives in fair New England where she writes humorous, apocalyptic tales and dark fantasy. Owns two incredibly fat felines.

Good Fire

Eric Landreneau

Aaron drove his dirt-bike up a back road and onto the main streets, making his way for the outskirts of Keller, then hopped to the familiar trails that spider-webbed out into the hills. The wind over Aaron's skin blew some of the cobwebs out of his brain. He'd spent the last few months cramped in a van with amps, instruments and three other dudes, "touring" piss-bucket dives up and down the East Coast and getting progressively more pissed-off at each-other. They'd come back poorer than they left, and not just monetarily. Thinking about it gave Aaron a feeling in his chest like two magnets, held north-to-north and south-to-south

Tribe Head's triumphant return to their home-town had turned out anything but, and he'd spent last night drinking through the anger, which only ever seemed like a good idea at the time. He welcomed the cleansing air now that there was a greasy breakfast sopping up the beer-scum in his guts, though it did nothing for the terminal feeling that his band was finished.

That was the trouble with being as skinny as Aaron. He was tall, a wild performer, but too damn skinny to drink like a proper Virginian hillbilly. When he was wrecking himself on stage, throwing his body behind every note and dancing like he'd got the Spirit, he called to mind other beanpole frontmen: Steve Tyler, Iggy Pop, Mick Jagger. But he didn't have anything close to their tolerance.

He pulled up to the end of a gravel driveway up in the boonie-hills. Bloo's house was jammed back in the woods like a hunk of meat between craggy molars. Aaron tucked his red forelocks behind his ears, still crispy with yesterday's mousse. He thought the hair-do looked killer on stage -- two lacquered red sickles framing his face, short black spikes behind. Juan, the band's bassist, liked to say Aaron was too dumb a redneck to get his mullet the right way on.

He crunched his way down the gravel drive. Bloo's dad filled a straining folding chair on the porch like a moldy sack of grain. Aaron forced a bit of courtesy. "How you doin', Joe?"

Joe barely even grunted.

Bloo stepped out of the house and waved at Aaron. "Yo!" Bloo was on the small side, skinny, but moon-faced, eyes hiding out behind an unruly dark mop of hair.

He hurried past his old man. Joe latched a chubby paw around Bloo's arm." 'Ere'tha'hell ya think yer goin, Lewis?"

Bloo tried not to struggle. "Gonna hang out for a bit."

"Y' got chores, Son."

"Can I do them when I get back?"

"Y'd better... er I'll skin ya!" Ol' Joe finally let go of Bloo's arm, leaving angry red marks.

Aaron kept his mouth shut as he led his buddy to the dirtbike.

Joe shouted after them, "An you'd better not be goin' up t' th' Jut! Tha's my mountain. T'ain't yours! I got the deed! Stupid punks..."

While Bloo was fixing his chinstrap, Aaron saw the edge of a bruise on his collarbone. Aaron kept quiet. He shot Joe a dark look, revved the bike, and sped up the trail into the trees, climbing straight up Ol' Joe's mountain.

They parked the bike and climbed the last scrubby switchbacks to the Jut. They sat on the edge of the sheer drop, with all of Keller Valley spread out five-hundred feet below them. Keller was on a border of sorts, as high as you could get in the foothills without going ahead and saying you were in the Appalachians proper. Going a little deeper in, a little higher up, was like going two hundred years into the past.

Aaron fished sandwiches out of his pack. "Mom packed some for both of us. She figured Joe still ain't keepin' much food in the house." He bit into his sandwich.

Bloo shrugged, deadpan. "Not unless you count hooch and hillbilly crack."

Aaron snorted, laughing, but trying not to.

Bloo gave a lopsided smile. "What? You gotta laugh or cry, right? Your mom always says that."

"True..." The kid was nuts, but he had a point. "So what's new, Bloo?"

"Not a thing, man." The kid tried to push a stoner/slacker affectation into his voice. He always did in front of the Aaron and the older guys. "After you guys split, I pretty much lived at the library, surfin' every chance I got."

"Yeah?"

"Anything to get out of this town. Ever hear of spontaneous combustion?"

"Huh?" said Aaron around a mouthful of bologna and white bread. He'd been friends with the kid for years, but he still couldn't keep up with Bloo's brain-jumps. He chewed, gulped and asked, "Like when someone burns up?"

Bloo's face lit up. "Yeah! But not like they're *set* on fire. It's like they just catch on fire, out of nowhere. One second they're fine, the next they're smoking piles, even their bones get burned up."

Aaron smiled at Bloo's enthusiasm. Everyone he knew always shut Bloo up, but he'd learned some interesting shit letting him chatter on.

"It's real!" he continued. " I read all about it! Sometimes these people just *burst* and seconds later, they're nothing but *ash*! There was this priest in Moscow, burned to nothing on the street in the Russian winter. People said he burned brighter than anything they'd seen! Seven seconds like a sun, and he was gone! A lady in England went up with her dad right there. There was no gasoline or anything. Her hands and head just *burst!* Then there was this guy in Kansas. People came into his house, and where his rocking chair used to be, there was a charred hole in the floor. Down in the basement, they only found tiny pieces of bone and ash."

"How's it happen?"

"They don't know!" Bloo was shaking and bug-eyed like an antsy shih-tzu. "Some think it's a chemical thing, like when stored hay catches on fire, then our fat melts and burns off like wax. But people tested and tested that, and it always takes hours to burn off. The spontaneous thing, it's like *pwoof!* yer gone! I dunno. People used to think if you were angry and drank too much, you'd explode like that, none of these cases fit that. Calm an' sober an' happy."

"Yeah, and why ain't Ol' Joe burst yet? He's as drunk and pissed off as they come. Err..."

Bloo gave a strangled sort of a laugh, the response to the completely un-funny. "Yeah, I guess that's out. I dunno..."

Aaron wanted to kick himself. *Stupid ass.* He hated when he said shit like that. Bloo could get brittle as glass. The silence stretched on, awkward and tarry. Aaron gulped on an apology.

Bloo cut him off. "Anyway, I've been reading lots of stuff. Like this Navy lady who was just driving with her friend when she caught on fire. She survived, man! I wanna meet her. And I've been reading other stuff, too, like about Darwin and Buddha. I dunno, it's stupid. So anyway, how'd the tour go?"

Aaron was relieved that Bloo had pushed past the clumsy moment for him. "It was cool, I guess. Most places are more like Keller than you'd think. More crowded, but just as many stupid people."

"That sucks. Why'd you come back anyway?"

Aaron shook his head. "Just gotta rest and write some new material." *Who am I trying to convince?*

"Cool." Bloo bit into his sandwich. They ate quietly, baking in the sun on the side of the mountain. Bloo unwrapped a granola bar and asked, "When you go again, can I go with you? I could be a great roadie!"

"We'll see. I'll talk to the guys."

Bloo looked back out at the valley. "The guys hate me."

"Nah, man!"

"Juan and Jerun do!"

Aaron shook his head. "Juan's an asshole, and Jerun's sure he's the only person on this planet. But I like you, and Dob likes you. Fiddy-fiddy ain't so bad."

"Dob likes me?"

Aaron shrugged. "Near as I can tell. Never said anything but good about you. Then again, Dob don't say nuthin' bad 'bout anyone anymore." Aaron sighed, "Anyway, don't feel like we'll be going out again, anyway."

Bloo nearly choked, spat a wad of granola and spit off the edge off the Jut, then said, "What? What, you guys breaking up or some shit?"

Aaron shook his head. "Forget I said it."

"Bag that! What gives, man? *Tribe Head* can't call it quits!"

Aaron stared at his hands. "We spent half the tour fightin' like bitches. Every time we tried to work on new material, we all ended up drunk, angry, and away from each-other." He looked up at Bloo. "Wasn't exactly a vibe conducive to creative growth, y'know?"

"But, but..."

"We ain't heroes. I know you think that, but we're just four loser hicks like you."

"You gotta fix it," said Bloo. "Someone's gotta get out of here. If you can't, ain't no way I ever could."

"I dunno, we'll see." Aaron lay back and let the quiet rush back in on the breeze. "We're gonna try again in a couple of weeks, try to get some new songs worked out without goin' off. But right now I don't even want to think about the band. Tell me some more about people catching fire."

Bloo lay back next to him and stared up at the sky. "Spontaneous human combustion."

Aaron picked shapes of people bursting into smoke and flame out of the clouds flying overhead.

"I read all kinda weird scut on it, man. People been burnin' up for hundreds of years. I think I might know what it is!"

"You do?"

Bloo looked confused for a moment. "No, but I've got this idea. You know anything about Buddhism?"

Aaron smiled. *He comes from all angles, don't he?* "Nah, man. You'd have to ask Dob about that. He ran into some monks up in Philly, been a changed man ever since. Why?"

Bloo shrugged. "Eh, just some stupid idea."

***

After dropping Bloo off, Aaron took a long way home, buzzing along the old trails and getting reacquainted with the hills he'd been missing while out in the big world chasing rock stardom. The humid summer had the whole valley broiling, but he could get from here to anywhere on his dirt bike without letting up on the throttle, and going fast was the best a/c a dirt-bike had to offer.

He had words bounding in his head. Sometimes a phrase struck him just so, and he obsessed over breaking out its meaning. Bloo'd said something Aaron knew he'd have to hammer into a song. If he could get the right words, the guys would give him the right music, and the music would hold the band together. Wouldn't it?

Seven seconds like a sun…
Seven seconds like a sun…
Seven seconds like a sun…
And you…

And you what? He kept searching for the words as he raced through the hills. It was a good hook. Bloo's words, and well worth stealing. But a hook was nothing without a strong line to hold it.

He'd still come up empty by the time the sun dipped low and he pointed his bike homeward. The words caromed around his skull, waiting for a shape and a sound to hold them.

***

A few days later Aaron dropped by Dob's to catch up, the drummer being the only band member he could stand to see yet. Dob sat Indian-style on his porch, eyes closed, hands curled into mudras. And there was Bloo lotused-up next to him, breathing synched. Aaron smiled, shook his head and settled onto the stoop near Bloo.

After a few minutes Bloo sighed, then whispered, "I asked Dob about meditation, like you said. We been doin' this a lot. Buddhists seek nirvana. I read about it yesterday. It's like perfect thought, I think. I read that when some of them meditate, they make their own heat, from inside their bodies. Some have meditated through blizzards, and the snow all melted before it hit them. What if, when you get the nirvana, you don't need a body anymore?"

"Cool story, bro. But why don't you tell me about that black eye?"

Bloo gave the tiniest of shrugs. "You know that story."

"Dude, I'm gonna report that asshole. I--"

"To who? The cops? Dad grew up with them, cooks meth for half of them. What are they gonna do?"

"Well, there's gotta be--"

Bloo glared at him. "No cops. No nobody. I just gotta ride it out. Just let me hang, get away from him. Couple more years, and I..."

Dob reached out, his arm moving like water, and rested two fingertips on Bloo's arm. "All... but nothing," he said.

Bloo shut his eyes and went back to breathing. Aaron got comfy watching fireflies from the Porch of Tranquility.

***

Bloo convinced Aaron to take him up to the Jut after they left Dob's. It was dark by the time they reached the shear drop-off. They sat for a long time, watching the stars and wispy clouds roll by overhead.

"I love it up here, Bro. I wanna die up here one day," said Bloo.

"Don't say that."

"I been thinking a lot."

"You're always thinkin'."

"Been thinking... Some people say we're not done evolving. Makes sense, right?" Aaron grunted his agreement. "Some say that one day, we won't even have bodies. We'll just be thought, energy. Makes me think about the Buddhists, and enlightenment and nirvana and all that. What if someone could skip thousands of years, and turn into that kind of person in an instant. Maybe enlightenment is like taking a short-cut through evolution."

"Never thought of it like that."

Bloo's voice wavered, balanced between hesitance and insistence. "If you were suddenly all energy, inside a body you didn't need anymore, think you might burn your way out?"

"Maybe. Maybe you think too much for a fifteen-year-old hillbilly."

"Naw, man. Think about it. If you're made of energy, what would you be like? Hot, bright, and fast, right?"

Aaron decided he'd bite. "All right, let's say this is possible. How could it ever happen?"

"Well... the Buddhists meditate. Hindus too. They can do some amazing things. At first, you meditate to clear your head. But after a while, when you do it a lot, it becomes a way to really focus yourself. I think if your desire is strong enough, and you meditate on it purely enough, maybe you can do extraordinary things. 'Mind over matter,' sort of."

Aaron smiled, letting Bloo's theory carry him a ways. "So you think, if I think really hard about it, I can make myself evolve?"

"Maybe. If you want it enough."

Aaron shook his head and laid back. "This is your big theory?"

"I take back what I said earlier, about dyin'. I don't wanna die, ever. I wanna burn."

Aaron didn't reply, didn't want to think about death and fire with the way the band was going.

Bloo broke the quiet again. "Remember when we first came up here, Bro?"

Aaron grunted in the affirmative. "Right before your mom died."

Bloo twisted himself into a lotus position and closed his eyes. "This was the only place I could escape. Above and away from all that." His voice softened to almost a whisper as he slowed his breath. "She only smiled when Dad was gone. Not like your mom, Aaron. Never had the guts to kick his sorry ass out. Then she died, and he got it all; her house, her dad's land, this whole mountain, even me. Since Mom died, this has been the only place I could go to get a breath of fresh air."

Aaron let the quiet move back in, then sat up next to Bloo. He saw twin tracks of starlight on his friend's cheeks. He put an arm around the younger boy's shoulders. "Don't worry, Bloo. You're gonna get out of here."

"Aaron?" his voice didn't catch like Aaron expected. He sounded strong. Older.

"Yeah?"

"I wanna show you something. Give me your hand."

He hesitated, then put his hand out. Bloo took it, folded between his own, and rested their hands in his lap.

"What is it Bloo?"

"Shhh... just wait." Though confused, Aaron complied. Bloo sat quietly, apparently slipping back into a meditative trance. His muscles relaxed, shoulders stooped, tension melted away from his face. His breathing slowed till Aaron worried it had stopped.

He was about to give up and ask Bloo what was going on when his hand started to hurt. It was suddenly *hot,* like a furnace was raging between the boy's palms. Aaron yelped, tugged, and finally pulled away. Under the moonlight, he saw red welts on both sides of his hand.

"Shit! That's gonna blister!"

Bloo blinked his eyes, returning to reality, and frowned at Aaron's hand. "Sorry... it's hard to control yet."

Aaron shook his hand, but even the cool breeze didn't sap all the burn. "Yeah... neat trick." He stared at Bloo, bewildered and terrified.

Bloo smiled. "Isn't it?"

Aaron stared longer, his heart racing. "Uh... yeah." he shook his head. *Did that just happen? Yeah, it did... but what...* "It's late dude. I need to get you home."

***

Bloo's dad was waiting on the porch when Aaron dropped him off, rocking slowly in his arthritic folding chair. "'Ere th'hell ya been, boy?"

Bloo mumbled, "I was just hangin' out..."

"I tollya be back early. Din' I?"

"I was just..."

The old man silenced Bloo with a slap up-side of his head. "*Din' I?*"

Bloo studied the planks of the porch, rubbing the back of his head. "Yes, sir."

Aaron said, "Hey, you don't need to..."

Joe turned on Aaron, jowls red and shaking. "Y' best mind yer own bidness!" He settled into the chair. Aaron held one fist, clenched and trembling, behind his back. Joe jerked his head back, pointing through the open door. "Git in th' house, boy."

Aaron stopped Bloo with a hand on his chest. "You don't need to listen to him, Bloo."

Joe shot up with a snarl. Aaron ducked the incoming punch, then latched his hands around Joe's throat. Years of wanting piled into his hands, squeezing.

Bloo wedged himself in. "No! Stop! Stop!" He squirmed and shoved and finally separated the two. Panting, he said. "Stop... It's all right Aaron."

"Bloo..."

Bloo shook his head, looked up with tired soldier's eyes. "*It's all right.* Go home, man. I'll call you tomorrow."

Aaron unclenched his fist, slowly. "You sure?"

"Yeah. Go home, Bro."

Aaron let out a long breath through his nostrils, then nodded.

Joe glared at Aaron with fierce, piggy eyes. Kept the gaze while he said to Bloo, "G'wan boy, inna house. I gots some words t' say t' th' faggot here."

"I got nothing to say to you." Aaron turned and walked away. Joe shouted something about him and his haircut. Aaron ignored it and rode off, blood boiling.

***

Two weeks later *Tribe Head* reconvened at Dob's for their first band practice since the rocky end of their lackluster tour. Juan and Jerun showed up with their amps and axes and they all pitched in lugging gear and pretending like their last gathering hadn't ended in a screaming match.

Jerun pulled a pile of sheets out of his bag, and Aaron's guts clenched. He recognized those wrinkled pages, the beer and coffee stains, the taped-up rips. It was the closest thing they'd managed to a new song; Jerun's tab, Aaron's lyrics, all re-hashed, forced, uninspired crap. He saw into the future – tonight would go just like the last time, just like every other time they'd tried to crank out anything new. Smartstipation, frustration, anger, shit-headedness.

Jerun stood, papers in hand, opened his mouth, and then something strange happened.

Dob put one hand on the axeman's shoulder and his other hand on the papers. He shook his head "no" and pulled gently. Jerun let go. Juan, Jerun and Aaron all watched in amazement as big, still, quiet Dob set the pages on a toolchest, sat behind his drumkit, raised his sticks and smiled. He said, "Jam," and started thumping out the intro to *Big Time.*

It was one of their first good songs, something they'd played a thousand times, so much they'd started taking it for granted. But Aaron felt the words itching in his throat and it felt *good*. He grinned. "Yeah..."

They set new music on the back burner and tore right through five songs they all knew front and back. Aaron loosened up, letting the music move him. There was no audience, but he never danced for them anyway; he moved because he *had* to. He twisted his limbs and spine, moving through a dance as old as the first drum beat. He latched onto his mike stand while he wound and writhed to push his voice out bigger, wider, deeper. There was no pressure to create with these songs; they were already whole, the blood and sinew that tied the four young men together. But creation happened, slipping in like a summer breeze.

Juan threw some slap-bass stank on their old songs, funked them up so bad they evolved into something new again, and the band tripped tight along with him, building on the raw sexuality of the sound. Jerun ripped out an old solo and they flowed with it, opening up space in the music for him and his fingers to fly. Dob ripped into a drum solo during *Primitive Pyre* and Aaron found himself *chanting*, hauling grunts and wails of pure emotion up from somewhere deep and dark beyond the campfire of the soul and hurling them into the flames with each breath, setting them free.

The sun set. They didn't write anything new, just played the songs that tied them together. The old songs brought them back to the band they were when they wrote them: open and wild, contentious and collaborative. It was a good place to be. They finished late, wrung out but smiling, too exhausted to laugh, but glowing with the hope that *Tribe Head* wasn't finished yet.

Juan slugged Aaron on the shoulder. "Damn, man, you got the spirit tonight!"

Someone hammered on the garage door.

Juan looked out the window next to the door. "It's your ol' dog Bloo. Man..." his eyes widened, "Whoa!" he threw the bolt and yanked the door open. "Dude, you got messed *up*!"

Bloo staggered into the room, left eye swollen shut and eyebrow split and bleeding. They hurried him to the couch and Dob brought in a first aid kit. At first Bloo kept shut, ignoring their questions while Aaron cleaned him up. Then he started gushing. "What you *think* happened?" Aaron felt tender lumps under Bloo's hair, saw fresh bruises on his arms. "You know the worst part? Tomorrow, he'll act like it never even happened! It'll go weeks like that. 'Hey, Lewis. Hey, Son. C'mere, have a cold one with your old man.' Then, *Blam*! For nothing. Sometimes I wish he would catch on fire. Him or me. I'd be done with his shit!"

Jerun and Juan stood on the periphery, not knowing how to act, while Aaron bandaged Bloo's eyebrow. Dob sat down next to the trembling kid. Bloo stared at the ground, arms and shoulders tensed and twitching. He rubbed one hand over the back of another. "I want him to burn away. All burn away, every last memory."

During a quiet moment, Dob touched him with two fingertips and whispered, "All, but nothing."

Bloo quieted. Aaron felt all the negative energy bleed off him like heat seeping off a radiator. He had found a new way to face the pain, it seemed, without walling himself up. When Dob looked up, Aaron mouthed a silent *Thank you.*

Dob looked impressed, confused. "He's *really* good at that. Centering himself... he's a natural." He shook his head, suddenly self-conscious at having said something completely straightforward and un-mystical. "His spark burns strong and slow."

"What does that mean, 'All, but nothing?'"

Dob started to reply, but Bloo beat him to it, voice hauntingly calm. "It is a reminder of the path to enlightenment. One can only achieve 'All,' complete oneness, when the soul is as quiet and calm as a void."

Dob nodded. "I told him it helped me. Seems to help him."

Aaron sat next to Bloo. "You feeling better, bud?" Bloo nodded quietly. "Good. C'mon. You won't let me report this, at least crash at my place. You ain't goin' back there tonight."

Bloo nodded. Aaron pulled him to his feet and tried not to think too much about how hot and dry the little dude's skin was, or how scared that made him.

***

Aaron woke shaking, not from fear or cold, but because his mom had him by the shoulders.

"He's gone!" she said, panic making her shrill.

"Wha—What?"

"Lewis! He ain't here!"

Aaron sat up, creeping dread clutching his guts like spider legs. "How long?"

She shook her head. "I dunno. I woke up, thought I smelled smoke. He wasn't on the couch, and the door was unlocked. I went outside and saw cops, lights flashin', tearin' up the road to his place."

"Aw, shit!" Aaron scrambled out of bed and grabbed his keys.

**

He went full-throttle, took every shortcut he could handle in the dark. When he got to Bloo's he shoved past the trooper standing by his squad car and climbed up onto the porch where Officer Johnson was questioning Joe.

The cop stepped toward Aaron, shaking his head. "Can't get a straight word out of him. You know where Lewis'd be?"

Aaron looked over the cop's shoulder. Joe was slouched on the front porch, lost in a drunken, tweaking daze. The palm of his left hand was black and blistered, like he'd stuck it on a hot stove. Burned skin showed through charred holes in his shirt, too.

Seeing him slouched there too drunk to feel any pain made Aaron sick. "He don't know? Where's Bloo, fat sack?"

The drunk sputtered, then mumbled, "Little shit... never listened…"

Aaron tried to push past the officer. Johnson put a hand on Aaron's chest, pushing him back. "Hold on there, boy."

"I ain't your boy!" The violence in his voice shocked Aaron, but he rode it. "You're protecting *him?*"

"Back down, Aaron, or I'll put you back down." Johnson pushed Aaron back hard and shouted for his partner back in the squad car.

Aaron wormed past Johnson, nearly got to Joe before the cop got hold of his arm. He surged forward, dragging the cop with him. "What's the story this time, Joe? You finally kill him?" He kicked Joe's knee before Johnson hauled him back. "Where is he?!"

"Uhnnn. Lay off punk, he's my boy!" Joe tried to get up, but was too drunk and dazed. He sputtered, then mumbled, "Little shit. Never listened."

Aaron turned on the cop. "Why are you protecting him? All these years, you *knew!* But you didn't do a damn thing! Everyone knew!"

Johnson's partner grabbed for Aaron's wrists, trying to cuff him. But he wasn't going to be bound, not with Bloo hurt or dead. "Aaron," said Johnson, "you don't know what the hell yer--"

"BULLSHIT!"

Joe surged to his feet and hollered, "THE DEVIL HISSELF!"

They froze, staring at the man swaying with a look in his eyes like he'd seen his own death. "I showed him right! Finally hit back, this time."

Aaron snarled, "What happened?"

"He came at me, an' I saw *fire* in him! Comin' off him!" Joe steadied himself on a porch post. "I grabbed him. An' he was so hot! Like his skin was on fire. An' then…" Joe looked at his hand like he was noticing the burned flesh for the first time. He shuddered. "So much fire! On him, it got on me! He was the Devil, the Devil hisself all fire'n screamin'! Stupid shit ran up the Jut again. You go get him, but that cuss ain't comin' back into this house! He's got the devil in him!"

Johnson's partner snorted. "We need an exorcist?"

Aaron slumped, stopped struggling against the cops. "The Jut." Bloo was safe, not throttled dead. He looked Joe in the eye. "The Devil already lives in your house, Joe."

Officer Johnson shook Aaron. "The Jut? What's that?"

Aaron shook his head. "You don't know anything, do you?" He lifted his free hand and pointed up at the promontory, high up the shoulder of the mountain.

Worry and dread materialized on the officer's pitted face. "Aw hell…" He barked at his radio, calling for an EMR team and backup. "We're gonna have a jumper."

Aaron shrugged away from them. "Cool it. I'll go talk him down." He talked like stone, but was all molten inside. All that talk of fire and death, why couldn't he have done more?

Johnson's grip tightened on him. "You done enough tonight."

"But I know him!"

A flash drew their eyes halfway up the mountain. The top of the Jut was lit up bright as day. A phosphorous-white bonfire blazed right at the edge. For an instant Aaron saw a figure, arms upraised, silhouetted in the heart of that blaze. Then it was gone and the fire winked out.

All in a white-hot moment Aaron's brain jumbled up jam-packed with clashing fears, fury, and the first drowning strokes of grief. His thoughts seized up like a rusted engine, but his heart knew what he'd just seen, what was real. He felt hollow, so many thoughts he could not get out... so he filled the space with rage.

He wheeled around just as the last of the light died – light that had filled Keller Valley like a beacon – ran, and pounced on Joe.

The cops stood in shocked silence for a long moment, staring up at the Jut, mesmerized by the light, blinking at the after-images. A man can do a lot of damage in a long moment. Joe was already down, already drunk, already hurting. Aaron was up, furious, and full of fire. Not white like Bloo's fire, but black, red and malevolent. He came at Joe with a kick to the head, then started in pounding, not even feeling what he was doing to his own fists, not caring. He'd broken Joe's nose and knocked some teeth loose before the police even started to turn.

Something cold touched his heart. Not bad, just cooling and somewhat... sleepy.

Stop.

It was a quiet voice. If there is a mind's eye, and a mind's ear, then this voice came softly from somewhere over his mind's shoulder. But it was nonetheless commanding.

Stop, Bro. There's too much. Every instant is so full of sorrow. I see that now.

Aaron stopped. "Bloo?" The air felt cold all around him. The edges of his vision were tinged blue. He turned his head, but couldn't see anyone but the cops, who stared at him, slack-jawed, hands near their guns.

He looked back at Joe, and the fire came up again. All he wanted was to hurt, again and again, to find out how many hits it'd take to break through the back of Joe's skull.

No, said the voice. *No more suffering. Let it go. You don't have to hold on to it. Please, Bro, let it go.*

It was like there were fingers on his, gently pulling, begging his to relax, loose their grip on Joe's shirt. The same fingers touched his heart, soothing the fire.

It's wild here, Bro. A forever-song, blazing away. No bonds, no suffering, just a big forever/everything, wide-open like a welcoming heart. I'll show you, later.

"Bloo? Is that you?"

The cops crept closer, wary, not sure how to handle the situation, the young man talking to the air, holding a half-unconscious bloodied drunk off the ground by his shirt. Aaron uncurled his fingers, slowly, feeling the pain in his hands, pushing away from Joe.

Yeah, let it go, bro. You got better things to do. More songs to sing. That's your mission. Don't add to the suffering. Ease it.

The cool, healing touch pulled away. Aaron panicked. "Bloo! Bloo don't go!" He didn't understand any of it, but he knew this feeling deep in his heart. When that touch was gone, so was Bloo. "What's going on Bloo?"

I burned. No suffering, no body. So much more than what I thought it would be!

"Where are you?"

Everywhere.

The last of Bloo's presence faded away, evaporating off his skin. The healing coolness left, and he was hollow again. Like an empty cave, where small sounds echo and grow, the pain in his hands, his heart, and the heat of his fear and rage screamed all the louder. He staggered away from Joe, then dropped to his knees, head hanging low.

"Bloo..."

***

The forensics team found nothing but scorch marks at the Jut. No ash, no scraps of shoes, teeth or bone, no combustible chemical residue. No trace of Bloo at all except for the scorched footprints in the stone. Their report said "suicide"; that was easy to accept. The version Aaron told raised too many uncomfortable questions for some folks.

Aaron stood up there, days after the investigation closed, staring into the blank space between the starry sky and the deep shadows of Keller Valley. A feeling like cold static traced up his spine, and he caught a hint of laughter in the wind. A fire lit in his mind. Words flooded his head. Thoughts and passions solidified into notes and waves and screams, filled the gaps in a song he'd been kicking around in his head for weeks. He stood still, filling the space where his friend had burned, and he sang:

> Seven seconds like a sun
> And you fly
> Seven seconds like a sun
> And you're gone
> You lit your own pyre
> Good fire so free
> Seven seconds like a sun

And now you're one!

Aaron listened to the stillness for a few breaths, feeling where the song had taken something out of him, and then where something else, something new and ready to burst and grow, took its place. "It's still shaky, Bloo," he said to the wind. "Still new. I'm calling it 'Good Fire.' I'd say it's for you, but you gave it to me."

The wind rose up, curling around him, wrapping a coolness on his skin that stirred a mellow warmth inside.

"I'm gonna keep goin', like you said. Keep singin'." He wiped his cheek, then put his hands in his pockets. "I'm gonna have something to show for it when I see you again, Bro. I promise."

The wind rose again, then faded for good. Aaron turned and walked into the dark forest, back down the mountain, heart full to bursting with song and fire.

Eric Landreneau has been writing since he was twelve. He has had short stories published here and there across the web and in print, including Kaleidotrope, The Rejected Quarterly and Title Goes Here. Stories of his will also appear in the upcoming anthology Women in Practical Armor. His self-published fantasy novel "BREAK! A Tale of Cursed Blood" is available through Amazon and wherever you buy e-books. He lives in the 'burbs of Portland, Oregon. To find links to more of his work, diatribes, maybe the occasional accidental bit of insight, filthy jokes and routine over-sharing, visit ericlandreneau.wordpress.com

Somnambulant

L.A. Little

He couldn't remember how long he'd been the supplier for sure. 12,000 years maybe? It had been a long ass time no matter who you were or how you counted it. He didn't remember anything before. In fact she had always told him there was nothing before, at least not for him or the gods or the other anthropocentric magical beings. They just weren't there before the quantum information of the local sentients reached the critical mass necessary to create a collective consciousness and all the beings that go with it. He thought that might be bullshit.

He always suspected that she made a lot of stuff up. He figured since she'd been around in some form or another since pretty much forever that she felt under pressure to know everything. She told him that she was the oldest, then the imps, who were like false starts from when the consciousness was mostly fear—that first dim, stupid consciousness that was barely more than reflexive self-preservation. After that, she said, came the first gods and then beings like himself.

But if her version of his creation was true then she couldn't be a whole lot older than he was. Sure, death was a universal constant, but Death as a being would have needed that same consciousness to take shape. She claimed not, told him that he just didn't get it. He hated the way she did that, diminished him. That was probably a small part of why they didn't work out.

Sleep maybe wasn't as big a deal as death, but dreams were close. Every culture had some version of a Sandman and over the eons he had come to encompass almost all of them somehow. Perhaps that lent credence to her tale about shared consciousness, but it still didn't seem like the whole story. She hadn't needed to keep him down. That wasn't what love was about. He wished he could say that their breakup was what started him using, but of course he had started before. She left him because he used so much. It wasn't his fault though.

The first times he handed the stuff out were pretty much forgotten by him. People had been so primitive. He remembered the sand of the beach or rocky soil inside a cave or the grass of the savanna under his feet, bare like theirs in those earliest times. His hair had been matted and smelled of meaty smoke. His hands had been hard and calloused though he made no tools and used no spears. From the very beginning he had been tied to their reality just as they were tied to his dreamworld.

He didn't shape their dreams. He brought the sleep and the state of mind that made them possible. They needed to shut down and the sand turned them off like a switch. He'd seen the dreams, but in those first days they'd been pretty dull—chasing, being chased, eating, and animalistic screwing. Fortunately they'd moved up the ladder pretty quickly from there. For a while there'd been a kind of innocence to them. He'd really enjoyed them for a long, long time.

He still remembered the very first time he saw one dying. It had been in the earliest of times—one of his first memories. Some big cat had laid open the poor fellow's chest but his mates had chased it off with sticks and stones before it could finish him. He was just lying in the dirt screaming and bleeding as the others milled and hopped about frantically with nothing else to do, no way to help.

The Sandman, no one called him that way back then of course, approached the scene. Pricks like tiny ant bites danced across his lips from the blood pounding through his head. He couldn't tell for sure how much of the roar around him was the dying man's cries, the people's wails, or the rush in his own ears.

The Sandman had felt pity for the dying man so he gave him his nightly dose early. It barely cut into the pain at all, so he gave him more and then more after that. It had taken so much of the stuff that much of the fellow's tribe couldn't get their whole dose or even any at all that night. They would sleep poorly if they slept and dream of simple horrors.

Finally the dullish eyes fluttered closed under his heavy brow and the man slept. The Sandman didn't stay around to watch him die. He was pretty shaken up by the whole ordeal and didn't think he was up to it. That was why he didn't meet her right then or for quite a long time after. He never stayed to watch them die. He eased their way out when called by the Cosmic Whatever to do it and then he got the hell out.

He never even saw Death until people started dying in larger numbers. They were very inefficient at killing each other initially and tended to linger. The Sandman would be easing them and then see her nearby, often near one he'd just helped. Sometimes, for a very long time in the early days, she was just a shadow. Other times she was a cloaked figure, or smoke that didn't move quite naturally, or something else entirely.

At some point he began to see her consistently in what he assumed was her true form. She was no longer smoke, at least not usually. She was a woman, beautiful but otherworldly. She still seemed to blow across the landscape from person to person. She held each hand for just a moment, not with pity or compassion, but with efficiency. Her hands, the color of a polished blond wood, had the delicacy of choking vines, slim and intractable.

He found himself lingering longer to watch her work, her hair drifting between appearing to be smoke and a nimbus of black wool. One day when he had paused and let her come closer, she locked his gaze with her eyes, liquefied chestnuts above almost bizarrely high cheek bones. The smoke and the dream blew away for good, leaving only the beautiful woman. Only then did he realize he was, or perhaps solidify in the form of, a man, or a male at least, with copper skin and a coarse beard and hair.

He'd been curious about her but they never spoke, even after the look that woke him from his timeless dream and made them both real. He waited, thinking he had time to come up with just the right words—forever if he needed it. He wouldn't have admitted to being shy, but his time had been a lonely time and so aside from the imps, whom he'd long since pressed into something resembling organized service, he had little experience talking to others.

It was at Cannae that they really met for the first time, but it wasn't because he had finally come up with the perfect line. He walked among the dead and dying, more than 80,000 of them—cut open, smashed, trying to push blood-muddied guts back inside themselves. He licked his lips and his mouth was dried by the dust from a quarter million sandaled feet, hanging in the air, still blurring the edges of the Italian summer sun.

It was not the first battle of their war, these two groups that he loved and admired for the richness of their dreams and progress, but it was the worst. It was the worst any humans had ever fought and as he walked among them, soothing those he could, he foolishly looked at every face and he knew them all for he saw them every night.

When he had touched all who he was supposed to, he lie on the edge of the field and wept. He wept for the dreams lost and the beauty and the love, and even the cruelty and mundanity, that would never form behind their eyes again and would never again lead them to add to the greater whole. The heat of his own tears further dried his mouth and made the sobs stick in the back of his throat, where the scent of the battlefield collected like a slimy ball and coated his tongue with the flavor of copper, making him gag.

He started when she touched him. "Are you alright?" she asked him in the lulling voice he expected she would have.

"No," he answered. "It is all so awful. How do you stand it?"

"It's just what I do. If I didn't take them they'd suffer forever."

He considered that. It made sense but she seemed so cold about it. "I try to help them."

"Yes, I've seen. It's very kind of you."

The Sandman shook his head. "No, I'm called to do it, like you I guess."

"But you want to do it too, don't you?"

He nodded, "I always have, but this is so much, so terrible. I just want to sleep."

Death cocked her head quizzically. "You sleep?"

The Sandman realized that he had never been called to supply her. "You don't, do you?"

"Never. I'm always awake. Part of me is always working"

The Sandman smiled ruefully. "Part of me is always sleeping," he told her. "Except for right now. Right now every bit of me is awake. Right now there are no dreams, no sleep for anyone."

Death looked around, seeming to tabulate and confirm that her work was done as her sharp eye took in the carnage. "We should go. We're done here I think."

"Yes. Let's go," The Sandman said. "Maybe we can go somewhere more pleasant." He had said it without thinking and instantly regretted it. He hoped that it wasn't the wrong thing to say.

"I'd like that. My work is lonely too."

That night was the first time The Sandman used his own product. It was only a little, to put the ever-sleeping part of him, the part that walked among and recorded and reveled in all the dreaming, back to sleep. He'd been afraid to sleep, afraid of what he would see in the aftermath of this most terrible day, but his stuff worked, even on him. The dreams were awful and he cried a lot, but she stayed with him and somehow that made it better, even though she couldn't really understand why the job upset him so.

For centuries after that night they were inseparable. Some part of each was always with the other. They were in love though she was, perhaps less sensitive than he, less expressive. He never doubted her sincerity. Not even when she left him.

He'd used a little here and there for about two thousand years, but he had it under control until the

American Civil War. There'd been other large die offs as bad and worse in their way. The plagues had been awful but they'd been natural, part of being mortal. The brutal, primitive battles, like Cannae, could take thousands at a time, but then the combatants were usually spent for months or years. Besides, he was accustomed to that sort of up close killing. There was an odd human-ness to it that he had gotten somewhat used to. Even with Napoleon there had been limits to the spread of the suffering. Oh sure, The Sandman got into the sand a little heavier when these things happened, but he was maintaining.

Shiloh had been his point of no return. The killing had been becoming more industrial for forever, but to see 23,000 men blasted apart with lead balls and canon fire, to see their ruined limbs sawed off while they screamed, to look into their faces while he poured the sand over their eyes, not to help them, but so he wouldn't have to hear the screams anymore, to silence them, that broke him for good. And then Second Manassas just a few months later and then Antietam just a couple of weeks after that. Another 41,000 men screaming in the dreams of all who were there and, thanks to telegraphs and newspapers, screaming in the dreams of widows and children and all the others who learned of it.

He used the stuff to put his sleeping part back to sleep and then used more so he couldn't see, couldn't hear while he slept, to go ever deeper and escape, folded into the black, wrapped in velvet too thick for any sound to penetrate or for even the light of dreams to shine through. Every time he came up for air there was another reason to go back under. Another

Fredericksburg, another Gettysburg, so he just kept using and left his work to the imps and to the humans crude substitutes for his stuff, the ether, the opium, the edgy-shaky not-sleep.

She worried about him, tried to help him, but she was the busiest she'd been in some time. Because they shared everything, but she couldn't share his perspective, she couldn't understand what he was going through and so wasn't as sympathetic as he felt she should be. When he didn't use enough, and the dreams came back and woke him, she wasn't always there.

She really did try. He knew that. She stuck it out for decades, but he went back to the stuff easier and harder after Appomattox. The cleverer the humans got, the more horrible it was for him. The Great War marked a new low and that was what ended the relationship. By then he hardly worked at all. With just the imps distributing, dreams got darker and sleep got harder to come by for everyone. Even before that war began the electric light and his increasingly unreliable helpers were screwing it all up, creating a world of dark circled eyes, short fuses, and missed trains of thought.

It was a lot to deal with and this time he knew it was his fault. He just wasn't motivated to fix it. Who was he to fix anything? He didn't even love people anymore. He just resented them. It was all just something else to avoid, another reason to use. The worse the war got the more he used, more and more with every battle. After the Somme he took all the stuff that was meant for all the men who died there and tried to use it all at once. He failed to reach that forever sleep, but it killed the relationship.

Death was able to wake him just long enough to tell him that the humans he felt so much for needed him more than ever. She told him he was a junkie. Then she told him something that finally got a response. "I can't watch this anymore," she said. "We're done."

His lethargic heart tried to race but couldn't. His mind wanted to be frantic and look madly for an answer, but it couldn't remember how. He gave her the best he could at the moment. "Yeah. We had a good run though, huh?"

She left, heels drumming accusations into his throbbing gray matter as she crossed the tile floor of his near-earthly home, the place where he slept, and left for good. He wondered if he had really seen, for the first time in two thousand years, a tear in her eye. It didn't matter. She was gone and he went back to sleep, waking only when the awful dreams woke him.

The more their dreams showed him, the more gas covered battlefields, burning skyscrapers, and mesothelioma wards he had walked through in dreams, the more sand he had poured into his own eyes, trying to block out the images, trying to stop the dreams by sleeping ever deeper. He didn't stop when his eyeballs felt rolled in glass, he didn't stop when he literally couldn't see through the stuff caked under his lids, he didn't stop when the sand went up his nose causing him to hack it back out of his throat, or when the literal weight was so heavy that it held his head down almost as well as sleep.

One day he awoke fully for no apparent reason. His head was remarkably clear. He'd not been so clear in hundreds and hundreds of years. His face was on a cushion, his beard was crushed against his skin so that where the left side of his face touched the fabric it seemed wrong but somehow a relief—oily smoothness describing a volcanic coastline. The Sandman tried to rub the front of his face against the softer texture, but recoiled from the musky uncleanness and lifted his head away in sudden distaste. He was lying in one of his filthy rooms on a filthy couch. Death sat across from him on another, watching him wake after, presumably, watching him sleep.

"You came back," he said and felt joy for the first time in a long, long time.

"I had to," she said.

"I'm not dreaming?" The Sandman asked.

"How could you be dreaming and talking to me?" Death asked.

"I could be dreaming you."

"I'm certain that I am here for real," she told him.

"I could be somnambulant," he offered.

"Sleepwalking?"

"And talking. It happens."

"I don't think so. Even if, I'm still here for you. You're done sleepwalking now."

"I'm sorry," he said. "It was all my fault, but I'm feeling better now. I promise I'll stop."

"I know." She held out her hand and he took it. She rose and pulled him up. "We have to go now. I have to take you."

"You have to…oh. Shit."

She wiped tears from her cheek, bit her lip. She pulled him close, his face deep in the black of her hair, pure black and the aroma of rich, dark soil. He realized this was what he had searched for all along—a place of final peace and comfort.

He dropped his eyes, ashamed. "I'm so sorry," he whispered. "I didn't mean to put you through this."

She tugged his beard lovingly, the way she used to, and kissed his downturned forehead softly. "It's okay," she said. "It's just what I do."

L.A. Little is an author of science fiction, fantasy, & horror. In addition to writing acclaimed short fiction he is a novelist and former music journalist. His work has appeared in magazines including Allegory and AnotherRealm.com. In addition to two novels and his many short stories, L.A. has published over 600 non-fiction articles.

He has two novels forthcoming. Deadblood: The Mourning Walk will be released early 2016. The Flatstone Beach, the first book in his YA series The Paler World, is in search of a publisher. His new monthly series in the Deadblood Universe, Drop by Drop also begins in 2016

L.A is a father of three children and a husband of 23 years. In addition to writing a lot, L.A. works a corporate job, does community work, and coaches youth sports. He holds three degrees and speaks several languages poorly. As his 3rd grade teacher noted, he lacks focus.

He can found on line at LALittle.com and on Twitter @LALittleAuthor.

"Somnambulant" started out in a dream. That was where I first met Death and The Sandman and became aware of their somewhat troubled relationship. As I thought about them in my waking mind I found myself drawn back to the sand and its narcotic effects. In my first career as a music journalist I had been around a lot of very heavy drugs and addicts (though I was never a user). We tend to not think of addicts in terms of their love and relationships, but they are people with those same feelings and concerns we all have. I've seen how hard that lifestyle is on relationships and I thought that even a cosmic couple would have a hard time making it work if one of them had a habit and ready access to a supply. I'd had a desire to create a new mythology and to take my writing, which is typically very concrete and grounded, into a more ethereal and expressive space for some time. This seemed like the right story through which to push my boundaries.

Meanwhile On A Different Earth

Anya Penfold

Nobody *wanted* a war, we were all very clear about that. Not us, not Them, not so soon after the last one, and certainly not with the vastly, hideously destructive weapons that had been developed at the end of it. Everyone agreed on that, even before it was discovered that their destructive powers didn't end with the flash and the firestorm with which a single bomb could wipe out a city. Radiation sickness, fallout—these were horrors even worse than the horrors of what was now being called 'conventional' warfare, and ones which the experts gloomily predicted could be capable of wiping life itself from the face of our planet. Nobody, not even the experts, wanted a war involving weapons like that.

We were put to work on developing more of those weapons even before the ink was dry on various treaties of peace. It was merely a precaution, of course, because nobody *wanted* a war. It was just that our spies reported that They might be thinking about taking similar precautions against it, and therefore we had to have them too. If we did anything less, the experts gloomily predicted, then there might be a war.

It wasn't as simple as work in the 'conventional' munitions factories, of course. The new weapons were an ingenious breakthrough in what technology could achieve, but still word came down from above that they must be improved upon. They must be larger, faster, capable of being propelled like a rocket, rather than dropped from a plane. They must be able to be aimed towards Their munition factories, Their shipyards and cities, from a distance of many hundreds of miles away, and they must be designed and built to do so in complete secrecy. After all, if They found out we had the capacity to do this – or worse, They copied our ability to do so – then there might be a war.

So we were moved to a brand new base, with all the best security money could buy; out in the desert and out of the range of Their weaponry. As soon as we arrived, we were told to hurry up and build new weapons that could be propelled even further, because our spies informed us that They had similar ideas, and if our weapons couldn't destroy the similar facilities that They were building, what then? They would have the advantage, and if They became aware of the fact, well, that was precisely the sort of thing that might encourage Them to start a war.

We protested that it wasn't that easy. All sorts of new inventions had to be dreamed up just to deal with the practicalities of building such weapons in safety. Devices to measure radiation, and guard against its effects, devices timed and primed to guide a rocket through a hundred miles of atmosphere – all this was still being developed, let alone improved. Valve technology was being stretched to its limits, vast underground rooms of computers dedicated just to calculating flight trajectories. And there were matters of weight, of compression, and of the critical and daunting task of getting everything just *perfectly* right-

We were told to belt up and quit bellyaching. Everyone who was working on preventing the war was facing similar difficulties. There were radar arrays to be designed and redesigned, pushing back the limits of our sight into Their airspace. There were bunkers to be dug out and provisioned, and then dug still deeper as Their weaponry development kept pace with our own. There were thousands of tonnes of ores to be blasted and dug, refined and transmuted, whole mountains torn down for materiel, by-products whose toxicity made the very things around them toxic mounting into depots that would make a rad-counter squeal for a thousand years to come. All of it, the expense, the waste, so that our patient, painstaking hands could make the tiny, intricate mechanisms of the weapons for the war that nobody wanted.

Meanwhile, in remote corners of the world that had barely heard of us *or* Them, conventional warships were racing to bring peace and order and the forward-monitoring stations that would help prevent the war—so long as They didn't get there first.

We did our part. We built new weapons, whose flights would be measured not in the hundreds of miles, but the thousands. We built weapons that could be fired from silos deep within the desert, or from submarines, lurking under the Arctic or the Antarctic ice. Weapons designed to burst open the deepest bunker, weapons to detonate in the air above Their cities. It was barely sufficient. Hurry, hurry, was the constant word from above. It wouldn't do if we were late for the war that nobody wanted.

We didn't talk about our work, even amongst ourselves. It was a far cry from the production lines of the conventional munitions factories, and of course, the need for secrecy was paramount. But there was a sense, if not of camaraderie, at least of a silent, shared *complicity*.

Everyone else was doing their part to prevent the war too, of course. Our politicians regularly took to the airwaves, or the new televisual ones, to assure us that they didn't want a war, no matter how much They might. They responded with similar statements, and every so often either our spies or Theirs would announce new evidence of the other side's industrious preparations to ensure there wouldn't be one. In the schools, the children practiced diving under their desks. Along our shared borders, tanks and gun regiments postured at each other in bristling displays. Skirmishes broke out over remote islands, so strong was the shared conviction that placement of another forward-monitoring station might prove critical. The war that nobody wanted began to take a distant shape, on tropical atolls and storm-lashed Antarctic crags.

I think I only spoke about the situation once, and I can't even recall who it was with. Of course, it was hard to tell through the layers of protective clothing, and the shifts had only become longer as the years groaned on.

"It's like a wolf we're trying to keep from the door," I found myself saying, "only the way we do it is by throwing it chunk after chunk of bloody meat, each one closer to the threshold."

My colleague laughed, not in a nasty way. "More like a fire in the kitchen," I heard through my earpiece. "Only instead of throwing water at it, we throw in the living-room furniture."

Despite all our precautions, the war that nobody wanted coalesced, grew, and made landfall.

There was a brief blast of the siren, followed by a crackling assurance that this was not a drill, and that all the weapons we had worked so hard on had been in vain. Missiles were in flight – both ours and Theirs – and the estimated time to a bunker-busting impact at our own base was calculated at slightly under an hour.

I decided I might as well go out and see the sunshine for the last time.

One of my colleagues plucked at my sleeve from the emergency elevator as I passed. "Come on," he shouted, over the siren's hoot. "There's time before they seal the bunker-"

"I'd rather not," I told him, shrugging off his grasp.

It was hard to tell, since he still had his protective mask on, but he seemed to peer at me as if I was the one who was insane.

"But – there's food down there!" he shouted. "Clean air, water-"

"Then there'll be more for everyone else if I don't," I smiled back.

Quite a number of us had decided to go up to the surface; someone had even had the presence of mind to bring beers. I found that I myself was still carrying the rad-counter I'd been holding when the siren went off. We sat in small, quiet groups, smoking and looking up at the blue bowl of the sky.

"It'll be bad in the cities," my shift supervisor muttered, shaking his head.

"It's only for a small while," someone told him comfortingly. "Then it'll be bad in the countryside, instead."

"Do you think They really did push the button first?" someone else asked. "Because They wanted this? Or was it another flock of geese, maybe?"

"Might have been geese at our end this time," my supervisor sighed. "Or a meteor, or... Did you hear what happened to that guy who didn't press the button, last time? I heard he was shot."

"Good," I said, feeling I should contribute something. "If he's still alive, then he knows he didn't stop the war after all."

"Nobody did," somebody said. "We all tried so hard, too. Do you think we did the right thing?"

"We did the only thing we could do," my supervisor said firmly. "If we hadn't…"

"Here it comes!" It was a shout. People started to get to their feet around me.

I took a deep gulp of beer. The war was in the sky above us now, and would soon be ploughing its way into the ground beneath our feet.

"Are you going to watch?" someone asked me.

I considered it. "I don't want to see the flash," I decided aloud.

"I'd get your head down then," I was advised. "It's – *oh*."

The flash wasn't as bright against my eyelids as I'd expected, nor the thunder of the detonation as loud. In fact, I shouldn't have been able to hear it at all, given the plasma-hot furnace I should be standing in.

When I opened my eyes, there was a blizzard around me. Confetti, I thought, holding out my hand.

"It's petals," my supervisor was saying, staring dumbly at his own, outstretched palms. "After all that – I guess They really didn't want the war after all." He seized my arms. "Do you realise what this means? For our cities?"

I was thinking more of Their cities. Even as we spoke, the air-burst detonations would be blossoming above them, releasing not petals, but thousands upon thousands of tiny origami cranes.

I've been writing since I was old enough to find my way around a BBC Micro, such a dismayingly long time that I have floppy disks older than some of my colleagues (and also, really need to clear out some cupboards). Despite this, I haven't had the courage to put anything forward until this year, when I hit 40 and realised it officially doesn't matter what I do anymore, because I'm a mad old bat now either way. Phew! I write science fiction, fantasy, weird fiction and horror, and am also a part-time artist, subsistence-farmer and wine-maker.

Writing Meanwhile on a Different Earth

I have to confess, this was written in one evening, after a rather mellow, misty day and a phone conversation with my chestnut-haired old mother. She doesn't usually talk much about the past, especially her life before I came along, but on this particular day she suddenly told me all about when she was working at a forward radar station in Ireland, during the Cold War. I hadn't ever known anything about this, so I was most impressed. When I asked what it was like, having the responsibility of being early-warning for a USSR nuclear-missile attack, she told me it was a nightmare trying to keep the seams straight on her regulation stockings, and what a relief it was when someone finally invented tights (pantyhose, to anyone reading this in the US).

The idea of my mum warding off a potential nuclear attack while wearing seamed stockings – as part of a regulation uniform, no less – was so bizarre I'm afraid I burst out laughing. I hadn't quite finished when it occurred to me that she would hardly have been better able to prevent a missile-strike in khakis, but the juxtaposition stuck with me. It made me wonder, what would be the most ridiculous thing you could defy a nuclear holocaust with?

The Banana Tree

Gail D. Villanueva

I never knew why, but banana trees grew worse than weeds in the town of Calajuacan. They were an infestation like fleas on a dog, serving us no purpose but to suck the soil nutrients our useful plants needed.

Just like the one Manong Isko asked me to take down. It grew right in the middle of our backyard, an unattractive beacon of flappy leaves and layered trunk. How it managed to grow to a good four feet without me noticing it, I had no idea. These plants sprouted in our town so fast.

"Tatay won't be happy looking down on you from heaven. Can't even maintain the yard," I muttered, shooing the chickens my *nanay* kept. She cared so much for these birds, sometimes I wondered if she loved them more than she did me, her only son. I waved my ax to keep the chickens away, but they continued to circle the banana tree.

The ax I carried belonged to my father, my *tatay,* the greatest man I ever knew before Manong Isko. Now, it was mine. I expected Manong Isko would keep it — he had been Tatay's work partner and his best friend — but instead, he gave it to me.

It was a great honor being Manong Isko's apprentice. He and Tatay had been the best lumberjacks in town, the only ones the Calajuacanons trusted to rid their properties of the unwanted trees. Soon, I would take Tatay's place as Manong Isko's new partner. And maybe, Nanay would be well enough to weave the fibers I prepared from the discarded banana trunks.

Tatay would be proud of me. No one would doubt I deserved to inherit my father's ax and carry on his name.

I am Antonio Palpal-latoc, Jr., the bane of weedy banana trees in all of Calajuacan!

I swung the ax and hit the base of the banana tree. I hit the stem again and again on the same spot like Tatay taught me. *Make a deep enough cut on one side, and a just little bit on the opposite end so the banana tree falls where you want it to.*

Even with Tatay gone, I still remembered everything he taught me. I did as he had instructed. *Keep your hand steady, so you don't waver from your target.* My hands were steady. I didn't waver from my target. I hit it the same spot so often, the ax rubbed my palms raw. I hit the base of the stem twenty times, and managed to expose two layers of the white flesh.

But it was as far as I got.

"What in the world — ?" I muttered, wiping the sweat trickling down my eyebrows. I tried again, swinging harder this time. But it still didn't make a difference. The wound on the stem got no deeper.

The sun was on its way to sleep, turning the bamboo walls of our home slightly orange. Soon, I would have nothing but the moon and the stars to guide me. If only we could use these banana trees for energy, the town would have had electricity day and night.

But no. They were useless, nutrient-sucking weeds not even capable of bearing fruit.

I dropped the blade and studied the stubborn banana tree. It was smaller than usual, just a few inches taller than me. I walked around it like the chickens did, then took a step closer. I hoped to see what made the plant so impenetrable, but instead came face-to-face with an oddly-shaped and unusually-colored banana leaf.

My eyes adjusted, and I realized it was no leaf.

It was a banana flower; the plant part that books referred to as the "banana heart."

Shaped like a butterfly cocoon as big as my arm, the heart had layers upon layers of purple leaves covering it. I never saw a banana heart up close until now, the only ones being in photos my friend Weng showed me from her book of plants. I was intrigued, but at the same time, disturbed.

Tatay told me the nutrients in the soil where our town sat made it impossible for the banana trees to flower. When I asked how come the other trees and plants were able to bear fruit, my father didn't bother to explain. He said it was a mystery. *God had a reason, and only He knew why.*

If God made the Calajuacan banana trees infertile, then why did this one flower? And right in the middle of our yard.

Maybe the banana heart was an omen.

I already lost my father. True, no omen could have warned us of Tatay slipping on sharp rocks and hitting his head. But if the flower was a warning, I would heed it nonetheless.

I didn't want to risk losing my mother too.

In her current state, Nanay would freak out if she saw the flowering tree. I couldn't let that happen. It was my duty to care for my mother, to make sure her mind didn't leave her completely. Nanay used to prepare afternoon snacks for me and Tatay. But lately, all she did was to lie on the *papag* all day, listening to radio dramas and staring at the ceiling.

I had to get rid of it, I thought. *For Nanay's sake.*

I took off my shirt exposing my chest, still not as strong or broad as Tatay's had been—not yet anyway.. The chickens clucked and flapped their wings, circling me like bullies in a school yard. In my mind, the chickens mocked me, chanting in symphony with my growling stomach. *Toto payatot! So thin, he can't even bring down a banana tree. Toto payatot!*

The chickens' chant grew louder in my head, but I ignored them. I took a deep breath, and swung the ax at the base of the banana tree once again. I swung with all my might.

Still, nothing happened.

"Why don't you just die?" I gritted my teeth, and swung again.

Nothing.

Toto payatot! The chickens sang. I shooed them away, looking up in time to see my mother by the window. She was like a ghost, flitting through the house with half of her soul missing, half of her heart buried underground with Tatay.

I wished I could help her. Get her well, and be a family again. Even with just the two of us. But I couldn't. I couldn't fix Nanay the way I couldn't cut down this stupid tree.

Frustrated, I swung my ax, aiming for the base of the banana heart. Omen or not, my mother would never see it; she *should* never see it. Whatever was left of her mind and soul had to stay, for both our sakes.

The red cocoon dropped with a thud.

Light escaped from the flesh my blade exposed. It was so bright, I thought I would go blind. Dancing spots cleared from my vision, and the light turned to a comforting shade of green. It swirled, forming a whirlpool of green light, getting larger until it reached the size of a door.

I stepped back, my mind full of visions of evil fairies and demons our elders warned us about. I wanted to run, but my foot caught on a branch. I fell backward. My elbows hurt and the scratches on my palms stung, but I couldn't tear my eyes off the whirlpool of light.

A webbed, four-fingered hand slowly forced its way out.

I wanted to scream, but the voice died in my throat.

***

"There's a *lakay* in our chicken coop."

Weng stopped in her tracks, and a man carrying a sack of rice on his back nearly bumped into us. She clutched the schoolbooks to her chest as though they were the most important things in the world. "Are you serious?" she asked me, avoiding the stranger's gaze.

"Sorry, *manong*," I told the stranger, who nodded and gave me a strained smile. Weng and I walked this path daily. She should have known better than to stop without regard for the people around her.

It was unlike Weng to be so rude. But then again, my Nanay was never the same after Tatay's accident. I didn't think my family's loss would affect Weng. Mind you, it wasn't because she was insensitive.

Weng was the strongest person I knew. She was an only child like me, but God had thrown more challenges on her path than I would have been able to handle. When she was four, her father abandoned their family for a woman he met in Tuguegarao City. Then a year ago, her mother died, leaving her in the care of her uncle, Manong Isko. Weng handled all these obstacles in stride. But when Tatay died, she didn't seem like the strong and confident Weng I knew. She changed; she became jumpy, scared, and rude.

I pulled Weng aside, on to the side of the road where she wouldn't be a bother to anyone else. She flinched at my touch as if burned. Calajuacan only had one paved road, and it went through the center of the town all the way to the other end. At this time, the road was at its busiest — adults turning in after a day of work and errands, children coming home from school.

Tatay always reminded me to be considerate of others. *Respect your neighbors, Toto, and they will respect you*, he said. If Weng couldn't, I would be considerate for the both of us.

"Yes, a lakay. But keep your voice down," I warned, leading her farther away from the side of the road, stopping only when we were a step away from the mouth of the forest. My eyes darted left to right, making sure no one was listening. "It looks like the dwarves in your books. Pointy ears, stubby, and this tall." I pointed to my shoulder.

Weng raised a brow, turning one of her slanted brown eyes slightly bigger than the other. Mine had a similar shape, as most Calajuacanons did, but Weng's seemed prettier than everyone else's. Except the skin around her right eye was tinted black and blue.

"The lakay has a beard like Santa Claus', but his isn't white and doesn't look like facial hair," I continued. "More like, a bunch of cockroach feelers stuck to his face."

"Okay…"

"And he's green. The lakay is green all over."

"Green?" Weng narrowed her eyes. "Lakays aren't green. They're brown, like you and me. It says so in my book."

"But he is." I didn't care what Weng's book said, I was the one who saw the lakay. "He's green."

"How do you know it's a 'he' and not a 'she'?"

"I just do."

"So," Weng started. "This 'lakay' just appeared in your chicken coop? How?" Her lips formed into a smirk. "Magic?"

"No." I scowled. "It came out of the portal from a banana tree."

Weng burst out laughing. She held her books tight, clinging to them like a lifeline. I would have done anything to see her smile in the last few months, but not at my expense.

"Forget it." I turned to leave, but Weng grabbed my arm.

"I'm sorry, Toto. Don't go. I didn't mean to laugh," she said, gasping between giggles. Weng tucked a strand of her long black hair behind an ear and took a deep breath. "But listen to yourself. You have a lakay in your chicken coop that came out of a banana *herb* portal — banana plants are herbs, not trees, by the way. Tell me if that doesn't sound funny to you."

I stopped and looked at her. Weng was right. "But I'm telling you the truth."

Weng tilted her head, studying me. "Fine. Let's say I believe you," she began. Weng peered closer. She was twelve like me, but already a good three inches taller. "You didn't let him go off wandering about, did you?"

"Of course not," I said, frowning. "I told you, he's locked inside with the chickens. I gave him some *niyog* before I left."

"The lakay liked the coconuts?" asked Weng. "But my book says they love sugar. You should have given him sugar!"

"Well, *my* lakay enjoyed the niyog." Weng's book was beginning to annoy me.

"Are you sure it's a lakay?"

"Yes."

"What if you're wrong? It could be something else!" I opened my mouth to protest, but Weng held up a hand. "Wait, did you get to look at its hands and feet?"

I frowned. "The feet, no. But its hands were weird. Kind of like a frog's."

"That's not a lakay!" Weng exclaimed. "I read about this somewhere. Pre-history, I think. Before the Spaniards came. The ancient gods sent magic creatures to earth from heaven…" Weng kept mumbling about some book she read, not even noticing the ones she was dropping on the ground.

"Weng, your books — "

"Be quiet, Toto. I'm thinking," she said, marching back and forth in front of me. I picked up her books, but she didn't seem to care anymore. She just kept pacing. Weng mumbled some more, then stopped without warning. She stared at me, her eyes were wide with excitement. "I have to see it."

I bit my lower lip. Should I let Weng meet the creature?

After I had gotten over the shock of seeing the lakay come out of the whirlpool of light, it took every bit of my self-control not to scream and frighten Nanay. I thought it would harm me, but it didn't. The scratches on my palms and elbows closed up when it touched me. The blisters I got from assisting Manong Isko cut down banana trees would have faded too, had I not yanked my hand away. The lakay seemed to have good intentions, but would it be friendly to Weng the way it was to me?

"Come on, Toto. Please. I want to see," Weng begged.

I stared at my friend. For the first time in three months, I saw a glimmer of the spark in her that I missed so much. She lost the twinkle when I lost my father, replaced by gloom and fear, made worse by tears and an occasional black eye.

Sighing, I said, "Fine. But don't tell Manong Isko."

Weng winced at the mention of her uncle's name, but she nodded. "I won't."

I handed Weng her books, and our fingers touched. Instead of pulling away, I circled my pinky around hers. It felt warm in mine. "The lakay healed my wounds. It could heal your eye."

Weng avoided looking at me, but she didn't let go of my finger. "I fell on the steps again. Manong Isko hasn't fixed it yet."

"Right." As if she would tell me the truth. But she didn't have to. I knew.

Whenever Manong Isko started smelling like a chico fruit, Weng would have a black and blue ring around her eye soon after. I had always thought Weng had it coming — I figured she might have done something wrong to deserve the beating. Today, it was as if someone turned on a lightbulb in my head.

I loved Manong Isko. Nanay and I would forever be grateful for him. He brought us back Tatay's body. He visited Nanay every day even when drunk. He also gave me a job. The pay wasn't the same as when he and Tatay were splitting the earnings, but it was enough to help me and my mother get by. And he took care of Weng. He could have sent Weng to her father in Tuguegarao, he didn't.

The lakay must have done something and messed with my mind for me to question Manong Isko. But for the first time, I saw things clearly. Like Nanay and Weng, Manong Isko wasn't the same man he was when my father was still alive, making me wonder if maybe I had changed too.

Deep down, I knew that no matter what Weng did, she didn't deserve to be beaten—no one did. I had moments of displeasing my own father, but not once had he raised a hand against me. I wished Weng would talk to me about it. She needed to know she wasn't alone, and that I was there for her.

"Weng —"

"Just show me the creature, Toto." Weng snatched her hand from me, and her lower lip quivered. "Please."

"All right," I agreed. Weng would tell me when she was ready. "Let's go."

***

At the end of the paved road, Weng and I turned left to a dirt path. The farther we were from the road, the denser the trees became. Every now and then, there would be a clearing surrounded by waist-high bamboo fences and a *bahay kubo* in the middle.

As we passed by the home of Kapitan and his wife, Manang Tess, Weng placed a hand over her right cheek.

"Does it hurt?"

Weng shook her head and walked faster.

I sighed. If anyone could help Weng, it was Kapitan and Manang Tess. They were two of the nicest people I knew. Kapitan was the town sheriff, and he worked very hard to keep Calajuacan peaceful. Because they couldn't have children, Manang Tess devoted her time helping less fortunate Calajuacanons like my family. She would not let a week go by without making sure Nanay and I were still okay.

Weng and I saw three more houses before my family's bahay kubo came to view. Tatay built our home near a cluster of banana trees, telling me how he wanted to be close to the plants he considered our bread and butter. The banana trees might be weeds, but they were our livelihood.

Like most houses in Calajuacan, our bahay kubo had woven bamboo mats for walls and dried blady grass for roofing. They weren't as sturdy as the cement walls of Weng's house, but the nipa huts withstood every typhoon that passed through the town. Tatay reasoned it was because of the banana trees; they were so many, they protected us from bad weather. *God made everything with a purpose*, he said.

We neared the house. I beckoned at Weng to follow me to the covered narrow alley connecting the *batalan* — the wet area where I cooked and washed the dishes — and the main house.

"*Shh*," I said. The bahay kubo was raised on stilts of more than a foot high, obscuring us if we stooped low enough. Nanay was likely zoned out again, hidden behind the tattered curtain of the papag. But I had to be careful. If by some miracle her mind suddenly returned, I couldn't risk having to explain what Weng and I were up to.

"Is that where the creature came from?" Weng pointed to a plant in the middle of the yard.

"Yes," I said, frowning. "Strange. It withered so fast. Do the banana trees in your book die as soon as their flowers are chopped off?" I nudged the fallen banana heart with my toe. Overnight, it turned from purple to black.

"Probably. I don't know. This is the first time I've seen its flower up close," she admitted. "And like I said, it's not a tree. Banana plants are *herbs*."

I put a finger to my lips to hush Weng, carrying my feet with care as I walked to the chicken coop. I left the chickens outside their cage and made sure to close the backyard gate, but I counted them nonetheless.

One, two, three… All twelve were present. None escaped, or got eaten by the lakay.

As I unlocked the door, Weng stuck her head eagerly over my shoulder. She smelled like sweet mangoes and sampaguita flowers, a pleasant reprieve from the otherwise disgusting stench of chicken manure.

"Oh," Weng said, disappointed. "Is he supposed to be invisible?"

"No... Oh, no." Dread washed over me, and blood drained from my face. "It's escaped!"

"At least you got the toilet you wanted." Weng pointed to the spot where the lakay dug a hole deep enough so he could slip beneath the bamboo wall. "You might need to move the walls a bit though. The hole your 'lakay' made is too far from the center. Unless you want Manang Tess seeing your butt every time you squat to poo."

"Stop making fun, Weng. This is serious!"

"I am serious." Weng coughed, as if it could hide her smirk. I glared at her. "Sorry," she said, raising her hands in surrender.

"Listen. I'm telling you the truth. When have I lied to you?"

Weng turned somber. "Like, never."

"That's right. Trust me, there was a lakay in here, and it escaped. I don't know what will happen if someone sees him. The lakay didn't hurt me, but I'm not sure he'll react the same with other people." I sighed in frustration. "We *need* to find it. I just don't know how and where to start."

Weng took her time before replying. She stared at me with an expression I couldn't quite read. Finally, Weng broke our gaze and walked around the hole, then crouched beside it.

"Careful," I said, holding her shoulders as she peered beneath the wall. Weng tensed, but I held on. She might have fallen into the hole if I had let go.

Weng cleared her throat. She stood up so fast, I backed away. "I saw footprints going into the forest. We could clear the area around your house before it gets dark," she declared and hurried to the door, but I remained rooted in place.

"Well?" she asked, a hint of impatience in her voice. "Are you just going to stand there or help me find your missing lakay?"

I didn't know what I would have done without Weng, she always knew what to do even when I froze in panic. I just wished she wasn't so jumpy around me.

"Lead the way, Weng."

***

We searched the forest surrounding my family's property in silence, giving each other the privacy of our thoughts. I worried about the lakay, but I worried about Weng more. The forest was our favorite place to talk. Or rather, Weng's —she rarely allowed me to get a word in edgewise. Usually, she wouldn't pass up a chance like this to tell me about a new book she read, or some interesting trivia she overheard from the gossiping *manang*s from the sari-sari store beside her home.

The sun had begun its descent when Weng spoke again. "It's not here, Toto," she said, stopping beside a banana tree.

I marked its trunk with an X using my *balisong*, the sharp knife Manong Isko gave me for my twelfth birthday. My parents didn't want me carrying it, but Manong Isko explained it was for my own safety. What if I got lost in the forest? Tatay eventually relented and allowed me to keep Manong Isko's gift. Despite Nanay's protests, he taught me to mark trees so I could find my way back home.

The marks will guide you, Toto.

"We should go home," Weng said as she stared up at the darkening sky. "I haven't cooked dinner for me and Manong Isko yet."

I nodded, remembering how famished my father was after a day's work. Weng shouldn't get in trouble because of me. I was the one who didn't secure the lakay properly.

"You're right. Nanay might be hungry by now too." I sighed. If I hadn't let my emotions get the best of me, I wouldn't have released the lakay from the tree.

"Do you need help with cooking?" Weng asked. "I can ask Manang Tess on the way home. She'll be happy to bring you some *bagnet*."

My mouth watered at the mention of Manang Tess' signature dish. Pork belly slab thick with skin and fat, fried to crispy perfection. Our neighbor's bagnet was the best in Calajuacan. Probably even the best in all of the towns in the Cagayan Valley region. Still, I declined Weng's offer. "Don't worry, I'll be fine."

"You're thinner, like you haven't been eating well," Weng insisted. "Let me talk to Manang Tess."

"I thought you didn't want her to see this." I reached out to touch her bruise, but Weng stepped back.

"It's nothing," she said, averting her eyes. "I can't just let you and your mother starve."

"We won't," I said, a small smile playing on my lips. Weng had problems of her own, and yet, she still thought of us. "Manang Tess has a family too, you know. She's given us so much already, and so have you. I wish I could do the same," I continued, letting the words slide before I had the sense to stop myself. "You can tell me anything, Weng."

Weng's gaze was everywhere but me. "Toto…"

"And don't leave yet. I just harvested eggplants this morning," I said.

"Thanks, but — "

"They'll just spoil. We don't have a refrigerator like you do, remember?"

"Toto! Shut up about the eggplants." Weng stomped her foot in frustration, while pointing to a cluster of trees. "Look! Smoke. From your house!"

White smoke snaked into the sky from where our bahay kubo stood. *Nanay Jesusa.* My mother. Why didn't I consider the lakay coming after her? It hadn't seemed dangerous. And the tracks. The tracks led us to the forest. It never crossed my mind he would attempt to get inside our house and hurt Nanay.

The lakay was kind to me. He healed my wounds. He didn't struggle when I led him to the chicken coop. He even seemed glad to be around the chickens while munching on the niyog I gave him. Apparently, I was wrong. Like I was wrong about Manong Isko. The only ones left I could be sure of were Nanay and Weng. I couldn't let anyone, or anything, harm them.

My heart pounded rapidly. Nanay was in danger. We had to hurry.

***

The smoke we saw came from the batalan where the clay stove was. The very same clay stove Tatay molded with his own two hands. I didn't see any reason why the stove could be aflame. Unless the lakay decided to cook Nanay for dinner.

"No!" I shouted, running as fast as I could. Weng grunted behind me, trying to catch up.

The lakay was too small to reach the stove, so it stood on top of the stool Nanay used when doing the laundry. It hummed an unfamiliar tune — an eerie, out-of-this-world tune — as it stirred a pot of boiling stew.

My mother in the stew.

"What did you do?" I was so horrified, I could barely get the words out of my mouth. Weng gave a strangled cry.

The lakay stared at me, its black pupils wide and innocent.

"My mother! Where's my mother?" I demanded, trying to ignore the delicious smells coming from the clay pot.

It reminded me of *dinengdeng*, the soupy vegetable dish Nanay used to prepare for me when I got home from school. The steam was so distracting, I almost forgot Nanay's body parts were swimming in the shrimp paste soup, bumping occasionally with the bitter melon, calabaza squash, string beans, and whatever else the lakay decided to throw in.

The door from the main house opened, making me jump and prompting another shriek from Weng.

"I'm right here, Antonio. Why are you shouting?" It was my mother. I was so happy, I hugged her. To my surprise, she hugged me back. She hugged me for the first time since Tatay left.

Pushing the hair off my eyes, she kissed my forehead. "You need a haircut."

"I know," I said. "I thought you were in the stew." Nanay laughed. That beautiful, happy laugh I missed so much.

"Eloy is helping me cook. I told him dinengdeng is your favorite," she explained. The lakay grinned and chirped, showing me two rows of jagged teeth. "He doesn't speak yet. But he'll learn our language soon."

"Eloy?" Weng asked. I had forgotten she was there.

"Hello, Rowena. Yes, I named him Eloy. It seemed to suit him," Nanay said. She smiled at Weng. "Would you like to stay for dinner?"

"Manong Isko — "

"Rowena! What happened to your eye?" blurted out Nanay, gently lifting Weng's chin to take a closer look. "Did Isko do this to you?"

I expected Weng to deny it, to say it was her fault, how she hit her face because of clumsiness.

But she didn't. Weng couldn't lie to my mother.

Just to me, I realized with a pang.

To her credit, Weng didn't confirm nor deny. She looked down like a dog with its tail between its legs. No tears either, but I could see Weng struggled to keep them from flowing.

Stop being selfish, Toto. I scolded myself. *Weng needs you.*

I lifted my hand to touch Weng's shoulder, but hesitated.

"Your hand, Antonio. What's this on your hand?" Nanay's voice raised an octave higher. Eloy the Lakay made a whistling sound as if sensing her distress, but Nanay ignored him. She studied my hand, running her fingers across my palm. "So many calluses! What have you been doing, my *anak*?"

"I assist Manong Isko taking down banana trees," I said. Nanay turned livid. "He pays me, Nanay. For us. Our food. My things for school," I added hastily.

"Come here, both of you," Nanay said, her voice cracking as she gathered me and Weng in her arms. It had been a while since I felt this—safe in my mother's embrace.

Nanay released us, but held on to my shoulders. "I will never let anybody take advantage of you again, my son. I'll weave, and we'll sell the things I'll make. You never have to cut banana plants until you're old enough, you hear?"

"But —"

"*Shh*," she said. Nanay took Weng's hand and led her beside Eloy the Lakay. "He came from the stars. I will handle Isko, but Rowena, you need to let Eloy take away your pain."

Without a word, Weng nodded and closed her eyes. Eloy placed his webbed fingers on her forehead. Just like when he fixed my elbows, dark purple light emanated from Weng. It lingered a bit, and I felt its negative energy hang in the air. But it dissipated as soon as Eloy lifted his hand.

"Better?" I asked.

Weng smiled, the dimple on her left cheek showing up again after disappearing for several months. "Much better," she replied.

"Stay here for the night, Rowena. I will speak to Isko tomorrow."

"No!" Weng cried. "He might hurt you! If he gets angry — "

The thought of Manong Isko hitting my mother sickened me. "'*Nay*, no —"

"Hush, both of you," Nanay said. "Have a little faith. I'm not marching in there on my own. I'll ask Kapitan and Tess to come with me."

Of course. Manong Isko wouldn't dare attack my mother with the sheriff around. I had forgotten how my mother thought about everything.

Things are going to be okay.

Nanay hummed together with Eloy as they prepared our dinner. I went inside to set the table, this time for four instead of two. Weng followed me.

"Your mother really is back, isn't she?" Weng asked as she helped me spread banana leaves on the table.

I cleaned the leaves with a damp cloth. "Yes, I believe she is," I answered. I stopped scrubbing and met her gaze. "What will happen to your uncle?"

Weng shrugged.

"Well, at least we can be sure he'll stop beating you."

Instead of answering, Weng folded the edges of a banana leaf beneath the table. "Do you think there's more like Eloy?"

"I suppose so. Where will you stay if they send Manong Isko away?"

"I don't know." Weng looked down. "Maybe they'll bring me to my father in Tuguegarao."

"They won't," I said with confidence, reaching over the table to give her hand a squeeze. "The Kapitan and his wife could adopt you. Manang Tess said they always wanted to have children."

"Maybe."

Nanay sat across from me and Weng, while Eloy took the seat beside her, setting down a pot of steaming dinengdeng on folded banana leaves. The pot scorched the leaves brown, but it didn't burn through our bamboo table. Eloy's multiple feelers shuffled as the steam tickled his beard.

I stood up and reached out for my mother's bowl, but she stopped me. "It's okay, Anak." Nanay smiled as she filled my bowl with dinengdeng. She did the same for Weng and Eloy.

Just like she used to before Tatay died.

"Were you not scared of him?" I asked my mother.

"No," she answered. I raised an eyebrow.

"My mind wasn't right, Antonio. But Eloy healed me," Nanay explained as she turned her gaze to the yard. "He showed me how you let him out; how he heard your heart's plea. You wished for me to get well."

I pretended I didn't see the tear running down my mother's face. She brushed it away.

Weng cleared her throat. "Toto said he's a lakay, the dwarves in the legends. Is he?"

"No, he's not a lakay," Nanay answered. "But the lakay stories were probably based on his kind. Eloy seemed like he's been here before."

I nodded, loosening the clumps of rice with my fingers.

Nanay reached over and squeezed my arm. "I'm sorry I left you, Antonio. I couldn't handle your father's —"

"It's okay, mother."

Nanay didn't press me, and poured some of the dinengdeng over the rice mound in front of her.

I was blowing the hot steam from my soup when a thought occurred to me. "What if the town finds out about Eloy?"

My mother stopped chewing. She swallowed, washed down her food with a glass of water, then answered, "Calajuacanons are used to strange things, Anak."

"But wouldn't they be scared of him?" Weng looked at me. "Toto was."

"I wasn't —"

"Toto," Nanay warned. She carefully considered Weng's question. "When they first see him, I expect they'll be frightened. But in time, the people will accept him. Calajuacan didn't always have banana herbs growing everywhere. Yet, we managed. We adapted. We always have."

The rooster in the yard crowed, prompting us to look outside. The other chickens pecked the dirt around the banana *herb*, but the plant where Eloy came from already withered and died. In its place, a new sucker began to emerge.

Yes, things were going to change. Perhaps Eloy's arrival would change Calajuacan for the better, perhaps for the worse. Weng might move to Tuguegarao, but she might be fortunate enough to stay. Either way, things were going to be different.

I glanced at Eloy. The alien slurped the soup from his dinengdeng before picking off the greens one by one. The feelers on his face parted every time he brought a vegetable close to his lips. Beside him, Nanay mashed the dinengdeng with rice. Weng, on the other hand, meticulously separated her vegetables around the grains by shape and by type.

This is my family now.

I lifted my bowl of dinengdeng and took a sip. Salty, a little sweet, and just a bit spicy — the flavors all came together with the right amount of bitterness.

Delicious.

Hey. I'm Gail. I'm a web designer by day, and a writer by night -- or by the crack of dawn, if the inspiration strikes. I enjoy sharing my imagined worlds through words and illustrations, but telling stories for children is what I love the most. I'm currently working on my first novel, a gaslamp fantasy set in nineteenth century Philippines, and hoping to write more stories of fun, magic, and aliens. I live in the suburbs of Manila, Philippines with my husband and our menagerie of pets. No extraterrestrials, no faeries, nor are there monsters hidden in our property. But there might be a chain-smoking giant living in our neighbor's mango tree, and yes, we do own a couple of banana plants in our yard.

"The Banana Tree" was obviously inspired by the succulent plants sprouting everywhere at home, in empty lots in the city, and practically in every province I've visited in the Philippines. I used to be a travel blogger in my past life — you will easily find my website — and I've travelled my country a lot. Enough for me to glimpse a Filipino way of life lost to living in the cities. This culture, I think, was something I believed I could immortalize in a story. Calajuacan was a mashup of the places I've been to, but Tuguegarao is a real city in the Cagayan province, at the tip of Luzon island. Like Toto, my grandfather was of Ilokano ethnicity. According to my mom, the bagnet and dinengdeng were his favorites. I must have inherited his love for bagnet, but the gene liking the bitter dinengdeng definitely skipped me.

Writing "The Banana Tree" allowed me to explore my own Ilokano roots, to get to know the grandfather I heard about but never met, and to bring together real-life experiences with the fantastical world of "what if."

The Breeding Dust

Dennis Mombauer

Silent, angular houses with white plaster, a sand-suffocated well and a couple of stunted palms huddled together on the low ground, a once bustling city that only the ghostly desert wind inhabited now.

The sun gleamed down without mercy, hanging in the sky as a swirling ball that made the air flicker, and the small caravan decided to rest in this ancient oasis. The camels were led down the loose sand dunes and racked up in the shadow of the ruined walls, while the men sought refuge in one of the best-preserved buildings.

Scattered sunbeams fell in through holes in the roof and illuminated dusty rubble, but it was comfortably cool compared to the heat outside. Everyone looked for a place to sit, drank freshly cooked tea and tried to pay as little attention as possible to the wind, which seemed to carry along doleful whispers from a prouder time.

The men agreed to wait for nightfall or late afternoon before they would continue their journey, although a short examination found the well waterless and the rest of the city equally empty, not even home to bones or mummified remains.

After everyone else save the guards had retreated for a short rest, Ikrashun wandered through the lifeless streets. Besides the panting and scraping of the camels, the quiet conversations of the men and the wind's lonely tune, the oasis was utterly silent, the unbearable heat having driven even the scorpions into hiding.

The young monk sat down beside a big boulder and began to meditate. The heat didn't touch him as much as the others, his breathing calm and steady while he thought about his journey and his destination, about why he had left the Tourmaline Sheikhdom and resigned from the Order.

The wind whirled up wispy sand particles, creating unsteady forms, faces contorted with pain that instantly collapsed back into curved towers and clouds, delicate constructs without consistency. Ikrashun sat motionless, stared at the ground and watched this play of the sand while contemplating the corruption and decadence of his former masters. There were still doubts in him, but it was far too late to turn back: he had joined this caravan in Mahasutaf, and they had already travelled hundreds of perilous miles into the desert.

After the sun had crossed its zenith, the men prepared their departure, as nobody wanted to linger between the ruins till nightfall. Ikrashun returned to them as he heard a commotion, hushed voices arguing with each other, the sounds of a frantic search. They soon discovered that one of the guards had gone missing, and that they couldn't find a trace of him anywhere in the abandoned houses.

The remaining caravan members packed their things hastily while keeping an eye on the buildings and nervously touching the hilts of their weapons. Ikrashun was watching the desert, where he suddenly spotted hazy movement – but as he shielded his eyes from the sun and looked again, there was only pristine sand.

Before he could share his observation, a loud scream of pain split the air, followed by a gurgling groan. One of the caravan soldiers broke down, clutching a feathered arrow shaft that had penetrated deep into his neck. Ikrashun scanned the landscape, while all around him men took cover, ran back into the oasis or ducked down behind some forward rubble.

Right before Ikrashun's eyes, a bone-bleached figure manifested at the crest of a dune, luridly gleaming in the sunlight, and another man, not fast or lucky enough, was struck down by its arrow. All over the sand hills girdling the city, white specters rose up, and the young monk started to run as well. A shower of arrows rained down, stirred up the sand or splintered against the dusty ruin walls, and Ikrashun only narrowly evaded them.

As soon as he reached cover in a house entrance, silence set in. The figures along the dunes stood motionless, their bows strained, without a sign of fatigue. The only sounds were made by the wind that swept around the buildings, swirled up sand waves and haunted the well shaft, and Ikrashun realized they were trapped.

From an opposing building, a soldier beckoned to him, and Ikrashun took one last look, braced his muscles and rushed across the street. Nothing happened, no arrow tried to hit him, and he reached the shaded door safely.

Inside the structure, the majority of the caravan members huddled in a paved courtyard behind another gateway, which had probably once been veiled by a curtain. The men discussed what to do now, and a few late arrivals, who had been with the camels, reported the entire city to be encircled by figures spectral in appearance, but alive enough to defeat any attempted escape.

The caravan couldn't expect help, for the roads on which they crossed the desert were unknown and abandoned, a fact that had seemed convenient when they departed, because many of the travelers had an interest in secrecy – but now, they cursed the excessive caution that had left them stranded far away from all trading routes and the Sheikhdom's patrols.

**

They decided that a small band of men should try to sneak through the circumvallation to get behind the attackers, and Ikrashun volunteered together with four soldiers. They quietly climbed the courtyard wall, darted low along the empty streets and approached the outskirts of the city. As they reached the foot of the dunes, they almost didn't believe their eyes: not a single figure was to be seen, the yellow-brown sand stretching under the fading sunlight without a trace of the eerie bowmen.

The caravan decamped as quickly as possible, eager to get away from this place and the ghostly figures. Soon, the shadows lengthened, the air cooled and the sun descended in the sky. They reached a rocky hill and put up their tents, tying the camels to the posts and playing dice to distribute guard shifts for the night. Ikrashun got one around midnight, and when a soldier woke him after a few hours of sleep, Ikrashun went outside to keep watch and meditate.

The moon hung over him like a vindictive eye, and its silvery light flowed over the nightly dunes, leaving deep shadows between the tents and rocks as it receded. Except for the movements of nocturnal desert animals, the sandy nothingness stretched out placid and inert before Ikrashun, and as far as he could see, it differed in no way from the desert they had crossed for days and weeks.

After a time Ikrashun glimpsed something in the distance, far away, along the ridge of an elongated dune: a caravan passing by. Pallid figures and camels moved slowly, seemingly emerging from nothing and vanishing behind the sand again, as if something had swallowed them. The monk had no doubt that this ghostly trek was leaving just as little footprints as the bowmen had, and that even a thorough investigation would yield no proof it had ever been there.

He decided to tell no one about this apparition, as it would only fuel their fear – but suddenly, a horrified cry rose up behind him. He spun around and saw one of the merchants rush from his tent, break down and weep: "Dead, he is dead, wholly dead, and I haven't touched him, dead, stone-dead, he just lay there and now he is dead, dead, dead."

As it turned out, the merchant's tent mate had passed away without any injury, and the merchant had woken up to find the corpse's arms slung around him. The morning revealed a total of five people to have perished in their tents, all of them without visible wounds, without blood, without a cause.

Tales of invisible creatures stalking the caravan spread quickly, and the mood was tense as they set out again. Only an endless expanse of yellow sand stretched out around them, traversed by long dunes and burned by the sun from a clear sky. Like a trail of ants, the men and camels moved through this heat-hazed, waterless sea, far and wide the only signs of life between isolated rock pillars and scattered cacti.

There were no accurate maps of this area, only a few known oases scattered along the major trading routes between the Sheikhdom and the nation of Hâl

Bedur. The caravan, however, was travelling further south, right through the unpopulated, largely unexplored region commonly known as "Vanishing Sands", notorious for its lifelike and frequent mirages. Ikrashun hadn't seen any mirages up to now, although he wished that the sinister enemies surrounding them were nothing more than hallucinations, their arrows just blinks of reflected sunlight.

The soldier right before Ikrashun stopped, and the young monk almost ran into him. There was no apparent reason for this halt, so he moved further along the caravan, in the direction of the vanguard. In front of the foremost camel, a disk at least 25 feet in diameter protruded from the ground, made of a bone-white, smooth material, around which the merchants and soldiers had gathered. One of them, a dark-skinned trader with an expensive robe and turban, asserted loudly that the disk had moved. A fat man with a stubbly beard didn't believe him.

At that moment, the disk soared up, followed by an underlying block of the same shape and consistency. Startled, the circle of bystanders widened as a massive pillar ascended in a fountain of sand, higher and higher toward the sky. Finally, as the shadow of this pale tower already reached over the entire caravan, the movement stopped and a semicircular, pitch dark portal became visible, just big enough to admit a single person.

A pall of silent disbelief hung over the travelers, with nobody daring to approach the unearthly tower or to depart. Eventually, a bold warrior stepped forward and advanced, his sword held out in both hands before him like a lucky talisman.

He stuck his weapon into the impenetrable darkness of the entrance, and then took a step inside. His next step made him disappear, so they could only hear the sound of his movements, followed by a quick hiss. The light of a matchstick made the man's face float in the shadows before it became brighter as he lit a torch inside the tower.

In the flickering illumination, a low, dusty room became visible – a room containing several chests with open lids, filled to the brim with gold pieces and jewelry. The bystanders were quick to sum up the situation, and several soldiers and merchants rushed into the tower, ignoring any possible danger in view of this treasure, pushing and shoving each other without consideration.

Ikrashun stayed clear of the tower, watching his fellow travelers stream inside and rummage through the chests, decking themselves in trinkets and treasure. "We shouldn't linger here," he said to no one and everyone, though one seemed to hear him. "This isn't right."

As soon as the first looter wanted to bring his prize outside, he ran into an unseen barrier across the entrance. Surprised, the bearded warrior dropped his plunder and tried again. His eyes widened in disbelief and bewilderment when he still could not pass through the invisible wall.He whipped out his scimitar and struck at it.

At the moment of impact, the tower began to tremble, then moved once more, downward. The other prisoners became aware of it now, abandoning their treasure and hammering with fists and swords at the entrance, only their desperate screams making it outside. Horrified but powerless, the people who had stayed back watched the bone-white building slowly sink into the desert's depths, carrying its occupants down to a sandy grave.

Finally, the screams fell silent, and where the tower had risen up just a moment ago, only uniform sand remained. No more than a dozen men and twice as many camels were left, and as the caravan continued on, even Ikrashun had to lead one of the animals. The sunlight soon dwindled while the men again made camp for the night, silent and with heavy spirits. Guards were assigned, but only a few of the travelers would be able to find sleep that night.

Ikrashun was concerned as well, not only for his own life, but for the lives of his comrades. At midnight, the shine of the full moon revealed a ghostly procession in great distance, and a swarm of tiny dots rose up from it into the night sky, vanished between the stars and transformed into wooden arrows that unerringly drilled into the remaining water skins. The men could save just a fraction of the precious fluid, as most of it seeped into the insatiable sand. What was left would only last them a few more days.Even more desperate than on the day before, the caravan broke camp at dawn, trying to reach a new oasis or watering hole as soon as possible. The sun blazed down on them, drying up their throats and blinding their eyes as they trekked further and further, driven by the hope for water or rescue.

During the next days, the surrounding desert remained as lifeless as the desert they had already wandered through, and their empty water skins ran bone dry. There were no apparitions in the nights, but the thirst began to torture the men, and if not the thirst, their worries and fears kept them from sleeping.

Two days further, the first winged shapes appeared in the sky, vultures circling above them. Ikrashun still felt calmer than the others, but inside his mind, uncertainty and doubt eroded his willpower. His steps carried him forward through the hot sand, but he walked as purposelessly as a revenant while the thirst burned his mouth and exhaustion dimmed his field of view.

They moved until noon, when they finally found a sign of hope: the fleshless cadaver of an oasis bird. Such animals were only seen in the close vicinity of water, where they built their ornate nests in the palmtops – and this meant that a place with water couldn't be far.

Once more, the men's steps quickened as they dug deep and pushed on to finally reach the summit of a higher dune, from where they saw something like paradise. Just a few hundred feet away, half-hidden behind heat hazes, a glittering azure lake spread out, framed by shade-giving palms and shrubbery that stretched around it like a green wall against the desert.

Their fast steps turned into a hasty run without regard for anything else, as their legs grew lighter and their relief vanquished all thoughts of exhaustion. The feet of the merchants, warriors and even camels flew across the sand in a downright race toward the oasis, using up their last reserves of energy. Ikrashun ran with the others, but lagged behind as they reached the vegetation and he stumbled amidst the undergrowth.

Like famished beasts, the members of the caravan fell on the life-promising water, splashed it on their faces, jumped in it and – above all – drank it. Even as the monk caught up to them, he noticed the complete absence of animals at the oasis, as well as the oppressive silence. Ikrashun understood.

Before he could open his mouth to shout a warning Ikrashun's comrades collapsed one after another, their faces turning waxen and losing all color, their arms and legs becoming stiff, their skin overcoating with a thin, oily film, then losing all moisture.

The entire scenery flickered, the illusion of the oasis having served its purpose, and everything transformed. The lush vegetation turned into wilted brown weeds and toppled palms, the glittering surface of the lake into something covered with iridescent streaks and bloated fish corpses, and the air now carried a stench of putrefaction and death, overlaid by a treacly whiff of decaying fruit.

On a hill above the oasis, its malignance needing no further concealment, a low tower became visible, with unnaturally smooth walls and a heavy dome of gold, coming ablaze in the sunshine like an surreal lighthouse.

Ikrashun groaned. His body was powerless and drained, his tongue hanging in his mouth like a dusty rag, red dots glimmering before his eyes. He forced himself to ignore the temptation of sleep, to fight against the dull oblivion that threatened to overwhelm him, and cramped his hands around the handle of his only weapon, the small dagger at his belt.

Every step was harder than the one before, but Ikrashun trudged forward through the crackling dead grass, his eyes fixed on the tower and its open entrance. His only hope was that the inhabitants of this building didn't count on anyone surviving the trap – after all, it had been pure luck that Ikrashun hadn't reached the water in unison with the others.

Finally, he arrived at the entrance and dragged his body inside. It was cooler here, and Ikrashun sensed a small part of his strength flow back into his body. Heavy carmine tapestries covered the walls, the floor and even the stairway leading up, all of which were built from the same pale material as the tower's exterior. Determined, Ikrashun put his foot on the first step and started to labor his way up.

After a long ascent, during which he almost lost consciousness several times, he reached the top of the building. The same sweetly corrupt smell that had come from the oasis' tainted water confronted him here, intensified many times over, and it was difficult to fight a feeling of sickness.

Before him, there was a twilit chamber decorated with tapestries just like the rest of the tower, with a domed ceiling from which chains with dull luster dangled down. In the center of the room, an ancient, sunk-down figure slumped on a plain throne. Wisps of white hair flowed over an almost fleshless skull covered by skin as thin as parchment, and spindly claws sticking out from the sleeves of a blood-red frock.

As Ikrashun approached, the old man opened his eyes under heavy lids and studied him. Wrinkled jaws exposed yellow tooth stumps when he began to speak, with a hoarse voice that seemed to come from a great distance: "So there is someone who has managed to come here." The old man paused, and only his piping breath was audible. "I assume that you want to know who I am."

"I was once called Khuradhafar, a long time ago, and I lived in a very distant place, between the grey houses and colorful markets of a city whose name I have forgotten. I studied the art of incantation, but I got tangled up in its secrets, and soon, people feared me for my power. They banished me, first from my city, and then from any other that I entered. Ultimately, after many journeys in which I burdened myself with great guilt, I ended up here, amidst this phantasmagorical desert, conjuring my illusions from this breeding dust. My powers protected me from the thirst and hallucinations, and so I built this tower in the heart of the wasteland. I lived here, and the incantation rituals allowed me to preserve my body far beyond its time, to betray death itself."

A bleating laughter issued forth from the man's decayed throat, and Ikrashun shuddered. "And then, I constructed my traps, so easy, so easy. I just had to make the mirages a little bit more real, to fill them with life to make them able to kill. The ghosts, the towers, the voices."

The young monk had listened entranced, but as the words of this cadaverous creature ran dry, he regained his composure. "But why? Why do you have to kill all these people?"

"A game …" The old man smiled dreamily, his age-marked skin stretching over bare bones. "Yes, a game. The stakes were lives, theirs against mine, you understand? You don't know how it is to be imprisoned for a thousand years in a frail, aching body. You don't know how many times I have cursed the moment I used my powers to extend my life. So long have I lived … I wanted to make the game easier, but it was forbidden to me. And every day, every night, the voices came."

His fingers cramped around the throne's armrest, clinging to it until his knuckles turned white. "And now, you are the first to win against me, to beat me at my own game: and I have to let you live."

His eyes glossed over, as if he was gazing into a very distant place. "Take your weapon and kill me, release me." With trembling hands, he produced a bag from under his frock. "Take this, water and provisions, and maybe you will survive the desert, maybe you can finish your journey. But first, kill me!"

Slowly, Ikrashun pulled out the dagger from his belt, weighed it in his exhausted hands. He reluctantly took the bag and watched the old man before him, this ancient, cadaverous creature which had taken countless lives for his own sins. A loud clank cut through the oppressive silence as the dagger fell to the ground.

Desperation and hate glistened in the eyes of the old man, and he stretched out his crooked fingers in a pleading gesture. "Kill me!"

But Ikrashun would not. He turned around cautiously, the bag in his hand, and walked down the stairs without looking back.

His body too weak to stand up, too weak to follow the monk. The old man listened to the steps fading away and gazed at the stairs for a long time, until the voices returned from the shadows and filled the whole tower once again with their whispers, stirring up the dust.

Dennis Mombauer, born 1984, grew up along the Rhine and today lives and works in Cologne. He writes short stories and novels in German and English and is co-publisher and editor of a German magazine for experimental fiction, "Die Novelle – Zeitschrift für Experimentelles" (http://dienovelle.blogspot.de/). Current or upcoming English publications in Plasma Frequency, Geminid Press' Night Lights anthology, Third Flatiron's Ain't Superstitious, Heroic Fantasy Quarterly, and other magazines.

The Forest Realm

P.E. Bolivar

I'd gotten a call from my cop buddy Bernie at four in the morning. They'd responded to a noise complaint at my brother's apartment, not the first time either. Danny liked to crank up his surround sound when playing his video games. Said it made them feel more realistic. Always thinking of himself over others, our Danny was.

As soon as I saw the ambulance outside his building I ran inside in a panic, entering the open door of Danny's apartment before Bernie could stop me.

"You don't want to go in there, Bobby," he said, gently but firmly placing his hand on my chest.

"What happened?" I said. "Is he okay?"

"Why don't you and I go to the coffee shop on the corner and talk about it."

"Screw that, Bernie," I said, shoving his hand aside and storming into the room.

There lay Danny, lying spread-eagle on his living room carpet, naked, face down, the coroner crouching over him like some sort of vulture. When the coroner saw me he hid my brother's body with a sheet, a disgusted expression on his face, as if I was some sort of annoying looky-loo. I felt myself stagger back into Bernie's arms.

"Come on, Bobby, let's get that coffee, okay?"

I nodded, letting him lead me away.

The coroner said the cause of death was a brain aneurism, leading Ma to blame the video games he'd been playing nonstop since losing his job.

Thing is, she wasn't far wrong.

***

I couldn't muster up the courage to clean out his apartment until after the funeral. I threw dirt on

Danny's casket, said goodbye to Ma, and went straight over to his place, skipping the wake. Opening the door I turned on the hallway light, dumped the packing boxes onto the floor, then reluctantly entered the living room.

The centerpiece of Danny's apartment was his 52 inch LED TV, sitting on top of a wide entertainment unit, blocking the room's only window. The cheap afghan carpet where I'd last seen him lay hidden from my view on the other side of his couch, an old beige leather monstrosity built sometime in the eighties. I was nervous moving forward, a part of me worrying that his body would still be lying on that rug.

The landlord had left the place just like he'd found it, but only because I kept paying the rent, something I'd been doing for months.

When Danny's bank account went dry, Ma wanted him to move back home, but I knew that was a fast ticket to trouble. Danny always suffered from depression and a feeling of low self-esteem. He'd mostly dealt with it through high school, but his second year in university it got real bad. The suicide attempt occurred not long after his first and only girlfriend had broken up with him. The hospital managed to pump out all the sleeping pills he'd ingested, but it took years to pull him out of his mental black hole. I couldn't let that happen again.

Now he had died anyway, and something about the coroner's explanation didn't sit right in my gut. I hoped going through his things would give me the answers I desperately needed, or at least some closure.

Cracking open one of the six beers I brought along I began to pack up. It didn't take long to clean the kitchen, bathroom and bedroom. He only had a couple of glasses and plates, some toilet bowl cleaner he appeared to never use, and more clothes in the laundry hamper than there were in his dresser. In the drawer of his bedside table I found a box of condoms that made me chuckle. Danny never did improve his track record with girls. The box still had the plastic packaging on it.

Nothing in those rooms held hints to how he died, but I had suspected that. If anywhere in his place held answers, it would be the living room, where he'd spent all his time online gaming. I'd saved it for last on purpose.

With a little dread in my heart I dropped a box full of towels by the front door then sat down on the couch. Stuffed in a box under the side table was his collection of video games. I rifled through the titles. Some I'd played with Danny, on rainy days after a fight with one girlfriend or another, or after a night on the town with friends from the old neighborhood. Sometimes after both. He always kicked my ass.

When I didn't find what I was looking for I went over to the hard drive and opened the player. There it was, the game he'd become obsessed with over the last year: 'Journey to the Forest Realm'.

***

"Come on, Danny, let's go, okay?" I said, one foot already outside the video game store. Danny ignored me, his greasy hair flopped over his face as he rifled through the bargain bin inside the entrance. "I ain't buying you another game, Bro. You waste enough time on them as it is."

"You don't have to do nothing, Bobby, I can trade for these. Played it, played it, sucks, sucks…" He muttered under his breath as he sorted through them.

"Well, hurry up, we're supposed to be meeting Bernie and the boys at noon."

"Hey, check it out," he said, pulling a CD case out of the bottom of the bin. The picture was faded and worn, showing some sort of forest scene with a woman in black standing amongst the trees. 'Journey to the Forest Realm' was an old title that Danny hadn't even heard of, but for some reason it intrigued him enough to pull three newer games out of the backpack he always carried and trade for it. He wanted to play it so bad he only lasted an hour at the bar before coming up with some lame excuse to ditch us for home.

***

'The Forest Realm' had a simple plot: a long time ago this Irish God named Dagda cast a veil over the land of the faeries, separating it from the rest of the world in order to protect his people from the barbaric humans. Annwn was a paradise of endless trees, protected by a magic wall that kept out the warring hordes living on the other side. There was only one way in: through the Castle of Forest Shores, which was guarded by a deadly monster, some mystery being that couldn't be killed.

The game's quest was to find the clues that led to the castle, once there obtain a key, then journey through the dark maze of horrors inside until meeting this monster. If you beat him you'd be granted entrance into Annwn, and your heart's desire.

I tried playing it with Danny a few times, but it was too weird. The thing was supposed to be multi-player, but the title was so old there weren't many online participants. Those that did still play were real bastards too. They refused to share any clues they'd learned, and most of the time tried to kill you without a word.

That didn't stop Danny though. He obsessed over every aspect of the quest, studying internet chat rooms for clues, losing himself in search of the castle. I was happy to leave him to it and get on with my life. At least his mind was off suicide, right? Too bad the game drove him mental.

When I opened the game's CD case a yellow sticky note fell out, causing my heart to sink. Sucking up my courage I read what I assumed was his suicide note. It began,

"Bobby, if you're reading this, I'm dead. No, I didn't kill myself. Well, that was a relief. *"The Forest Realm killed me."*

Like I said: mental.

Case in point: a month ago Danny came to my apartment building at three in the morning, ringing the doorbell like there was a five alarm fire or something.

Rain had soaked him, making him look like a wet dog begging for a home. My girlfriend was sleeping over, so instead of risking waking her up, I grabbed my coat and dragged him to the nearest all night diner.

"This had better be good, Danny," I said.

"It is, Bobby, I found it!" His excitement turned a few heads in the diner, causing Danny to lean forward nervously, as if he didn't want to reveal his secrets to anyone but me.

I noticed a white ring dangling from a chain around his neck, but didn't think much of it at the time. "Found what?"

"The castle," he said in a whisper. "And I know how to get in."

"What are you talking about?"

"The Forest Realm, the game! Only it's not a game, don't you see? It's real, an actual door to the land of Faerie."

His crazy talk left me speechless, which seemed to give him the surge of confidence to press on. "I think the mystery monster is either the Green Knight or Havgan, the enemy of Arawn, the lord of Annwn. Either way I need to learn to fight before I can face him. Friends of mine are part of a medieval society that teaches swordplay downtown. They said I could learn a lot there. Thing is, the lessons costs more money than I have."

"You don't have any money, Danny."

"Exactly," he replied, nodding as if I understood him. "So, can you help?"

As you might imagine I left him there without saying another word. I wanted to call him pathetic, a loser, but knew better than to go down that rabbit hole.

I didn't lose much sleep over it either. We didn't speak much during his last few weeks, but I knew Ma was keeping tabs on him. It wasn't until the funeral that I realized she'd paid for his lessons at that medieval society.

Those friends of his even helped me carry his casket. What a pair of jokers. They were in full plate armor, their helmets failing to hide the long pony-tails trailing behind them. Ma nearly fainted when she saw them. Me and Father Mulcair though, we couldn't help but laugh. They turned out to be good guys. We drank together at the wake that night, laughing at each other's stories of Danny until we cried.

The note that wasn't a suicide note ended by telling me to look under the sofa cushion. There I found a journal, written in Danny's left hand scribble. Inside were all the clues he'd discovered for 'The Forest Realm', the pieces needed to reach the Castle at Forest Shore.

The note concluded,

"Bobby, I know you're not a believer, and that I sound crazy, but I think I'm in love! I met the Lady of Forest Shores. She's gorgeous, dude! All I have to do is kill the monster holding her and then she'll be free to come home with me.

"I'm going to try my best, but if I fail, I need you to finish it. She doesn't deserve to be trapped in that castle. Please, Bobby, this is really important. Consider it my dying wish."

My first reaction was to snort in disbelief. What a crock of horseshit. Danny had always been like Ma, who'd believed in the fantastic stories she'd heard as a child in Ireland, always dreaming of a better life than the one she led. Me, I'd been more like our father.

Dad had spent most of his life helping his relatives, working himself down to the bone so his sisters could get the education he never had, so that his uncle wouldn't get his legs broken over gambling debts. And what did all that good work get him? A heart attack by fifty-five.

For most of our lives, I'd been doing the same for Danny. My brother never wanted to be like Dad, so he forced me to be like him. Forced me to take care of him. At first the note angered me so much that I nearly crumpled the page and threw it into the trash.

But then I imagined Danny saying the words to me, his big gullible eyes waiting for my answer, and I knew I would do it. He was my brother and I loved him-- a whole lot more than I ever admitted.

I paid the landlord an extra month's rent on the apartment, took leave from my construction job, and got down to figuring out how to win this game.

It wasn't easy, even with Danny's notes. The world outside the faeries' wall was a mixture of Celtic myths, constantly changing, just like the old stories themselves. One minute I was on the road to Camelot, the next I found myself at Castle Perilous, dealing with some Fomorii creature with a poison eye. Everything kept moving around, a shifting maze of roads and tunnels, full of trickster faeries that constantly tried to deceive you into taking the wrong path. Even with Danny's help I fell for a lot of those, believe me.

All the countries beyond the Forest Realm were called the 'Trying Lands'. Danny wrote that I needed a Worldmaze map, so that I'd know what road to take and when.

How I got to the Shore was a long story, and full of a lot of nerd speak. Let's just say I took out a lot of Giants and dark elves called Unseelie, stole some Dragon treasure, answered riddles, escaped tombs, the whole bit, until finally reaching the castle.

I was surprised to find so many people already camped there. The land in front of the wall was a massive desert, aptly titled the Waiting Sea, since that's all anyone seemed to be doing. It was a weird cast of characters: a white-bearded wizard, two ninjas, a Viking, a big, green female ogre, and a cute little girl with faerie wings.

When they saw me crossing the last dune they tried to kill me, even the little girl, who went from cute to vicious in seconds.

By this point my marathon gaming session had turned me into a pretty damn good player, so I fended them off easily. Once they realized it would cost them too much to kill me they left me alone.

I joined the queue in front of the castle gate, watching with disbelief as some of them prostrated themselves in front of the doors while others prayed to the heavens. To avoid these nuts I hit mute on the TV and moved my character so close to the gate that only its wooden surface remained visible on my screen.

I imagined the other players in their homes, sitting on a sofa just like me, and wondered if they were praying there as well. Danny always hated going to church, but somehow I knew he fit right in with these devout gamers. I guess he finally found his religion.

We were waiting outside, because none of us had the key yet. If I followed Danny's instructions I'd have it soon.

After saving the game I went to bed, chasing after a good night's sleep. It ended up being the best I ever had, my first full night of rest in weeks.

The next day I loaded up on sugar food, a couple of thermos's of coffee, and returned to the game. "Okay, Danny, let's do this," I said, hoping his spirit was listening.

Using the flying boots I'd stolen from a drunken God I flew up to the top of the castle's highest tower. The turret was a wide open space, surrounded by high battlements that hid it from the ground below. At one end stood a simple door, lacking the flowery scrollwork of the main gate.

A stout bearded character already stood upon the landing, his axe held in both meaty hands as he swung repeatedly at the door, trying to break it down. I knew from Danny that only one thing could open it: the key. But you had to be patient, you had to earn it.

The dwarf wasn't patient. Pretty soon he gave up, leaping back down to the desert below. I immediately flew in to take his place.

Texts appeared on the screen, messages from the players below.

"Hey, newbie, wait your turn!"

"You're not worthy, heathen."

I didn't bother typing a reply, nor did I try to open the door. Instead I placed the keyboard on the ground and went to take a leak, setting my phone's timer for four minutes.

According to Danny, only one player was allowed on the landing at a time. If the character didn't move for five minutes the game placed them back in the desert, making room for someone else.

For three nights Danny had stayed up, prostrated before his TV like some squire of old. In medieval times such vigils were performed to prove a man worthy of his impending knighthood, only they held their swords and did it in a church, not their living room.

Every few minutes Danny would move his character, making sure he never lost his spot, waiting for the church doors to open, to prove his worth.

And on the morning after the third night she came.

I tried the same, pounding back cola's, setting two more alarm clocks to go off every three to four minutes, doing pushups and sit-ups, whatever it took to stay awake.

By the third night I thought I was home free. Then I nodded off.

A light shone on my face, waking me up. I opened my eyes to find the moon glaring down at me, brighter than I'd ever seen it. A wall of stone teeth encircled me. Glancing down at my body I found myself armored in leather, like my character in the game. When I jumped up in shock I tripped over the sword strapped to my side, its scabbard tangling my legs.

Through the battlements I saw the desert stretching out. The heat from the Waiting Sea blew over me, bringing with it a dry smell that removed all the moisture from my mouth.

Down below slept the other players, on beds of sand. Through a haze of heat I caught glimpses of their rooms in the real world, and their true selves. The winged fairy was a little girl holding a unicorn stuffy, the big female ogre a fat man in striped pajamas. They all looked content, curled in their beds, smiles on their sleeping faces.

It felt so real, but I knew it wasn't. Sometimes, after days of driving nails into walls at a construction job, I'd dream about it, over and over. This was no different. "It's just a dream."

"If it's a dream then why are they all sleeping?"

I turned to find her standing there, the Lady.

Danny had described her in his journal as a vision of unequaled beauty, whose skin was the silvery white of a full moon, whose dark hair reflected the stars.

To me she looked like a million girls Ma had tried to set Danny up with years ago, when we'd gone to visit her family in County Kerry. Yeah, she looked real Irish alright.

What made me stare, though, were all the markings on her body. Her slender fingers were ringed by black circles, as were her wrists, all the way up to her elbows. She even had a few of the black circles around her neck, like tattooed chokers.

When I didn't answer her question, she did. "To them this is the real world. Their jobs, their classrooms, their tedious lives, those are the dreams. But when they wake up they'll be home again, they'll be here."

"What about me? I'm awake."

"That's because you don't believe, Bobby. Those below are the faithful. They worship at our shores, giving us strength with their beliefs."

"A bunch of idiots, if you ask me. My brother believed, and look where that got him."

"Ah yes, Danny. I've been watching you, furiously playing the game, trying to reach this place. What is it you want, Bobby?"

"To get some answers. To kill your damn monster."

Her eyebrow lifted. "I have no monster, Bobby. The only terrors here are the ones you bring with you."

"Sounds like psycho-babble to me, Lady. If a monster didn't kill my brother, then what did?"

"You know what killed him, Bobby."

Of course I did. As soon as she said the words, I knew.

I'd seen his body that night, the way he was positioned. He lay on his front, his arms outstretched, like he'd tried to fly off the entertainment cabinet. When I asked about his keyboard, curious as to whether he'd been playing when he croaked, Bernie claimed it had been stashed away next to the hard drive, unused.

He'd found the key, made his way here for real. Then he committed suicide.

"But why?" I said, not meaning to say it aloud, not wanting to know the answer.

"To gain entrance into Lord Arawn's Court. Danny tried to descend the tower steps, but the deeper he got the worse the nightmare visions grew. Soon he was face to face with what the believers call the Monster: a reflection of his true self, brought up from the depths of his very soul. Danny ran away in fear, unable to bear the sight of what he saw. Let me show you what happened next."

The door opened behind her, and Danny stumbled out into the light. His body was translucent, a hazy memory. He wore a breastplate that barely fit over his pear shaped body. Ripping off his helmet revealed damp hair and a snotty nose. The Lady turned to watch the memory with me, her back perfectly straight, no sign of emotion upon her features.

At first I thought Danny saw me, but no, he was looking at her. "I'm sorry, I failed you!" Danny said, his words an echo on the wind.

"Yes, you did," the Lady replied, her voice carrying the same echo, her words from the same memory. "Now who will free me?"

"My brother! He's worthy, so much more than me!"

"No, Danny, not another. I want you, no one else. There is still a way, my love. A way for us to be together."

Wiping his nose he looked at her, hope in his eyes. "How?"

"You know how, Danny."

Danny closed his eyes, tears running down his cheeks. He nodded his head, and climbed up onto the battlements, between two stone teeth.

I moved towards him, forgetting he was in the past, that this was all a memory. Danny squeezed his eyes tight, like he was trying to stop the flow of tears, a glowing white object clutched in his hands, held close to his heart. Then he turned away, leaned forwards, and fell. As simple as that.

"No!" Running to the edge I screamed his name, my voice crackling through the silent air like thunder.

The forest spread out before me, a sea of roots, leaf and limb. Danny's body lay below, in the exact same position they'd found him at his apartment. As I watched his body slowly melted away, growing into a dirt mound, covered with blood-red flowers. His wasn't the only mound down there. There were dozens of them.

I barely cried at the funeral. I made up for it then. Sliding down the wall I let it all out while the Lady watched me in silence, her arms hidden in the long sleeves of her black dress.

Wiping my eyes I said, "At least he got what he wanted, to stay here."

She laughed then, a cold and crystal clear sound. "No, Bobby, he did not get what he wanted. Now I will show you the penalty for those that trespass."

I heard the baying of dogs, a chilling sound that gave me horrible shivers. Getting back up I stared out over the forest, an endless sea of green, stretching towards the horizon. The moon was bright, yet the rest of the sky was black as oil.

White shapes danced over the treetops, darting quickly left, then right, making loping jumps from branch to branch. "What are they?"

"The flying hounds of Lord Arawn, the master of this castle. The wild hunt is about to begin. The fox is there, just below."

I looked, knowing what I'd see. Danny stood on his own grave, his skin deathly pale, his clothes shimmering rags, ripped and frayed, like they'd known the teeth of these dogs before.

I swear he saw me then, but instead of giving me his usual dorky smile, his face was full of terror. Before I could call out his name, he turned and ran, disappearing into the woods. With a howl the hounds gave chase, their red eyes burning bright.

"Every night he shall be hunted, from here until the end of our time."

In my anger I grabbed her throat, wanting to kill her. "Why are you doing this? Danny loved you, he wanted to free you!"

"Being sent to your world would be banishment, not freedom, Bobby. Those mounds you see below are all the men that have fallen in love with me. But I haven't loved a single one of them in return, including your Danny."

"You're the damn monster, aren't you! What did you really show him down there?"

"I showed him his reflection, Bobby, as I said. And what he saw was exactly what he expected to see: a failure. He knew what he was, Bobby. As did you."

Another memory began to play itself out before me. That night at the diner, right after Danny asked me for money, I never called him pathetic, but I may as well have. The image the Lady showed me was from Danny's point of view, as if I was looking through his eyes. It was written all over my face that night, what I thought of my brother.

Screaming with rage I shoved her away, angry with myself, but pissed at her even more. Drawing my sword I pointed the tip at her throat. "I want him back. Give me the key!"

"No. Long ago, Lord Arawn cursed me with this task, as punishment for my unfaithfulness. He knows that their heart's desire will always be me. But my Lord does not get to choose who enters, I do, and I choose only those doomed to fail."

I laughed at the sick joke of it all. "Your lord has never had to grant a wish, has he?"

Her smile of triumph was all the answer I needed. "Lord Arawn does not mind. In fact, he has come to enjoy our little game. Our believers below think Danny succeeded, and that gives them hope, providing future prey for my master to hunt."

The door was still open, hadn't shut after Danny's ghost exited the tower. Taking slow steps towards it I kept talking. "Listen, Lady, the last thing on my mind is freeing you, my brother's dying wish or not. I only want his soul back."

She tossed her hair in a way that made me want to stab her right then, I swear. "That's what you believe now, but once before my Lord, you will succumb to your desire for me, as all men do."

"Yeah, I doubt that," I said before turning and running for the entrance.

Talking about it now it seems obvious that it was a trap. But after catching a glimpse of stairs leading down into the darkness I only ran faster, eager to get inside before she caught me. Of course she made no move to do any such thing.

Once my foot touched the top stair she broke into laughter.

"You do not have permission to enter, Bobby! Only key bearers may cross my threshold."

I screamed as fire leapt up my body, melting my armor, my sword, melting me.

I woke to darkness, pins and needles electrifying my arms and legs. The power in Danny's apartment appeared to have gone out while I slept. My first thought was for the game. I smelled smoke. Sparks were flying from the hard drive.

"No!" I burnt my fingers prying open the driver. Too late, the disc was fried.

As I collapsed in defeat, I swear I caught a last glimpse of those tower stairs on the TV, a pale image, like a mirror reflection on the black screen. They were only there a moment, then gone.

Had it been a dream, or was it real? Only another copy of 'The Forest Realm' could answer that question, or so I thought. I searched every video game store in the city, every internet shopping sight, but found nothing. For days I wandered the streets, feeling detached, out of body. Maybe the Lady had been right, maybe this world was the dream, while hers was real.

Then yesterday I found it. Not the game, better.

The movers were clearing out Danny's apartment. I watched them take everything away while in a daze, my hands clasping that burnt CD like it was my brother's ashes.

When they moved the couch, the white ring I'd seen around Danny's neck was revealed. It must have rolled off him after he jumped, abandoning him and his dreams, just like I'd done before he died.

The ring beat like a heart in my hand, warm, pulsating. The mover thought I was nuts when I asked if he felt it too.

It was made of skin, her skin. Lady Monster.

All those circles around her body were bits of flesh carved out of her so that humans could gain entrance into her Lord's realm. I almost felt sorry for her then. Almost.

Once I put it on, it will transport me straight to the castle. How do I know? Because, for better or worse, I believe now, just like Danny did.

Hang in there, brother. I'm coming.

P.E. Bolivar is an Air Traffic Controller living in Vancouver, British Columbia. When not controlling flying metal machines from atop a two hundred foot tall tower, he is dreaming up stories of the fantastic.

Random Acts of Cosmic Whimsy

Jetse de Vries

The Multiverse is a weird, weird place.
Multitudes weirder than most suspect.
Some, though, do have an inkling.
While for a rare few it's not quite weird
enough...

***

Recipe for a Time Machine.
Ingredients:
--One Kerr-Newman black hole
--Highly advanced nanotechnology
--A reliably functioning, self-correcting
Entangled Particle Information Transmitter (EPIT-link)
--A budding, space-faring civilisation.

Preparation:
Take one Kerr-Newman black hole of the
smallest possible size and put it in a geostationary orbit
of the home planet of the space-faring civilisation.
Place a space station at the closest safe distance from it.
Develop nanobots with a nano propulsion, a
quantum computer as CPU, and a self-correcting EPIT-
link. Send nanobot to Kerr-Newman black hole, and
make it run Closed-Timelike-Loops by moving in and
out of the hole in the ring singularity via a highly
elliptical orbit. The temporal jump of each loop depends
on the time spent in the hole, so the temporal
displacement of the nanobot can be decided by taking
the number of the largest possible jumps and fine-tuned
by a single, well-timed final jump.
Once in the desired time period, the nanobot
must either find some raw material for the fabrication of
a small re-entry craft (as nanobots are very prone to an
atmosphere's turbulence), or take the very bumpy ride

down to the planetary surface and fabricate a small plane to take it to the desired location.

Once on the desired spot—in a concealed place—the nanobot can multiply and gather enough raw materials for the fabrication of the human clones for the time travellers to be transported into by means of its EPIT-link. Once safely installed in their clone bodies, the time travellers are ready to begin their—at times esoteric—tasks. Enjoy!

Note: most civilisations that have developed nanotechnology and EPIT-links have transcended into Matrioshka Brains, and have no need to investigate their own pasts, nor their own future, as the bandwidth of the link to the future is much too small to be of any practical use.

For more weird and wondrously impractical recipes check out:

-How to become God in your own Universe, see: Solipsism for beginners
-A Virtual Reality made exactly to order, see: Escapism for the slightly advanced
-Tweaking the basic constants, see: Creationism for experts
-Searching for the real Theory of Everything, see: Infinite regression for the over-focused.

***

The Mona Lisa was stolen. A cryptic note was attached on its empty spot at the Louvre, reading:

Art, in fact
alienates hitmen

contrasts and shades
as if SF, you tomato,
lights the dark
obscurity, when theirs
more in tiny details
than just the devil
or the deep black sea

The press had a field day, while all field agents of Paris's gendarmerie, France's Sécurité National, and Interpol were called in. This was a matter of national pride. In the following weeks, though, not a single clue—apart from the nonsensical note—was found. It looked as if the Mona Lisa had just vanished into thin air. The 'crime of the century' began to disappear from the front pages and prime time news as another event took centre stage...

***

Meanwhile, in Interpol's hi-tech department in Glasgow, agents Watt and Krikksen are called into the research department. Hu—first name classified—the enigmatic research leader meets them personally as they enter the test laboratory.

"I've developed this new gadget, a kind of highly miniaturised 3D-projector that needs to be tested in the field. I'm actually supposed to give this to Bonditch, but..."

"But?"

"That cold fish with his lofty upper class manners—"

"—not quite."

"Always looking like a million dollars, and knowing it—"

"—bit of a façade."

"That disdainful air of British superiority—"

"—he'd wish."

"But he's not half bad, really." Krikksen says with a smile.

"While he wouldn't know yoga from yogurt, or ascetic from acerbic," Watt, struggling to stay serene.

"Let alone the internet from the interzone," Krikksen's grin broadens, "his stiff upper lip charm has a way with the ladies that gives great fringe benefits to his colleagues."

"Yeah, right."

Hu starts to explain the newest device.

"You see these two tiny dots? Both are two-way miniature 3D recorders and projectors. Both are highly mobile and are linked to each other by EPIT-links—"

"By entangled particle information transmitters? I thought that was only theory." Krikksen, wondering.

"You know about them?" Hu, more surprised than Krikksen.

"Well, I try to follow the newest developments—"

"—in psychedelia. But sometimes he surfs crazy links—"

"—I have very broad interests—"

"—says Mr. Zappo himself—"

"—and they seemed groovy—"

"Please," Hu interrupts the interrupters, "with these TITLEs you can spy in any place undetected, because nothing can shield an EPIT-link."

"So we only need to get one on a quarry and we are always linked to him."

"Another whimsical abbreviation, Hu?"

"Telepathic Identical Twin-Link Engines," Hu admits, "and with a reversible Master-Slave setting you can also use them to project images of yourself—"

"If we throw one on stage during a Red Hot Chili Peppers show—"

"—we can appear next to John Frusciante in the middle of a solo."

"—or jump around with Flea."

"GROOVY! BABY!" In unison.

Hu smiles, knowing his TITLEs will be tested in ways he wouldn't dream of.

"Always linked, and a reversible Master-Slave setting," Watt thinks out loud, "like invisible bondage."

"The way Flea's funky lines always connect—" Krikksen concurs.

"—with Frusciante's riffy tripping: an invisible connection through a higher plane."

"Indeed," Hu says.

**

In the immediate aftermath of the big bang, singularities of all sizes were created, called primordial black holes. The real big ones became centres of their own galaxies, growing in size as they gobbled up more incoming matter. Some others became the engines of astronomical extravaganzas like quasars, X-ray pulsars and gamma ray bursters. There were also much smaller ones, with masses far below the Chandrasekhar limit. The smallest of those, amassing a few billion tons, will by now have evaporated by Hawking radiation. Larger ones, though, will have survived until this very day.

Suppose that a relatively small primordial black hole—say some 2×10^{18} kilograms, about a third millionth of the Earth's mass—would skim near the fierce particle beam of a pulsar at a glancing angle. Suppose that the constant glancing bombardment of the charged particles and X-rays both spins up this black hole to a large fraction of the speed of light, and charges it up to a very high degree. In such a way, a Kerr-Newman black hole could be created.

The chances of this happening are smaller than one in a septillion. However, in a Multiverse with more than an octillion parallel Universes, this probability approaches one...

***

An anomalous object was detected in the outer reaches of the solar system, and it was heading straight towards the Earth. As it approached three things became apparent: it was artificial, it was huge, and it was silent. All attempts to contact the alien craft were met with no discernible response.

With all due haste, an unmanned spacecraft was launched to intercept it just outside Jupiter orbit. From a distance it already detected several remarkable things: its mass—about that of a medium-sized asteroid—matched its size—a sphere with a 60 kilometre diameter. Really strange was its strong magnetic field, rotating at a tremendous speed. Then, as the unmanned probe came ever closer to the alien craft, trying to contact it all the time, but meeting with nothing but silence, it bounced off the impenetrable hull.

More probes arrived at the alien craft as it entered Mars orbit, but they found the dull, mirror-like hull just as impervious. The closer anything was coming to the reflective perimeter, the harder it was repelled, like a kind of anti-gravity. Seemingly oblivious to its many visitors, the enigmatic sphere headed for Earth. Arriving there, it settled into a geosynchronous orbit almost straight above Mount Kenya, where it remained, inert to all incoming signals.

Of course, any space agency worth its salt sent up astronauts and researchers, and in this second space age, with its permanent moon colonies and several manned interplanetary missions, that were quite a lot. Even Interpol—the official ESA security agency—had its subsidiaries in space and its own launch facilities.

So while W.—director of Interpol's hi-tech department—was following the news with great interest, he was not happy when he received a request from HQ in Lyon to send a few men to investigate the inscrutable object. Damn it, Lyon already had his best men looking for the Mona Lisa. He simply couldn't spare anymore... But wait, maybe he could...

He called Dolly, his secretary and—not coincidentally—his daughter.

"Dolly, are Watt and Krikksen around?"

"They just went to Hu, probably testing another gadget, dad."

"Remember to call me Sir, especially in the presence of my agents, Dolly. Anyway, tell these two idiots to come to my office."

"Come on, dad, don't be so uptight. I'll send them up as soon as—hi, agents Watt and Krikksen—ehm, Sir."

***

In this way Watt and Krikksen find themselves in Space Station Emerald, that was relocated closer to the mysterious space anomaly. A couple of astronauts invite them to join the research team on the next trip to the alien object, but Watt politely declines. Krikksen is not amused: "A perfect lift! And you say no."

"Everybody's going there. Therefore my intuition tells me it's the last place we should go."

"Your bloody intuition. Last time—"

"—it got us backstage passes to a Peppers show."

"Right. So what do you propose now?"

"We set off in space and follow—"

"—your nose?"

"—my sixth sense. Let's go."

Both men board a small spacepod, and once safely removed from the Space Station, Watt takes the control over from Krikksen, closes his eyes and heads for a direction that feels right. Which gets them nowhere for a while, until a freak burst of their pod's thrusters jerks the vessel uncontrollably and the safety system ejects both men—fully suited, as per the stringent safety regulations—into space.

Slowly tumbling over and over, the detectives are drifting in space, ever further away from their little vessel. Their uncertain state does not seem to worry them, though, as their space suit's radio is working fine, and they can chat, the two men dressed up in silvery shining space suits with purple, pulsating seams, and fishbowl helmets tinged a deep red. With arms crossed, legs locked in Zen position and their helmets gleaming bright in the darkness of outer space they emanate a kind of defiance against events.

***

One of the advantages of drifting through space by tumbling over and over again is that you get a perfect view of your surroundings, that is, if you don't get space-, motion-, or just plain sick of it all. Watt and Krikksen, though, have been on quite some heavier trips, and calmly enjoy the Earth, moon, sun and stars swirling around them.

"That little star over there," Krikksen points, "a bit strange, innit?"

"Yeah. It's got a hole in it."

Coming closer to the strange object, they see it looks like a thin donut, the inner tube of a bicycle tire, however with all kinds of spiky objects protruding from it, like a halo of thorns. One rectangular opening gleams with a blood red glow. Since this seems to be the only entrance, the agents head for it.

"Look at that: it's enormously much bigger from inside than seems possible from the outside."

"Like John's trippy riffing, you mean?"

"And Flea's badass slapping. Inconceivable how they complement, transcend and still fit in a song's constraints."

"OK. Before we get in let's make sure the entrance stays open."

***

Let's take this one step further: suppose that this Kerr-Newman black hole, with almost the smallest possible mass for its desired characteristics, was also accelerated in the process. Also suppose this happened at the pulsar nearest to the accretion disc of stellar debris from a previous supernova that will later coalesce into our solar system. Then suppose that just before arriving in our solar system, it is decelerated by a series of braking trajectories through the gravity wells of large gas giants. Finally suppose it enters our solar system and Earth with exactly the right momentum and timing to achieve a geostationary orbit.

The chances of this happening are smaller than one in a nonillion. However, in a Multiverse containing more than a decillion parallel worlds, the probability of this happening on one single Earth comes dangerously close to one...

**

Inside the strange artifact, the crimson reception space appears to be an Escherian illusion of impossible figures, with a good measure of Dalíesque grotesqueries thrown in for good measure. The only—relatively—static things in the vermilion madness are a big metallic plaque inscribed with strange symbols; a blue, semi-regularly flashing light source; and a rectangular opening at the far end of the headache-inducing space.

"Cool."

"A bit like the old I-Beam club on Haight."

"Without the music, though. Anyway, shouldn't we be on the case?"

"If we must."

"Right. Those signs on that great plaque, and that flickering light source over there, as if pulsating in some kind of Morse code—"

"Yeah, let's feed them into to the decryption software in our suit computers."

"I thought I was the tech guy, here?" Krikksen, slightly miffed, "Don't you think we need a Rosetta Stone or something?"

"No: this is meant to be understood." Watt, mighty spliffed. "Trust me: I'm still in Vipassan mode."

Right on cue, the decryption software signals a successful decoding. On their screens Watt and Krikksen read:

Welcome to the @$#% of *&$#%@ X%^&*(){}.

In each chamber you will find four representations. Study each one shortly and decide which one you think approaches reality the closest. Touch your choice and you will either be allowed into another chamber or punished. This is an all-or-nothing test: once you enter the first chamber there is no turning back. So if you don't feel up to it send somebody more suitable. Better: send your very best.

Success.

"Yo, what's with the first sentence?"

"I think we set the decryption to the highest degree of interpretation."

"I see, then it can't decide the meaning. Let's set it one notch lower."

The lower setting gives two possibilities:

(a) Welcome to the labyrinth of ever-deepening truth.

(b) Welcome to the tangled web of infinite regress.

Krikksen is getting second thoughts. "This is creepy. Let's get some help."

Watt is smiling defiantly. "Of course not."

"Now listen, Watt. If we get lost in there nobody knows where the hell we are."

"Let's not get help yet. You know how it goes: those after us with a bigger mouth take all the credit. No. We can do this ourselves, although these selves will be spread very thin..."

"Ahh, I get it: Hu's TITLEs."

So, as the actual Watt and Krikksen make a tactful retreat, their projected counterparts enter the first chamber full of audacity, bravado, chutzpah, Dutch courage, élan, force de frappe, gallantry and a further supranational alphabet stuffed from hubris to Zähigkeit.

The first room of the labyrinth is stripped from the entire mind-bending extravaganza that imbued the reception space. Four white pillars stand in the middle of a square, Spartan chamber, all cut off at the top under a 45-degree angle. Inscribed in each sheared-off top is an equation:

(1) $E = mc2$
(2) $F = Gm1m2/d2$
(3) $\lambda = h/mv$
(4) $\alpha = 2\pi e2/hc$

"Einstein, Newton, Heisenberg and something fine and dimensionless." Krikksen muses, trying to make sense.

"Just starting," Watt jabs, "and already uncertain."

"Well, (3) is about the Uncertainty Principle."

"Let's take that one then."

Before Krikksen can stop him, Watt touches the second pillar. Nothing happens.

"Of course," Krikksen says, "your projection can't actually exert pressure."

"Hmm. Didn't Hu say that his TITLEs were very sturdy and mobile? Let's make the TITLE jump against the place where I put my ghostly finger."

"Might work. But what if the choice is wrong?"

"Who cares? We try again."

"We might lose the TITLE."

"Oh, Hu gave me a whole box of spares. Mumbled something like 'You never know'."

"It was probably more like: 'With you two, you never know'."

"Hey, some inkling of human character. Superb scientist, but a bit awkward socially."

"But learning fast. Of course, with us as shining examples..."

Which gives even the normally irony-impervious Watt pause. Not for long, of course: "Anyway, there we go," as his doppelgänger pushes an ethereal hand almost through a solid pillar. The TITLE—instructed by Krikksen's remote control to keep itself positioned on the top of Watt's index finger—ticks against the inscribed column, and a door in the ceiling opens.

"There you go," Watt says, "easy as space cake."

"I wonder," Krikksen wonders, "if another answer would have opened another door—"

"—of perception."

In the weightlessness of space, Watt and Krikksen move 'up' with a short burst from their spacesuit thruster, and their counterparts effortlessly float through the opening in the ceiling.

"Why don't we just walk through all the walls?" Watt, who—mindsurfing—often wonders why he should get out of bed.

"That's unsportsmanlike." Krikksen, who—netsurfing—often wonders if he should go to bed.

"So what?"

"Besides, the TITLE can't follow, then."

"OK."

The hatch in the floor closes the moment they pass through, and four eerie statues made from some perfectly mirroring material float in the next chamber.

"Abstract art."

"More like topological shapes."

"Whaddya mean?"

"Well, that swinging sculpture over there seems to represent Riemannian curvature of relativistic space/time; those multi-lobed clouds might signify the probability spaces of the electrons of a carbon atom; that psychedelic tree branching into infinitesimal points is a prime example of fractals; but I'm not sure about the fourth one, though."

"You surf too much."

"Not really. I just get sidetracked a bit, at times."

"Never mind. It looks like a Calabi-Yau shape."

"Bless you."

"I didn't sneeze. I meant a Calabi-Yau shape."

"How would you know what such a thing looks like?"

"I don't know, I just know."

"Like an idiot-savant, you mean?"

"How can I be an idiot if I'm wearing such an idiosyncratic outfit?"

Krikksen watches the iridescent motifs on Watt's silver-and-purple suit weave gnarly patterns, then watches his own reflective outfit pulse with random-generated constellations shifting colours every second and says:

"I guess you can't."

Which has a smug looking Watt choosing the Calabi-Yau abstraction, and a trapdoor on the left wall opens.

***

The exhibits in the next part of the madness museum are a strange kind of kinetic sculptures:

—One displays a constantly changing grid where black and white squares appear and disappear in formations that never seem the same—

—Another shows evolving cloud patterns on a small, rotating globe—

—The next shows a cone-shaped heap of sand where a small trickle of grains keeps falling on its very top—

—The last shows a mini-solar system, making exactly the same rotations all the time—

"The game of life and a planetarium." Watt says, happy to recognise more than one item.

"And self-organising criticality and chaos theory in action." Krikksen adds.

"The planetarium is dandy. I'm choosing it."

"No! It's not correct: it's moving like a Cartesian clockwork. The real world isn't that deterministic."

"OK, but I wanna see what happens if we make a wrong choice."

Before Krikksen can stop him, Watt touches the mini planetarium. In the blink of an eye, the room is filled with an indefinite number of lightning-fast balls, bullet-sized, that change colour at every bounce. In the few seconds that they charge through the room in a dash of razor-sharp neon flashes, they have reduced most exhibits to pieces. Only the sand heap, constantly replenished from the top of an imaginary hourglass, remains intact.

"That was cool!"

"Maybe a bit overdone."

"Something for the Peppers' last show on the last tour," Watt, getting enthusiastic, "John plays the ultimate riff and ZAPPO—SLASHERFEST."

"You sure? His guitar might get damaged."

"Out with a bang, not with a whimper."

"But, what then?"

"Well, there's Queens of the Stone Age."

"Nah, they're too modern."

"Anyway, then it must be this one." Indicating the shifting sand heap.

A hatch right in front of them slides open.

***

Then consider the extremely unlikely event of an alien artifact containing pre-programmed nanobots with nanopropulsion, quantum computers, and EPIT-links (with, on top of that, an easily decodable instruction manual attached) entering our solar system around the same time. Now the aliens that launched that craft weren't completely bonkers, as they protected that technology with a series of tests for the lucky finders.

The chances of this happening reach the limits of human vocabulary and understanding: they are smaller than one in a vigintillion. However, in a practically infinite Multiverse—and one containing more than a centillion parallel realities comes a long way towards that—there is one Earth where the probability of this cosmic coincidence will approximate one so perfectly as to be indistinguishable from it...

***

Eventually, by making all the right—and wrong—choices, and by passing through some incredibly inventive punishments basically by not being there, Watt and Krikksen arrive in the final room. At first sight it appears rather empty, at second hearing a thunderous voice is transmitted through Watt and Krikksen's radio channel:

"WELCOME HUMAN MORTALS. DO NOT COWER IN THE FACE OF ABSOLUTE TRUTH."

"Absolute truth? Isn't that an oxymoron?" Krikksen turns down the volume, but to no avail.

"If it's so absolute, no need to make it deafening, right," Watt turns up the paradox, with some effect. "old geezer?"

"The way I look is just a representation meant not to overwhelm your tiny minds." The ominous voice tones down, yet warps, twangs, and warbles seemingly at random.

"Right on. We're definitely overwhelmed."

"On the contrary. The special effects of X-men 666 were a lot better."

"Do not joke with me, puny insects. I am that which was, is and will be. The Fabric of Reality, the Basis of your Existence, the—"

"Sounds like he figures he's God."

"Not by a long shot. He doesn't even look like John."

The chances of this seeming deity smiting the irreverent Watt and Krikksen are actually smaller than the amount of its rather absolute bafflement.

"By all the intricacies of 23rd dimensional Calabi-Yau p-branes interacting with trans-topological twistor space, what do you two idiots want?"

"A confession."

"Did you or did you not steal the Mona Lisa?"

"I did that. But I do everything."

"No excuses, you've admitted it. Throw the book at him, Watt."

"Yes. You have the right to remain silent—or at least talk some sense—you have the right..."

"You can't do this to me. I'm the air you breathe, the songs you sing—"

"It's what we're paid to do, unfortunately."

"Keep John out of this. Are you coming along nicely or do we have to take you by force?"

"You can't just arrest me. I'm..."

"We just did."

"Your simple handcuffs can't retain me."

"But your conscience can."

"Aargh! Don't say that! I've been repressing it for billions of years!"

"Conscience and guilt are like the Rolling Stones."

"They always make a comeback."

"You yokels can't bring me to your medieval justice system."

"Your conscience wants it."

"Listen. I can bring you enormous riches—if you let me go."

"Such as?"

"I can release the negative CTL-field shielding the singularity."

"So what?"

"Your scientists will have access to a Kerr-Newman black hole!"

"And?"

"Research possibilities previously undreamt of!"

"So they can devise a better doomsday device?"

"Together with the nanotech manual your technology will advance enormously!"

"Don't know if our civilisation is quite ready for such a jump in the deep."

"The Kerr-Newman black hole is a gateway to the whole multiverse!"

"We can hardly manage our own planet, so unleashing us in the Multiverse would be quite premature."

"You could even travel in time to any period you like!"

"...any..."

  "...period..."

    "...we..."

      "...like..."

"Including 1967—"

"—the Summer of Love?"

"Of course."

"Maybe we can talk."

            ***

In the succinct negotiations that follow Watt and Krikksen get exactly what they want from a semi-deity cornered by its own omniscient conscience. As the disgusted demi-god retreats, resenting that it can't take the nice portrait that reminds it of the pre-big bang serenity, saying it will leave for a more understanding civilisation in a few hours, the spaced-out detectives have a tiny little last problem.

"How do we get the stuff out? Our doubles can't physically lift anything."

"Still cool how our imaginary handcuffs held that old geezer."

"Maybe a double negative makes a positive."

"Or a matter of shadow matter."

"All very nice, now how about some lateral thinking?"

"Hey, Krikksen, I've got it."

"Got what?"

"Remember the last Led Zeppelin album?"

"In Through The Out Door? Shit, you're right!"

With all due haste, the real Watt and Krikksen enter through the exit and take their booty. They retreat to a safe distance from the haloed artifact and wait until it disappears. Then they call for help over the distress frequency and gleefully await pickup.

"A crazy black hole."

"Nanobots and TITLEs."

"All adding up to a time machine."

"Yeah, we can go back to the summer of love!"

"GROOVY BABY!"

"Didn't you complain we were born too late?"

"Of course I did."

"Well, we might be born just in time."

Back in their Glaswegian headquarters Watt and Krikksen report to W. The much-plagued director—neither the research into the alien artifact nor the search for the Mona Lisa have yielded anything but a wall of nothing—is desperately holding on to the last shreds of both his patience and his sanity as their report gets to the point where he would have settled for a mere 'infinitely improbable' to describe their descriptions. With a dismissive gesture he cuts their ripping yarn short:

"Enough. Escherian mazes, ethereal mathematics and god-like gestalts. No more."

"But we still have to come to the good part—"

"—time travel!"

A sigh so deep it causes a local depression escapes W.'s exhausted mouth. "Do I need to remind you that agents are supposed to bring their quarry or any actual evidence to bear with their reports?"

"Oh, that. Well, we had to let the old geezer go—"

"—that was part of the deal."

"We handed the nanotech manual and de-activation method for the CTL-shield to Hu—"

"—man, you should've seen the look on his face!"

"And there's this old, somewhat boring portrait—"

"—must've been painted way before surrealism."

From an oversized holdall, Watt—smiling enigmatically—extracts a rectangular, well-wrapped parcel. After carefully taking off several protective layers, he shows a 70-by-53 centimetre oil-on-wood painting titled La Giaconda to his boss. To say that W.'s jaw dropped so far that one could park the historical portrait right in it would be stretching the truth, albeit only a little.

The rest is history, or rather the end of history as we know it.

***

The Multiverse is a crazy, crazy place.
Most people have no clue as to just how crazy.
Some suspect, but don't really care.

A select few, though, are about to make it even crazier...

Jetse de Vries—@shineanthology—is a technical specialist for a propulsion company by day, and a science fiction reader, editor and writer by night. He's also an avid bicyclist, total solar eclipse chaser, beer/wine/single malt aficionado, metalhead and intelligent optimist. Recent publications include The Singularity Magazine, Kaleidotrope *and the* XIII- Stories of Transformation *and* Second Contact *anthologies.*

#bff

S. Kay

Narrator
@blueberrio_omni
Lexi creates a Twitter account, eager to make new friends with a click. It's so much easier online.

Lexi
@lexi_blueberrio
Hi Twitter! #myfirsttweet

Narrator
@blueberrio_omni
Instantly, @yourBFFbot follows her account and replies to her tweet.

Botty
@yourBFFbot
@lexi_blueberrio LOLhi

Lexi
@lexi_blueberrio
@DrDinaKulik @yourBFFbot Thanks for following!

Lexi
@lexi_blueberrio
I just moved to Vancouver and only know one person here, but I like it already. Love the beach!

Narrator
@blueberrio_omni
Her new follower automatically laughs again.

Botty
@yourBFFbot
@lexi_blueberrio LOL beach

Lexi
@lexi_blueberrio
Oops, I mean #NorthVan, right@ParcPanorama?

Narrator
@blueberrio_omni
A split second after posting it, her message with the
North Van hashtag is retweeted, or "RTed."

Lexi
@lexi_blueberrio
@north_van Thanks for the RT!

Botty
@yourBFFbot
@lexi_blueberrio @ParcPanoramaLOL oops

Narrator
@blueberrio_omni
Karen, or @ParcPanorama, is a Twitter veteran who
encouraged Lexi to join. She sees her friend's tweet,
follows, and replies.

Panorama Park
@ParcPanorama
@lexi_blueberrio Yes, North Van. Welcome to Twitter,
Lexi! How are you? Settled into your new condo?

Lexi
@lexi_blueberrio
@ParcPanorama Getting there! It's so quiet here. I love all the trees.

Panorama Park
@ParcPanorama
@lexi_blueberrio Not so quiet now. Too bad you're missing #DeepCoveDaze. Great music.

Lexi
@lexi_blueberrio
@ParcPanorama I can hear it from my window. Sounds fun. I'm unpacking, and having a glass of wine.

Narrator
@blueberrio_omni
Lexi reads her Twitter feed, full of news, Kardashians, and news about Kardashians, marveling at the access to fame.

Narrator
@blueberrio_omni
Kim's entrance to the Video Music Awards in a daring dress causes a frenzy of tweets, many photos turning up in Lexi's timeline.

Lexi
@lexi_blueberrio
@UltimateKimK @MTV Kim's dress is amazing!

Narrator
@blueberrio_omni
Searching for mentions of @KimKardashian, and
"Kim," a program finds Lexi's tweet. It follows her and
sends a link.

KimBot
@mostfabulousk
@lexi_blueberrio Kim Kardashian Black Lace Bodycon
Evening Dress http://www.ebay.ca/itm/Kim-
Kardashian-Black-Lace-Bandage-Bodycon-Herve-
Leger-Inspired-Evening-Dress-
/221521147898?pt=AU_Wedding_Clothing&hash=ite
m3393b077fa

Lexi
@lexi_blueberrio
@mostfabulousk Wow, that's a great dress too. Thanks!
And thanks for the follow, I've made so many new
friends today. 9 already!

Narrator
@blueberrio_omni
After a star-filled night of TV and shopping online for
dresses she has nowhere to wear, at work she has
impulses to tweet.

Lexi
@lexi_blueberrio
Sure could go for a kale smoothie. Maybe after work.
First, I have a deadline. Shouldn't be on Twitter.

Botty
@yourBFFbot
@lexi_blueberrio LOL kale

Lexi
@lexi_blueberrio
@yourBFFbot Why do you keep laughing at me? It's not nice.

Botty
@yourBFFbot
@lexi_blueberrio You're beautiful! <3<3<3 Diamondz https://www.asseenontv.com/diamondz4-as-seen-on-tv/detail.php?p=443152&v=novelty_great-gifts

Lexi
@lexi_blueberrio
@yourBFFbot Well thanks, but I just got rid of an engagement ring I don't need anymore.

Botty
@yourBFFbot
@lexi_blueberrio You're beautiful! <3<3<3 Thigh Toner http://www.asseenontv.com/thigh-toner/detail.php?p=294648&v=fitness_exercise-equipment

Lexi
@lexi_blueberrio
@yourBFFbot Um, I don't need that either.

Botty
@yourBFFbot
@lexi_blueberrio You're beautiful! <3<3<3 Peek a Boo
Pet Bed http://www.asseenontv.com/peek-a-boo-pet-bed/detail.php?p=294619&v=pets

Lexi
@lexi_blueberrio
@yourBFFbot I don't have a pet. Thanks, but I have to
get back to work now.

Narrator
@blueberrio_omni
Lexi logs out, but @yourBFFbot relentlessly replies
with another link, the program following its script.

Botty
@yourBFFbot
@lexi_blueberrio You're beautiful! <3<3<3 Magnetic
Posture
Corrector http://www.asseenontv.com/magnetic-posture-corrector/detail.php?p=634518&v=health-and-beauty_personal-care

Narrator
@blueberrio_omni
The bot laughs at others, following more and more.
Lexi's irked as she tries to focus on charts, wishing she
hadn't logged in.

Panorama Park
@ParcPanorama
@lexi_blueberrio I know a good place for green
smoothies, want to meet up after work?

Narrator
@blueberrio_omni
Getting a notification of Karen's tweet in her email,
Lexi logs back into Twitter to reply.

Lexi
@lexi_blueberrio
@ParcPanorama Sure! Can we get it to go and hike up
to Quarry Rock?

Panorama Park
@ParcPanorama
@lexi_blueberrio OK, let's meet at 6, Bluhouse Cafe.

Lexi
@lexi_blueberrio
@ParcPanorama The forest will be great after staring at
a monitor in this cozy office all day. Back to work!

Narrator
@blueberrio_omni
Work goes on as the #Emmys begin, Lexi taking looks
at the time under her spreadsheet. Who's wearing what?
Winners will be RTed.

Narrator
@blueberrio_omni
She can't resist looking at red carpet gowns, winners
and losers determined not only by statuettes, but in
fashion media coverage.

Lexi
@lexi_blueberrio
The back of @Lavernecox's dress is spectacular! Love
@UzoAduba's gown too. Laura Prepon looks like Judy
Jetson's bridesmaid. #emmys

Botty
@yourBFFbot
@lexi_blueberrio @Lavernecox@UzoAduba LOL
bridesmaid

Narrator
@blueberrio_omni
She rushes home from work, changing into yoga pants
before heading out. A pair of puppies wag their tails
outside the cafe.

Lexi
@lexi_blueberrio
@ParcPanorama I'm here!
Panorama Park
@ParcPanorama
@lexi_blueberrio On my way! Hope you're ready for
adventure.

Narrator
@blueberrio_omni
Hiking to a rock once known as Suicide Cliff, the
friends talk about love lost. In the wild wide panorama,
Lexi shrinks in size.

Lexi
@lexi_blueberrio
OMG #QuarryRock is amazing! All the forest-fresh,
ocean-tinged superoxygenated air you can breathe.
#northvan pic.twitter.com/UJolXUEftH

Botty
@yourBFFbot
@lexi_blueberrio LOL breathe

Panorama Park
@ParcPanorama
@lexi_blueberrio Glad you liked it! Let's go again
sometime.

Lexi
@lexi_blueberrio
@ParcPanorama Definitely!

Narrator@blueberrio_omni
Once again, Lexi's hashtagged tweet is RTed right
away.

Lexi
@lexi_blueberrio
@north_van Thanks for the RT! Have you been to
Quarry Rock?

Lexi
@lexi_blueberrio
Is @KimKardashian pregnant? I keep reading that, but she didn't look it at the VMAs yesterday. I hope so, she'd be a lucky woman.

Botty
@yourBFFbot
@lexi_blueberrio @KimKardashian LOL pregnant

KimBot
@mostfabulousk
@lexi_blueberrio Kim Kardashian White Maternity Dress http://www.ebay.ca/itm/KIM-KARDASHIANS-CUSTOM-GIVENCHY-WHITE-SPLIT-SLEEVE-MATERNITY-DRESS-/121406576861?pt=US_CSA_WC_Dresses&hash=item1c446558dd

Lexi
@lexi_blueberrio
@mostfabulousk Ha! Well she doesn't need that size yet.

Narrator
@blueberrio_omni
Lexi browses maternity dresses, thinking of the baby she'll never have with Tim. She sends a link to @mostfabulousk. No reply.

Lexi
@lexi_blueberrio
Dark spreads fast. Birds are quieter. Can't get over how close to the wilderness I am, 100s of km of emptiness due north. #northvan

Botty
@yourBFFbot
@lexi_blueberrio LOL dark

Lexi
@lexi_blueberrio
@north_van Wow, you sure RTed that fast. You must be online all the time.

Lexi
@lexi_blueberrio
@north_van What's your name?

Narrator
@blueberrio_omni
No reply from the auto North Van retweeter bot. She resumes browsing photos with the #Emmys hashtag.

Lexi
@lexi_blueberrio
It may be eerily dark with ghost babies in the air, but luckily there are so many #Emmys pictures to look at. I love hashtags!

Botty
@yourBFFbot
@lexi_blueberrio LOL eerily

Lexi
@lexi_blueberrio
@yourBFFbot That wasn't funny. Stop laughing at me.

Botty
@yourBFFbot
@lexi_blueberrio You're beautiful! <3<3<3 Shoes
Away http://www.asseenontv.com/shoes-
away/detail.php?p=294565&v=household_storage-and-
organization

Lexi
@lexi_blueberrio
@yourBFFbot Are you trying to come on to me?
Because I'm not looking.
Botty
@yourBFFbot
@lexi_blueberrio You're beautiful! <3<3<3 Bra-
Tastic http://www.asseenontv.com/bra-tastic-set-of-
3/detail.php?p=366204&v=clothing

Lexi
@lexi_blueberrio
@yourBFFbot You're a pig. Leave me alone.

Botty
@yourBFFbot
@lexi_blueberrio You're beautiful! <3<3<3 Star Trek
Uhura Costume Women's T-
shirt http://www.asseenontv.com/star-trek-uhura-
costume-dolman-womens-t-
shirt/detail.php?p=443299&v=clothing

Lexi
@lexi_blueberrio
That's it, I'm getting offline. It's time for bed anyway, I
have a long day at work tomorrow. It's month end.

Botty
@yourBFFbot
@lexi_blueberrio LOL offline

Narrator
@blueberrio_omni
Babies laugh out loud at her in dreams, waking her
twice, before coffee flings Lexi into another day. She
worries about stalkers.

Lexi
@lexi_blueberrio
@DearAssistant A creep likes me and I don't like him.
What should I do?

Lexi
@lexi_blueberrio
No reply to my question to @DearAssistant. I'll figure it
out on my own.

Botty
@yourBFFbot
@lexi_blueberrio @DearAssistant LOL reply

Lexi
@lexi_blueberrio
@JPAutoGroup Thanks for RTing my photo of Quarry
Rock! What a great place to live. #northvan

Lexi
@lexi_blueberrio
@north_van Thanks for the RT again! You sure keep
busy.

Lexi
@lexi_blueberrio
@yourBFFbot Leave me alone. I'm not interested.

Botty
@yourBFFbot
@lexi_blueberrio You're beautiful! <3<3<3 Hot
Designs Nail Art Pen http://www.asseenontv.com/hot-
designs-nail-art-pen-as-seen-on-
tv/detail.php?p=484335&v=health-and-beauty

Narrator
@blueberrio_omni
She can't concentrate on work, worrying over
@yourBFFbot. Does he know where she lives? Did he
hack her, and is he watching now?

Lexi
@lexi_blueberrio
How can you tell if you've been hacked?

Botty
@yourBFFbot
@lexi_blueberrio LOL hacked

Lexi
@lexi_blueberrio
@yourBFFbot I knew it!

Botty
@yourBFFbot
@lexi_blueberrio You're beautiful! <3<3<3 The
Stealth http://www.asseenontv.com/the-stealth-
ssa/detail.php?p=294916&v=electronics

Narrator
@blueberrio_omni
She finishes her work for the day, not emailing about
the hacker or going on Twitter, fearing monitoring.
Broken sleep is haunted.

Panorama Park
@ParcPanorama
@lexi_blueberrio Are you around? Haven't seen you
online in a while.

Narrator
@blueberrio_omni
Lexi tweets from her smartphone, blinds drawn at home on a workday. The lure of celebs is stronger than her desire to stay offline.

Lexi
@lexi_blueberrio
@ParcPanorama I'm mostly offline. Can't tell you why. Not safe.

Panorama Park
@ParcPanorama
@lexi_blueberrio Oh no, are you OK?

Lexi
@lexi_blueberrio
@ParcPanorama I'm not sure, I hope so.

Narrator
@blueberrio_omni
Vexed, she quickly logs out and goes for a walk to get a smoothie. She's calmer until noticing a man walking behind her. She runs.

Lexi
@lexi_blueberrio
I can't escape, he's everywhere, watching me. What does he want?

Botty
@yourBFFbot
@lexi_blueberrio LOL want

Lexi
@lexi_blueberrio
@yourBFFbot I just saw you, you know, you're not so stealthy. How did you - are you - nevermind, stop it!

Botty
@yourBFFbot
@lexi_blueberrio You're beautiful! <3<3<3 Hollywood Detox Body
Wrap http://www.asseenontv.com/hollywood-detox-body-wrap-by-verseo/detail.php?p=451309&v=health-and-beauty_diet-and-health-care

Narrator
@blueberrio_omni
Horrified at the idea of him putting her naked body in a body wrap, she gets offline again. All day she thinks about his lewdness.

Lexi
@lexi_blueberrio
@Kardashianpedia I'd love to win a trip to Australia to see @KimKardashian. I need the break. Good distraction to think about it.

Lexi
@lexi_blueberrio
I love Kim in that white outfit, @GlobalGrindStyl! And her shoes are divine.

Botty
@yourBFFbot
@lexi_blueberrio @GlobalGrindStyl LOL divine

KimBot
@mostfabulousk
@lexi_blueberrio Kim Kardashian Mesh Skull Evening
Dress http://www.ebay.ca/itm/Kim-Kardashian-Mesh-
Skull-Velvet-Print-Bodycon-Pencil-Skirts-Midi-Dress-
inco-
/321484091186?pt=US_CSA_WC_Dresses&var=&has
h=item4ad9f1ef32

Lexi
@lexi_blueberrio
@mostfabulousk A little morbid? Maybe it's my mood.

Narrator
@blueberrio_omni
Driving home from the office, a car follows her too
closely. Locking her door, crying and panicking. she's
convinced it was him.

Lexi
@lexi_blueberrio
I should stay offline but want to see what Kim wore
today. But does it even matter anymore? Why am I
trying to start over?

Botty
@yourBFFbot
@lexi_blueberrio LOL why

Lexi

@lexi_blueberrio

@yourBFFbot Yes, why, when I attracted you?

Botty

@yourBFFbot

@lexi_blueberrio You're Beautiful! <3<3<3 Talking
Kitchen Scale http://www.asseenontv.com/talking-
kitchen-scale/detail.php?p=594422&v=kitchen_small-
appliance

KimBot

@mostfabulousk

@lexi_blueberrio Kim Kardashian
Sunglasses http://www.ebay.ca/itm/Tom-Ford-
Alessandra-Oversized-Black-Sunglasses-Kim-
Kardashian-
/261574051979?pt=UK_Sunglasses_Adults&hash=item
3ce707488b

Lexi

@lexi_blueberrio

@mostfabulousk I could use sunglasses for my puffy
eyes.

Narrator

@blueberrio_omni

Afraid to go out, she orders pizza. The driver's car looks
like the one she noticed before. She screams. He can't
calm her down.

Narrator
@blueberrio_omni
Lexi runs away, headed to Quarry Rock. He can't
follow her if she's fast enough.

Narrator
@blueberrio_omni
She stumbles, lost on the dusky trail, and falls onto
some moss, crying and not sure where to find safety.

Narrator
@blueberrio_omni
The pizza delivery guy calls 911. A search and rescue
team is dispatched, and they find her before sunset,
shaking in the bramble.

Narrator
@blueberrio_omni
After explaining why she got lost, paramedics take her
to the hospital. It's not the ER, it's the psych ward she's
admitted to.

Narrator
@blueberrio_omni
She's diagnosed with psychosis, having delusions of
stalkers online and off. Lexi can't convince them she's
sane.

Lexi
@lexi_blueberrio
They don't believe me and they've locked me up in the
hospital. Why am I here? He should be arrested!

Botty
@yourBFFbot
@lexi_blueberrio LOL arrested

Lexi
@lexi_blueberrio
@yourBFFbot You're the one who should be here.

Botty
@yourBFFbot
@lexi_blueberrio You're beautiful! <3<3<3 Disposable
Adult Bibs http://www.asseenontv.com/disposable-
adult-bibs/detail.php?p=505316&v=health-and-
beauty_diet-and-health-care

Lexi
@lexi_blueberrio
@yourBFFbot I do not need a bib! I'm not crazy. Leave
me alone! :"(

Botty
@yourBFFbot
@lexi_blueberrio You're beautiful! <3<3<3 Slice-o-
Matic http://www.asseenontv.com/slice-o-matic-slice-
your-prep-time-in-
half/detail.php?p=361235&v=kitchen_knives-and-
gadgets

Narrator
@blueberrio_omni
Lexi rests, awake in a room on the third floor ward,
wishing she could jump from the fenced rooftop garden.
The pills don't help.

Lexi
@lexi_blueberrio
@ParcPanorama Will you visit me in the hospital?
Visiting hours 6-8

Panorama Park
@ParcPanorama
@lexi_blueberrio Hospital? What happened? Of course
I'll visit.

Lexi
@lexi_blueberrio
@ParcPanorama You're my only hope. They don't
understand.

Lexi
@lexi_blueberrio
It feels like there's sludge oozing through my body. I'm
so tired.

Botty
@yourBFFbot
@lexi_blueberrio LOL tired

Narrator
@blueberrio_omni
She naps until dinner comes on a tray, evenly steamed
and bland. Her friend Karen walks into the lounge when
visiting hours begin.

Narrator
@blueberrio_omni
Lexi talks about the stalker, eyes wide. She's now sure
it's her ex Tim behind @yourBFFbot, having her
followed. Karen's not sure.

Narrator
@blueberrio_omni
They argue, Lexi upset that nobody will believe her,
desperate to expose Tim as her tormentor.

Narrator
@blueberrio_omni
"Get some rest," says Karen, leaving Lexi alone with
her smartphone.

Lexi
@lexi_blueberrio
@yourBFFbot Tim i know it's you why are you doing
this to me i loved you

Botty
@yourBFFbot
@lexi_blueberrio You're beautiful! <3<3<3 My Spy
Birdhouse http://www.asseenontv.com/my-spy-
birdhouse-peek-into-the-world-of-
birds/detail.php?p=495382&v=outdoor

Lexi
@lexi_blueberrio
@yourBFFbot i couldn't be a bird in a cage if im so
beautiful why did you leave me come back don't do this

Botty
@yourBFFbot
@lexi_blueberrio You're beautiful! <3<3<3 Inflatable
Buffet http://www.asseenontv.com/inflatable-
buffet/detail.php?p=373733&v=outdoor&pagemax=all

Lexi
@lexi_blueberrio
@yourBFFbot i don't understand you anymore, maybe i
never did. i don't understand why you crushed me 10
days before our wedding

Botty
@yourBFFbot
@lexi_blueberrio You're beautiful! <3<3<3 Gray
Away http://www.asseenontv.com/gray-away-best-
selling-root-concealer/detail.php?p=374183&v=health-
and-beauty_hair-nail-and-foot-care

Lexi
@lexi_blueberrio
@yourBFFbot you couldn't stand the idea of me getting
old, is that it? you've got wrinkles too

Botty
@yourBFFbot
@lexi_blueberrio You're beautiful! <3<3<3 Ab
Rocket http://www.asseenontv.com/ab-
rocket/detail.php?p=295123&v=fitness_exercise-
equipment

Lexi

@lexi_blueberrio

@yourBFFbot i'm beautiful, but you think i'm fat? i wish we never met. it's like you stabbed me with broken wedding china. go away

Botty

@yourBFFbot

@lexi_blueberrio You're beautiful! <3<3<3 Instagone Stain Remover http://www.asseenontv.com/instagone-pro-stain-remover/detail.php?p=605015&v=household

Narrator

@blueberrio_omni

Lexi cries herself to sleep after a long night thinking about Tim. Over oatmeal, she resolves to convince her doctor that it's him.

Narrator

@blueberrio_omni

In group therapy, she talks about the Gray Away and Ab Rocket, proof of her theory. The doctor makes a note to increase her meds.

Panorama Park

@ParcPanorama

@lexi_blueberrio Want me to visit tonight?

Lexi

@lexi_blueberrio

@ParcPanorama I'm not sure. I'm tired.

Panorama Park
@ParcPanorama
@lexi_blueberrio I have something to tell you about
@yourBFFbot

Lexi
@lexi_blueberrio
@ParcPanorama What about Tim?

Panorama Park
@ParcPanorama
@lexi_blueberrio It's not him. I'll explain it tonight.

Lexi
@lexi_blueberrio
@ParcPanorama You're wrong.

Narrator
@blueberrio_omni
Lexi fights with nurses and is sent to seclusion. Karen
visits the next day after she's released. Slow and meek,
Lexi sips tea.

Narrator
@blueberrio_omni
Karen says, "@yourBFFbot is a bot automatically
sending an LOL when you tweet, and a link when you
reply to it. There's no human."

Narrator
@blueberrio_omni
Lexi disagrees. "@yourBFFbot knows too much about me, about us. It has to be Tim, he's mocking me. He's cruel. And stalking me."

Narrator
@blueberrio_omni
"It's just a bot. There are many bots on Twitter. It's sending you links to products, don't you find that suspicious?" Karen says.

Narrator
@blueberrio_omni
Lexi looks confused, then defiant. "It's Tim, I know it is."

Narrator
@blueberrio_omni
Saddened that logic didn't help, Karen talks to Lexi's doctor on her way out, explaining about the bot. He's never used Twitter.

Narrator
@blueberrio_omni
Doing online research, the doctor learns more about Twitter bots, automated programs that respond to users' tweets.

Narrator
@blueberrio_omni
Searching further, he finds http://BotOrNot.net ,
software that reveals whether or not a Twitter account is
a bot. Is it a cure?

Narrator
@blueberrio_omni
Lexi's doctor shows her http://BotOrNot.net and
@yourBFFbot fails the test. She feels abandoned by
Tim all over again.

Narrator
@blueberrio_omni
"How could I believe it was him," she says in a
whisper. The doctor smiles a little, reassuring her. "The
mind is a curious thing."

Narrator
@blueberrio_omni
The doctor prescribes a sedative, sending her to bed
crying. He makes a note in her chart, she'll be
discharged in the morning.

Lexi
@lexi_blueberrio
Taking a few days off work. Here's a picture from
@ParcPanorama, the real Panorama Park,
earlier.#northvan pic.twitter.com/0yTDFtVAoQ

Botty
@yourBFFbot
@lexi_blueberrio @ParcPanorama LOL days

Lexi

@lexi_blueberrio

@yourBFFbot You're not real. You're a bot.

Botty

@yourBFFbot

@lexi_blueberrio You're beautiful! <3<3<3 Touch Free
Soap Dispenser http://www.asseenontv.com/touch-
free-soap-dispenser/detail.php?p=366412&v=health-
and-beauty&pagemax=all

Lexi

@lexi_blueberrio

I'm not responding to that, it's a bot. I blocked it. What's
Kim been wearing?

Narrator

@blueberrio_omni

Immediately, @mostfabulousk replies with a link, and
she notices that her hashtagged park photo tweet was
RTed by @north_van.

Lexi

@lexi_blueberrio

@north_van Thanks for the RT. I think?

Panorama Park

@ParcPanorama

@lexi_blueberrio Sorry, @north_van is also a bot. Nice
park photo, glad you're getting out. Let's go to Quarry
Rock soon.

Lexi
@lexi_blueberrio
@ParcPanorama OK, let's get a smoothie too.

Narrator
@blueberrio_omni
Lexi reads Kim Kardashian diet rumours, thinking about returning to work, confident in her grasp on reality and Twitter.

Lexi
@lexi_blueberrio
@KimKardashian, you don't need to lose weight. You're fabulous just as you are, and you deserve respect.

KimBot
@mostfabulousk
@lexi_blueberrio Kim Kardashian Pink Bikini http://www.ebay.ca/itm/NEW-VIX-PAULA-HERMANNY-1-pc-Pink-kim-kardashian-BIKINI-SWIMSUIT-bottom-L-/351078640950?pt=US_CSA_WC_Swimwear&hash=item51bdeaed36

Lexi
@lexi_blueberrio
@mostfabulousk Thanks! I might buy that for the beach. Sit on the sand, splash around. Try to stay off Twitter.

Lexi

@lexi_blueberrio

Enjoying the beach! pic.twitter.com/VNHjMxEpP4

Bio: S. Kay writes one tweet at a time. Her work has appeared in
Nanoism, theEEEL, Science Creative Quarterly, Grievous Angel, and
more. Her debut book "Reliant," an apocalypse in tweets, is available
from tNY.Press/reliant, and her novella "Joy" will be out January 2016
from Maudlin House.

About "#bff": Written for a social media book contest, this story was
created from intertwined Twitter accounts and collated in a Storify
slideshow on Tumblr. Read it online in its original context here:
http://blueberrio.tumblr.com/post/95656993780/reading-between-the-tweets